THE HARD WAY

W9-CYA-817

THE HARD WAY

New York Times and *USA Today* Bestselling Author

KATIE ASHLEY

Copyright © 2016 by Katie Ashley
Interior Formatting by Indie Pixel Studio | indiepixelstudio.com
All rights reserved.
No part of this book may be reproduced in any form or by any electronic or mechanical means, including information storage and retrieval systems, without written permission from the author, except for the use of brief quotations in a book review.

DEDICATION

To Shakespeare for his great love stories and tragedies that have inspired generations and for the words of wisdom to sustain us from day to day.

PROLOGUE

CADE

Alcohol…because no great story starts with milk. I read that somewhere on the Internet. At the time, I couldn't help raising my solo cup in agreement. It pretty much summed up my life's motto from the time I'd downed my first beer at fourteen to my post high school binges. Of course, I'd come a long way since the two high-end beers I'd snuck out of my father's office fridge had gotten me buzzed. Now I was twenty-one, a junior, and a starting running back at Georgia Tech. I didn't start feeling toe up until five or six beers in now.

This particular alcohol-related story starts after I had just finished up my sixth beer of the night. I'm sure you're wondering why I need to elaborate—I mean, we all have our drunk-as-hell stories, especially when you're a college student. None of them really amount to stellar storytelling unless it ends with waking up next to the crush you never had the guts to talk to when sober, or with a black eye from that bar fight when the alcohol made you feel ten feet tall and bulletproof. Let's not forget the legendary red-and-blue-flashing-lights alcohol-related story.

When it comes to my story, I owed everything to a hot-as-balls summer night and a six-pack of Bud, but I digress.

Anyway, Tech's summer football practice had ended, and two of my teammates—and coincidentally best friends—had gone back to my buddy Brandon's dorm room to help him pack up his shit. He was going to be living with me and our other bud, Jonathan, in our apartment a block off campus.

After packing up the truck and then unloading it at our apartment, we'd come back to Brandon's to celebrate with pizza and beer. Since we'd decided to crash at Brandon's that night and take the last load in the morning, we made it a *shit-load* of beer. We were stumbling out to the car with the last boxes when something caught my inebriated eye. Across the street, a bunch of dressed-up older people strolled down the sidewalk and into the one of the administrative buildings. The men in their tuxes and the ladies in their fancy dresses seemed out of place among the coeds packing up.

With a snort, Jonathan clapped me on the back before pointing. "Dude, there's your favorite professor."

A growl came low in my throat at the sight of Dr. Higgins. The bastard had given me my first C of my college experience. Yeah, I know what you're thinking: how's it possible a jock like me makes all As and Bs? Trust me, I'm not your typical jock. I graduated in the top ten at my prep school, and while most college football guys had their eye on the NFL, my future was focused off the gridiron. My sights were set on a sports medicine major. That's right, ladies—a doctor. You could call me a triple threat. I had looks, personality, and brains. How fucking sexy was that?

Anyway, it might've been a week since I'd seen my final grades, but I was still pretty steamed about Professor Cocksucker jacking my GPA—especially when it came to one of my science classes. I always aced those with high As. "So what's going on over there?"

Jonathan grimaced. "That would be the Academic Honors Dinner." When I blinked at him in confusion, Jonathan added, "It's where a bunch of professors get together and have dinner to celebrate that they're done teaching dumbasses like us for the year."

"They also give an achievement award, and this year it's going to Dr. Cocksucker," Brandon piped up as he shoved a box in the cab of his truck.

"You're shitting me."

"Sorry, bro, but it's true."

Jonathan shook his head at Brandon. "How the hell do you know this?"

Brandon glanced over his shoulder to give us a shit-eating grin. "I banged one of the TAs from the math department two nights ago. She was all in a panic when she overslept because she had to go work on the decorations."

"Shoulda known it had something to do with pussy," Jonathan mused.

"Holy shit!" I suddenly cried. My body tingled like I'd been hit with a taser—and yes, I knew what that felt like from firsthand knowledge, but that's another story for another day.

"What the hell is the matter with you?" Brandon asked.

At first, I didn't answer him; I was too busy processing the idea that had just hit me. It was one I probably wouldn't have entertained had I been sober, though that's not to say I haven't done some stupid shit when I wasn't plastered.

I waggled my brows at Jonathan and Brandon. "Who's up for some streaking?"

Brandon, who'd had the least to drink out of the three of us, stopped his OCD double-checking of the boxes in the back of the pickup truck and whirled around. "Did you just say streaking?"

I clapped my hands together. "Hell yeah."

His blond brows crinkled. "Through the empty dorms?"

"Nope." I threw an arm around his shoulder. "I was thinking more about through the honors dinner to ruin Dr. Cocksucker's big night."

While Brandon appeared horrified, Jonathan busted out

laughing. “Dude, that’s epic!”

“Isn’t it?”

While Jonathan nodded, Brandon shook his head. “This is a bad, bad idea—like one of the worst you’ve ever had, and that’s saying a hell of a lot.”

“Oh come on, man. Live a little.”

“And what happens when your bare ass gets caught?”

I whipped my shirt over my head. “I won’t get caught.”

“Newsflash, ace: they’re gonna see your face along with your ass,” Brandon countered.

“Well, duh, I’m not gonna let them see my face. Unless they’ve got cameras in the locker room, they’ll never be able to identify my ass.”

“Just how are you going to do that?”

I lumbered over to the cab of the truck and thrust my hand into the box Brandon had taken special care to put up front so nothing would happen to it. After rustling around in the box, I grabbed out his Dark Vader mask—the one Jonathan and I gave him shit for treasuring.

Holding it up, I said, “I’ll be wearing this.”

Brandon’s eyes widened. “Dude, you know that’s not to play with.”

Jonathan snorted. “You sound like a five-year-old.”

“I’m serious. It’s memorabilia, not a toy.”

Rolling my eyes, I replied, “Jesus, Brand, you’re an epic buzz-killer."

Brandon held his hands up to signal a timeout. "Come on. Let's just go back inside, finish the pizza, and sober up. Then if you're still hell-bent on revenge, we can find another way to get back at Dr. Cocksucker, one that doesn't involve you getting in trouble. Something slightly more…anonymous."

I wasn't sure if he was actually concerned about me getting in trouble or if his concern was more about anything happening to his precious Darth Vader mask. "Nope. It's on."

When Brandon opened his mouth to once again protest, I broke into a sprint over to the building. Of course, in my state, I ran like a kid coloring outside the lines. After cracking open the main door, I stuck my head inside and peered around to see if the coast was clear. The lobby was a ghost town except for two stiff-looking women at the check-in table. Everyone was already inside the ballroom.

It was now or never. It took me twice as long as usual to get my shorts off my hips. Usually I can get those off in record speed, especially if I'm about to unleash the beast for some sex action, but being plastered, I ended up staggering around to catch my balance. Once I had righted myself, I slid on the Darth Vader mask. It took me a few seconds to get my bearings with the mask on. Once I could breathe and see, I threw open the door.

One of the women at the table shrieked and clutched her chest while the other one rose out of her chair. "What do you think you're doing?"

"Dr. Higgins sucks mega cock!" I shouted at the top of my lungs as I barreled past them.

"Get back here!" the woman hissed.

I opened the ballroom door and charged inside. Through the mask, I could see about twenty round tables set up with white linen tablecloths, fine china, and crystal. On the stage, a few musicians screeched bows across the strings of violins and a cello. Ugh. It was a total pile of pretentious shit, which I knew all too well from my father's world of political fundraising dinners.

The pairing of a woman's scream and a man shouting "What the hell?" alerted everyone to my presence. I threw a hand in the air and fist pumped. "Dr. Higgins sucks mega cock!" I shouted again. A couple people in line for the buffet dropped their plates as I streaked by, which caused me to start laughing—like really crazy, maniacal laughter, the kind that would scare small children or get you institutionalized.

In my lunacy, I realized it was time to get the hell out of there. My attention was drawn to the door with the gleaming EXIT sign. It loomed in the distance like the end zone on the football field.

I almost made it, but I hadn't expected my sneaker to get lodged in an audio visual chord someone had tried to conceal under a rug.

"Fuck!" I grunted as I went flying through the air. The plastic Darth Vader Mask did little to protect me as I crashed at full speed into the metal door that also happened to be locked. A flash of light accompanied a searing pain in my head before everything went dark.

ONE

CADE

Sometimes you just know you're thoroughly and completely fucked. The mind-numbing, stomach-clenching dread slowly creeps over you until your entire body is drowning in it. It's all encompassing, and you can't shake out of it. You can try counting to ten, taking deep, cleansing breaths, or even going all kooky trying to find your zen, but there's no way in hell you're shaking that feeling.

It's the same dread as when you're down by thirty at the half, and it would take a miracle to pull a victory out of your team's ass. You know with absolute certainty you'll be trudging into the locker room with your tail between your legs.

That's exactly how I felt sitting in a hard-as-hell plastic chair outside the office of the dean of athletics at Georgia Tech. As my shoes drummed a rhythmic, anxious tapping on the floor, my mother placed a hand on my knee. “Cade.”

My toe tapping ceased at her admonishment. After being momentarily blinded by all the bling on her hand, I glanced up at her. A tight smile formed on the face that had been perfectly sculpted by one of the finest plastic surgeons in Georgia.

“It will be fine.” When I opened my mouth to protest, she gave a jerk of her blonde head. “Doesn’t your father always make things right?”

I couldn’t argue with her on that one, especially as a shit-ton of scenarios of me with my ass in a bind ran through my mind. In a weird way, my father was like my knight in shining armor when it came to getting me out of trouble. As a former corporate litigator, he sure as hell knew how to put forth a good argument. Now as a representative in the Georgia House, he had the power to pull strings if it came down to it.

On this particular day I needed his mad litigating skills more than ever before, and if necessary for him to pull strings like a fucking puppet master. The fate of my entire life was being decided within the walls of the dean’s office—well, it was really more the fate of my football career that was on the line. Considering I lived and breathed for the sport, I wasn’t exaggerating too much to say it was my life—at least it was until I finished undergrad. Then it was on to medical school.

I needed football like I needed air. It was the one true escape and high for me—to be more accurate, *one* of the escapes and highs for me, after drinking and sex. Although there were rules and a coach and teammates giving orders, I never felt freer than I did when I was playing football.

My mother pinned me with her blue eyes, the very ones I had inherited from her. "Of course, we both hoped that by now you would've ceased making such foolish and childish decisions. You're twenty-one now, Cade, a young man. You shouldn't be exhibiting the same irresponsible behavior you did as a teenager."

"It was just a little revenge prank. It's not like when I hacked into Dr. Emerson's laptop back in high school," I protested.

I mean, call me crazy, but I never imagined that a simple act of streaking would have my ass in such hot water. By the way Tech's athletic office was acting, you would have thought I'd set fire to the banquet hall rather than just flashing my junk. They obviously were a bunch of old farts with no sense of humor.

My mother opened her mouth to argue when the dean's voice rose loud enough for us to hear. "Representative Hall, by continuing to seek leniency, you seem utterly flippant about the complete disregard and respect for authority your son has illustrated. Hear me for the last time: the punishment this committee has agreed on *will* stand, or your son will receive a lifetime ban from the program."

Holy shit. The word *punishment* was bad enough, but banned from football? No more endorphin rush as I ran out onto the field to the roar of the crowd and the brass of the band. No more feeling the buzz of adrenaline as I executed a play. No more hero worship from undergraduates when I walked around campus. A lifetime ban meant I wouldn't enjoy any alumni benefits either. I wouldn't get to sit in box seats and muse with fellow teammates about how we were so much better back in the day.

I swallowed the bile rising in my throat. "Fuck," I muttered.

"Watch your language!" my mother hissed.

"There will be no further discussion on the matter!" A fist banged against hard wood. "Mrs. Murphy, bring him in now."

I'd barely had time to process what I had just overheard when the office door swung open. A middle-aged secretary beckoned me in with a quick flick of her wrist. "They're ready to see you now, Mr. Hall."

Since no one ever referred to me as "Mr. Hall", I remained seated in a stunned stupor, and I probably would have remained that way if my mother hadn't jabbed me in the side with her bony elbow.

"Cade, get up!"

I shot out of my seat and hotfooted it into the dean's office. Once inside, I skidded to a stop at the sight of not only the athletic board, but a sour-faced Dr. Cocksucker. When my gaze bounced over to my father's, the look in his eyes caused me to swallow hard. Oh yeah. I was in deep, deep shit.

Dr. McKensie, the dean of athletics, motioned to the empty seat next to my father. "Please sit down, Mr. Hall."

"Yes, sir," I replied.

After I eased down into the chair, I threw an uneasy glance at Dean McKensie, who was still standing. Both his expression and the way he was looming over me caused me to shift nervously in my chair.

He took off his wiry glasses and placed them on the table in front of him. "Your father tells us you've come here today to sincerely apologize for your actions and to plead for our forgiveness."

"Yes sir, I have."

"I can't help but find that very telling of your character."

I scrunched my brows in confusion as I leaned forward in my chair. "I'm sorry, sir. I don't think I understand what you mean. I thought I was here because you wanted my apology."

"What I meant is I find it interesting that only now are you apologetic. You've had an entire week to apologize to us—to plead for forgiveness." Dr. McKensie narrowed his eyes at me. "Why is it you've waited until today?"

With a shrug, I replied a little sarcastically, "Uh, I don't know. Maybe because this was the day of my hearing." When the members of the board glanced at each other, I softened my tone and added, "What I meant to say is today is when it mattered."

"It's mattered every day, Cade," Dr. McKensie replied.

Okay, this guy's holier-than-thou bullshit was really starting to piss me off. "Look, I was just doing what I was told to do."

"Exactly. I'm sure within an hour of the incident, your father and his handlers were guiding you through exactly what to say and do."

I tilted my head in thought. "Actually, it was more like I was in the ER an hour later making sure I didn't have a concussion."

Dr. McKensie pinched his lips together so tightly they turned white. "Perhaps it was after your recovery?"

"Well, yeah. What does that matter?"

"It matters a great deal, Mr. Hall. It shows me that you are unrepentant for disgracing Dr. Higgins's honor dinner. You are only apologizing now because you have been told that is what we want to hear. Moreover, you think an apology will save you from being expelled from the football program."

"I guess." When Dr. McKensie shook his head disapprovingly, I knew I had to start backpedaling. "Look, I am sorry, totally and completely sorry. It was a very stupid and immature thing for me to do, an act of alcohol-induced stupidity. If I had an issue with my grade, I should have made an appointment with Dr. Higgins to discuss it."

Bobbing his head, Dr. McKensie replied, "Yes, Cade. That is exactly what you should have done."

I threw a satisfied smile over at my father. I hoped he was glad I had managed to repeat the story we had gone over. He only gave me an exasperated sigh. Okay, so apparently he was less than thrilled with my performance. I don't know why I was surprised; there was seriously no pleasing my father. He was Mr. Perfect, and he expected his wife to be perfect along with his two children. They had managed to program the perfection into my older sister, but sadly, I hadn't quite mastered it. Even though I was a starting running back at Tech that usually made all As, I was still a fuck-up.

"So you do see that I'm sorry, right?" I questioned.

Dr. McKensie gave the same exasperated sigh my father had a moment before. "While you see the error of your ways, your actions still tarnished our university. Our football players are supposed to be leaders on and off the field, but regardless of the negative reflection on our program, it is you I am most concerned about." Dr. McKensie finally eased down into the leatherback chair behind him. "You have great promise, Cade."

I snorted. "Yeah, tell that to Dr. Higgins over there who gave me the first C of my life."

Dr. Higgins shook his head. "I don't 'give' grades, Mr. Hall. Students earn their grades, and while it might be hard for your inflated ego to grasp, you did, indeed, earn a C."

My fists clenched in my lap, and I fought the urge to leap out of my chair and across the table to smack the smug look off his face. "Whatever," I mumbled.

"Do you have any idea how blessed you are?" Dr. McKensie questioned. At first, his question took me off guard, and I was unable to reply. Then when I truly thought about what he was saying, I rolled my eyes and refused to look at him.

"You shouldn't respond to that statement so flippantly, but your reaction reiterates the sentiment that you haven't dealt with much of the world outside your social circle. You haven't had to see how harsh and devastating the world can be. You are unable to be grateful for the fact that besides being born into privilege, you have been gifted with both mental and physical abilities. While you excel at academics and football, you are morally and ethically bankrupt."

"Enough!" my father bellowed. He leaned forward in his chair and jabbed a finger at Dr. McKensie. "I will not sit by and let you continue making my son your moral whipping boy. Get to the point and tell him his punishment."

Dr. McKensie stared my father down for a moment before exhaling. "Fine." He then turned his attention back to me. "Cade, are you familiar at all with The Ark?"

Before I could make some smartass remark about only knowing Noah's Ark, my father anticipated me. He gave a quick jerk of his head before throwing me a death glare. "No sir, I'm not."

"I'm sure you're familiar with Atlanta's hometown sports hero, Amad Carlson?"

Just the mention of that name piqued my interest, and I leaned forward in my chair. "Amad Carlson who played for the Atlanta Falcons and shattered NFL records in rushing touchdowns?"

"Yes, that Amad Carlson. Ten years ago, he built a center where at-risk teenagers could go after school and during the summers. He dubbed it The Ark because he wanted a place for teens to find shelter from the dangers of the streets like drugs and gang violence."

I nodded; I vaguely remembered reading an article in *Sports Illustrated* about Amad's charity work. Although nowadays his multimillion dollar contract with the Atlanta Falcons meant he lived in a gated mansion off posh West Paces Ferry Rd, he hadn't forgotten his teenage years when he and his mother lived in some of the local homeless shelters. He was a hell of a stand-up guy to invest millions into the place that had once been a YMCA.

Dr. McKensie drew in a breath before speaking. "Since your father confirmed that you don't have a summer job, we have found you one at The Ark. You will be working forty-hour weeks for the entirety of the summer. You won't have a set schedule so it won't interfere with your practice schedule."

I held my breath, waiting for the punchline. "Excuse me, did you just say my punishment is a job?"

"Yes, Mr. Hall. I did."

"But I've never had a job before."

Dr. McKensie gave me a tight smile. "As the old adage goes, there's a first time for everything."

I leaned forward in my chair. "So this job is at a homeless shelter?"

"It's not a homeless shelter, Mr. Hall. It is a center for at-risk youth," Dr. McKensie corrected.

Part of me was slightly intrigued about working at Amad's

shelter. I mean, maybe I could meet him, and even though I wasn't planning on trying to get drafted to the NFL, he might like me enough to put in a good word for me or some shit. Medical school would always be there, but I wouldn't always have the opportunity to warm the Falcons' bench for a chunk of cash.

The other part of me didn't like the idea of being committed to forty hours a week during my vacation time. I had big plans of sleeping in after all-night parties and going back home on the weekends. During our practice break, I had planned to go down to Tybee Island to my parents' beach house to chill out for a week or two.

"Yeah, I appreciate the offer, but I have to decline. Volunteering just isn't my thing, and I have a pretty busy summer ahead of me. You'll just have to find me something else to do."

Dr. McKensie narrowed his eyes at me. "Either you take the punishment handed to you, or you will no longer play football for our program."

A shudder went through me at Dr. McKensie's words. I hadn't expected that hardcore response at all. In all these years, there hadn't been a situation I couldn't talk myself out of. Since I couldn't seem to get the job done, I glanced over at my father. "Dad?" I questioned.

My father turned to me. Instead of resignation, there was irritation in them. "There's nothing I can do, Cade. It's working at The Ark or no football."

Whoa. Not even my father could get me out of this one. Oh

yeah, I was screwed. My fists clenched in my lap as I inwardly shouted, *Motherfucker!* Gah, I was so pissed that these bastards had me backed into a corner. Although part of me wanted to tell them where they could shove their offer, I bit my tongue. Football meant too much to me.

I gritted my teeth. “Fine. I’ll do it.”

“I’m glad you decided to see it our way.”

What I didn’t know at the time was how that moment was about to change everything about me.

Two

AVERY

"Miss P, who do you think is hotter: Zayn from One Direction or Drake?"

I glanced up to see four pairs of staring intently at me. While the question was a welcome change from the ones my professors had thrown at me the past semester in my pre-law classes at Emory University, it was still a loaded one. I mean, to twelve-year-old girls, there's nothing more serious than your celebrity crush, so it wasn't something I could just blow off without hurting their feelings. I also teetered around ticking one of them off by choosing the wrong guy.

"Hmm, that's a tough one. I mean, they're both pretty hot in different ways," I replied diplomatically.

Serena flipped her intricately braided cornrows over her shoulder. “Zayn’s too much of a pretty boy for me,” she said matter-of-factly.

Renee cocked her head at Serena. “What’s wrong with pretty boys?”

“I don’t want some guy who takes longer to get ready than me, puttin’ all kinds a product and shit in his hair.”

I stifled my laugh at her comment while also not chiding her about cursing. At the recreation center—or The Ark, as it was called—we overlooked a lot of what usually wouldn’t have flown in school. We tried to cultivate an environment of brutal realness that fostered trust. Kids were more likely to tell you about a potentially dangerous situation if they felt they could do it without repercussions.

I had started working at The Ark my freshman year at Emory as part of a service scholarship I’d won. While I might have been attending one of the best and most expensive universities in the country, I still had some common ground with the kids. My mom had been seventeen when she’d had me, and besides seeing a few pictures, I’d never met my father.

Instead of the poverty of the inner city, my mom and I had lived with my grandparents on a farm in rural Floyd County, Georgia. Because of what the farm produced, I’d thankfully never known the pangs of hunger like most of the kids at The Ark. Within the walls of our multigenerational household, I’d been blessed with constant love and affection, which was also something a lot of our kids deeply lacked.

I used the foundation of love and affection I'd been given back home to interact with the kids at The Ark. I never sat around on my phone or hung around talking to the other college-aged workers. Instead, I immersed myself in the kids' worlds. It was why I found myself sitting at the arts and crafts table when I had absolutely no artistic ability whatsoever. While Serena, Renee, and the other girls sketched or painted, I worked on coloring a picture from my Harry Potter adult coloring book.

"Miss P, do you have a boyfriend?" Serena suddenly asked.

Talk about loaded questions. I mean, the immediate answer was no. I'd been single since back in March when I'd broken up with my boyfriend of two years. Hal was a great guy, but regardless of how hard I tried, I couldn't feel for him what he felt for me. Yeah, it was your classic cliché of *It's not you, it's me,* but it was the truth. I wished I could say I missed him, but the truth was I didn't. It was my past yet again screwing things up for me in the present.

After coloring in Hermione's hair, I finally replied, "Nope. I don't."

"But why not?"

As I forced myself to look into Serena's curious eyes, I couldn't bring myself to tell her the truth. Although I was sure she and the other girls would have enjoyed the juicy story, I didn't want to shatter what innocence they had left when it came to love.

Although life hadn't dealt them a fair hand, it hadn't completely altered their fairytale view of love and significant others. I didn't want to burst their bubble before they had the chance to learn for themselves. After all, that was part of what being a teenager was all about—although in hindsight, I wished I'd listened more to my mother's "men are pigs" and "love stinks" tirades.

Just as I opened my mouth to try to answer her, I was interrupted by raised voices across the room.

"Girl, if I catch yo' skanky ass lookin' at Antoine one more time, I will fuck you up! You hear me?"

The words, along with the *I ain't messin' around* tone, foreshadowed trouble. I threw a fleeting glance at the two fourteen-year-old girls standing in a challenging stance before I rose out of my chair. "Hang tight, girls," I said to the group before I hustled across the room.

When I got to them, I placed a hand on each of their shoulders. "Jasmine, Arianna, you two need to take a deep breath and step back."

Jasmine flung my hand off her shoulder. She transferred her death glare from Arianna to me. "But Miss P, this skank-ass bitch was just making eyes at Antoine."

Arianna's nostrils flared as she jabbed a finger in Jasmine's face. "Who you callin' a skank-ass bitch, ho?"

"Enough," I growled as I wedged myself between them. I tossed a warning glance between the two teenagers. "Whatever—or I guess I should say *whoever* you're arguing about isn't worth it. What's the rule again?"

The girls mirrored each other by crossing their arms over their chests and rolling their eyes to the ceiling. Now it was my turn to take a deep breath while simultaneously weighing the best argument to diffuse the situation. I mean, I wasn't in my third year of pre-law at Emory for nothing.

"Let me take a moment to repeat the rule for you: any center member involved in a physical altercation faces immediate suspension with the possibility of permanent expulsion." When they both turned their heads to me with *WTF* expressions, I broke down the inflated language by saying, "You throw punches and you're both stuck at the shelter all day for the rest of the summer—maybe even forever."

The rigidity of their bodies loosened slightly as I could almost see the wheels in their heads turning. While The Ark wasn't a country club, it certainly beat the shelter.

When Jasmine took a step back, I exhaled in relief. After flinging her hair over shoulder, she said, "Guess when you have a hot man, bitches gonna be looking."

Arianna rolled her eyes. "Get it straight. I wasn't looking at your skeezy boyfriend."

At Jasmine's fist clenching, I wagged a finger at the two. "Don't make me give you solitary time."

Solitary was something I had come up with when I'd started at

The Ark. It was a way to give kids time to cool off as well as working on their writing and communication skills, which most of them desperately needed. While it might've sounded like some harsh, prison-type torture, solitary at The Ark basically consisted of sitting in the director's office while writing a summary of what you did wrong. You also had to write an apology letter to the person or persons you'd had a conflict with. It wasn't so much that they were scared of Tamar, the director—she was a mother figure to most of the kids there—but more about the being alone and having to actually express their emotions without yelling or punching. I was going for the whole 'the pen is mightier than the sword' kinda thing.

Jasmine's lip curled in disgust as she spit out, "Sorry."

I motioned for Arianna. "Your turn."

"I'm sorry," she spat.

"Good. Now go do five laps around the track."

Both their eyes widened in horror. "But Ms. P!" they both protested in unison.

"Then what about watching something together on TV?"

"What's the catch?" Jasmine questioned curiously.

"There's no catch. You two just end up spending some quality time together without fighting." When they both continued giving me skeptical looks, I added, "Most of all, it keeps you away from the boys in the gym."

"Fine. The last thing I wanna do is have Antoine see me all hot and sweaty from being outside," Jasmine replied.

"Good. Then go enjoy the TV in the cool."

Although the girls didn't hug and make extra nice like in some sugary sitcom, they did at least sit down together to watch some trash TV on E! For the dysfunctional life at The Ark, you could consider it a happy ending.

I'd barely gotten seated when Renee asked, "Are you gonna answer my question now, Miss P?"

"Um, yeah. Sure," I replied.

"Avery, can I see you for a second?" my boss, Tamar Deegan, called from her office doorway.

A chorus of "ooh" rang around me as I thanked my lucky stars for being saved yet again. "Uh oh, Miss P. You's in trouble," Serena chided.

"She's not in trouble," Tamar countered with a grin.

I wagged a finger playfully at Serena. "Ha. Guess she told you."

"Whatever," Serena grumbled as she went back to her coloring.

After following Tamar down the hallway, I slipped inside her lavender-infused smelling office. She was a firm believer in the power of essential oils, and she had the calming lavender running through the diffuser from morning until night.

As the door closed behind us, I jumped. For a moment, my stomach coiled with anxiety like it was back in the day and I'd just been called into the principal's office. While I might've been called into the principal's office now and then, I'd never actually been in trouble; it was usually to tell me about an award I'd won.

I licked my lips. "You weren't just putting the kids off, were you? I'm not really in trouble, am I?" I questioned, my voice wavering with the trepidation I felt.

Tamar smiled at me, her pearly white teeth contrasting against her caramel-colored skin. "Honestly, Avery, I can't imagine there ever being a time when you would be in trouble with me."

The breath I'd been holding whooshed out in a relieved rush. "Really?"

"Of course. I can't even begin to imagine this program running without you. Why I even get a little anxious when I think about you graduating and leaving us."

"Oh, I see." Warmth rushed to my cheeks under her praise, and I ducked my head. The truth was I couldn't imagine my life without The Ark either. It wasn't just about the fact that the program was tied to one of the scholarships that paid a chunk of my hefty tuition and without it I probably couldn't attend the extremely expensive pre-law program at Emory University—not to mention the monthly stipend I received helped pay for my apartment—but it was also about feeling I was making a difference in the world through the lives of the kids.

I had chosen law as my major not because I would get a fat paycheck, but so I could have a career that would allow me to stand up for those without a voice. Growing up relatively poor, I had seen too many times how people in power and those with money took advantage of those without it.

I met Tamar's gaze and smiled. "Thank you for the compliments. It means so much."

"I meant every word." She shifted some papers on her desk before picking up a manila folder. She tapped it with one of her French-manicured nails before speaking. "The reason I brought you in here deals with a community service request I received a week ago."

"Oh?" It wasn't often that we were asked to fulfill court-appointed community service hours. Because The Ark wanted to bring out the best in the attendees, it didn't make a lot of sense to have undesirables hanging around them. Usually we got athletes from the hometown teams of the Falcons, Hawks, and Braves, and sometimes we even had some of the college guys from Georgia Tech stop by.

Tamar nodded. "The dean of the athletic department at Tech reached out to me to help with a player of his who got himself into extreme hot water with a prank involving one of his professors."

Hmm, that had to be a first for The Ark. "What are they asking us to do?"

"The young man has been assigned forty-hour volunteer weeks for the entirety of the summer. Of course, he is getting leeway to work around his practice schedule. He also has to work at least two Friday and Saturday nights."

My eyes widened in surprise. "Whoa. That must've been an extreme prank to get him in that much trouble."

"Yes, that's part of it, but it also seems this young man comes from a privileged background. The dean wants him to see more of the world to try to appreciate all he has been given and not squander his potential. He feels if this young man were able to interact with the kids here—to see their strength, resiliency, and hope in spite of hardships life has dealt them—that it might help."

The word *privileged* caused me to shift uncomfortably in my seat. I might not have ever met this guy, but I had a pretty good idea what he was like. While I came from a humble background, I'd been thrust into a very privileged world my freshman year when I'd left public school and entered Harlington Prep School. My grades and standardized test scores got me in on a scholarship program, which of course made me stand out among the other kids who were there because of their parents' money and social standing. I drove a beat-up pickup truck to school while they drove brand new Mercedes and BMWs. I didn't get to take vacations and they went to exotic locations.

While the majority of my classmates had been nice and welcoming, there had been a select few of the A-crowd who'd made my life a living hell. A pang entered my chest as I thought about one person…one guy in particular from that group who had almost ruined my life.

"At first, I told the dean no. Even though we're slammed in the summertime and we could use the extra body, I didn't think I had the time to take on the responsibility. Then I realized I had someone who could take on the job for me, someone who could be a good role model for this young man and hopefully get him to see the error of his ways." She leaned back in her chair and smiled at me. "So are you up to it?"

I blinked a few times. "Me?"

Tamar chuckled. "Yes, you. After all, you are our very capable day manager."

Bolstered by Tamar's confidence in me, I quickly replied, "If you want me to do it, I certainly will."

"I hoped you would say that."

A knock at the door interrupted us. "That must be him now. I hope Mr. Privileged won't be offended that we didn't roll out the red carpet for him." Tamar grinned before rising out of her chair and heading around the desk. I stood up as the door opened.

"Mrs. Deegan?" a masculine voice questioned behind me.

"Yes, I'm Mrs. Deegan, but please call me Tamar. You must be Mr. Hall."

Hall. The last name plus the inflection and tone of the voice rang through my ears before reverberating through my mind. My past and present collided violently, causing me to shudder. As the realization crashed over me, it felt like I plummeted into icy waters.

No, no, no! This couldn't be happening. The city was too big to possibly have our paths cross again. Surely the universe couldn't despise me enough to bring me face to face again with the nightmare that continuously haunted me, the one guy I couldn't seem to get out of my mind no matter how hard I tried.

"Cade, I would like you to meet Avery Prescott. As our day manager, she will be overseeing your tenure here."

When Tamar stepped aside, I finally confirmed my deepest fears. Three years had passed since I'd seen him last. One thousand ninety-five days. A million and a half minutes.

In all that time, nothing had changed about him. He still had the same short, sandy blond hair I'd once teased him about, calling him a metrosexual because he put product in it. His blue eyes were still as clear as a cloudless summer sky. His body remained impossibly built with muscles straining against his navy blue Georgia Tech T-shirt, and sadly, the same arrogant air of superiority swirled around him.

Like a flash of jagged lightning cutting across the sky, I was no longer in Tamar's office. I was spirited away across the years to a different place, a different time, a different me…

I eased my grandfather's battered Chevy Cheyenne pickup truck into my assigned space. A pang of grief speared my chest as I killed the ignition. He'd only been gone six months, and sometimes it felt like just yesterday…others it felt like an eternity. He had been the only father I'd ever known while at the same time showering me with love and spoiling me as only a grandfather can.

Buttoning my pea coat closed against the December chill, I started across the parking lot and into school. As I got jostled in the crowd of black and white standard-issue Harlington Prep uniforms, I craned my neck, searching for him.

Just the thought of him sent warmth through my chest and a flush to my cheeks. So much had changed since I had left school on Friday afternoon. My entire romantic world had undergone a seismic shift all because of him. I couldn't wait to see him again. To hear his voice. To see his smile. To feel his lips on mine.

On the way to my locker, conversations silenced to a hum. Some people pointed. Some stared. Some whispered behind their hands. The skin underneath my uniform prickled as if sunburned from the attention. What could they possibly be looking at? Had I tucked my skirt into my underwear and was mooning everyone? Did I have a milk mustache from breakfast?

When I got to my locker, my questions were answered. I recoiled in horror at the words that had been carved into the metal. Whore. Slut. White trash. Somehow everyone knew about him and me. I wondered how that was even possible since we hadn't been in school. Since we had been together in the privacy of my mother's shop, no one could have possibly seen us. I hadn't spoken a word of it to anyone, and I didn't want to believe he had either. After all, we'd made a pact. A promise.

And yet, they knew.

God, I had to get out of there. I had to get away from all their judgmental and hateful stares. My gaze spun frantically around.

When my eye caught the sight of the girls' bathroom, I started toward it.

It was then I ran into him and a gang of his friends. One of them snickered. "Oh don't look now, dude, but it's your girlfriend*."*

I glanced up into his eyes. For a moment, I saw in them what I had before: a reflection of what I imagined had once been in my own eyes—attraction, caring, and...love.

"Dude, did you really sleep with her?" his friend, Renly, asked with disgust.

At that moment, the emotion drained out of his eyes. It was like looking into the lifeless eyes of a shark. He was no longer who I thought he was—the one who had stolen my heart, as well as my virginity.

He jerked his chin up at me and pinned at me with an icy look that caused me to tremble. "Yeah, I did, but trust me, it was nothing more than a mercy fuck." He clapped a hand onto Renly's shoulder. "Think of it like throwing a dog a bone, but in this case, it was a boner."

I gasped as the roar of cruel laughter stung my ears while the enormity of his words pierced my heart. Although I tried not to cry in front of him or the others, tears pricked against the backs of my eyelids. Before I knew it, sobs rolled through me as my chest caved in from the jagged pieces of my broken heart.

Desperate to get away from him, I raced across the hallway to the bathroom. I slung my backpack and purse to the floor and started for a stall. I wanted nothing more than to hide myself away from the horrible accusations being thrown at me.

I pinched my eyes shut while desperately hoping to wake up and find that his rejection had all been a horrible nightmare.

Was that truly what is was? A mercy fuck? Had his declaration that he was falling for me just been a joke? After everything we had been through over the last four months, why would he lie to me like that? What had I ever done to deserve his heartless treatment?

Before I could hide, someone rushed at me and pushed me into the stall. Before I knew what was happening, a hand was at my neck and my lower back. "Stop it!" I cried. My plea for mercy was ignored as my head was placed precariously close to the toilet bowl.

My assailant and I fumbled around on the floor. "This is what happens to dirty whores who think they can fuck someone else's guy," a familiar voice whispered in my ear. The girl who thought he had belonged to her. The girl he had humiliated by momentarily appearing to choose me, even if it was nothing more than a fuck to him. It should have been him that was being treated like that, not me.

I screamed as my arms were painfully wrenched behind my back. The next thing I knew my head was dumped into the toilet water. I didn't know how long she kept me face down before bringing me back up. When I resurfaced, laughter echoed around me. "Drown the skank!" someone cheered before I was thrust back down into the water again.

Although I was fighting with everything I had in me to break free, a part of me wanted to give in. I wanted to succumb to the soul-crushing hurt and humiliation. To stop the flailing of my arms and legs as I fought against my captor. To widen my mouth and allow the water to overflow and overtake my lungs. To let the heart that had been betrayed and ultimately broken by him cease beating.

What chance of happiness did I have in the future if I had so misread his feelings? How would I ever be able to trust again?

The thoughts of defeat were intense but fleeting. They were chased from my mind by a stronger will to survive and overcome.

My savior came in the form of the bell ringing for first period. The arms and hands that held me bound released me as a flurry of activity came from outside the stall. I jerked my head out of the water and took in several heaving breaths of air. Then I began gagging before throwing up some of the water that had gotten into my mouth.

It was then I realized I wasn't completely alone. She was still there.

After she fisted a handful of my hair, she twisted my head back. "Even though he's made it clear that he wants nothing more to do with your pathetic self, I'll fuck you up even worse if you ever try anything with him again. You hear me?" When I didn't answer, she gripped my hair even tighter. "I said, do you hear me!"

"Yes," I croaked.

She released my hair and shoved my face to the floor then backed out of the stall and got her things. She calmly left the bathroom like nothing out of the ordinary had happened.

Although I literally only lay there for a few minutes, symbolically it would take years for me to pick myself up off that bathroom floor.

THREE

CADE

Fuuuuuuuuuck! This seriously was *not* happening. Just when I thought things couldn't get any worse, apparently the universe didn't just hate me, it fucking *despised* me. Not only was I stuck working forty hours a week at this shithole, but now I had the worst blast from my past standing before me. Avery Fucking Prescott.

In the world of every manwhore who seems to have no soul, there is one girl he regrets. One girl he thinks about from time to time. One girl he measures all the other ones against. One girl he even cries about when he's shitfaced.

Mine was Avery Fucking Prescott.

I couldn't help noticing that the Avery standing in front of me didn't seem the same. Sure, she still had the same long, dark hair swept back in one of those ponytail things, but gone were the glasses, which made it a lot easier to see her green eyes and the flecks of gold in them. Of course, there was also pure and unadulterated hate burning in them where back in the day, there had been love.

I had managed to kill that love by being a prick. Yeah, I'm sure you're thinking that isn't all too shocking based on the pure stupidity you've seen me exhibit so far. The thing was Avery had brought out the good buried deep down inside me, the good you needed a fucking bulldozer to unearth.

While there were slight differences in her appearance, her entire personality seemed different, and no, I don't just mean that she hated me with a fiery passion. She wasn't the wide-eyed, innocent farm girl who had seemed so out of place at Harlington Prep. It was like she'd had a personality transplant. It reminded of me of what had happened to my older sister Catherine the summer she turned fifteen and my mother sent her off to some glamour school shit to detox the awkward out of her. When she came back a month later, it was like she had become a Stepford Kid. Catherine no longer took the time to play with me. She had "more important" things to do like contouring her brows or preparing for cotillions. Things were never the same between us after that.

My ego couldn't help wondering if what had happened between us had caused the seismic shift in Avery, like I'd broken the old Avery with my actions and this was what had been rebuilt in its place. Another voice rationalized that unlike me, Avery had probably gotten her shit together in the last three years. College had matured her.

After a few moments of a silent standoff, Avery said, "Hello again, Cade." Her words might have been polite, but her voice was strained. I could tell it was taking everything within her not to go off on me.

"Oh, you two know each other?" Tammy—or Theresa, or whatever the hell her name was—questioned.

Do we know each other? Oh yeah, we know each other, like in the biblical sense. I can even tell you about the heart-shaped birthmark on the inside of her right thigh.

I knew I would mortify the hell out of Avery if I said anything like that in front of her boss, so instead I cocked my brows at Avery to indicate that she should take the lead on how she wanted us to respond to that question.

"A little. We went to high school together," she replied diplomatically. The wounded look that momentarily flashed in her eyes told an entirely different story—the story where I played the villain—but Tammy didn't seem to pick up on it.

"Well, isn't it a small world?" Tammy mused.

"Yeah," Avery and I said in unison.

Tammy smiled at me. "I was just about to sing all of Avery's praises to you, but since you know her, I don't need to waste my breath, right?"

"Right," I muttered.

"Well then, I'll leave you two alone to catch up, and Avery can show you the ropes."

"Thank you, Tamar," Avery said politely.

Oh, it was Tamar. Shit, I needed to remember that. "Yeah, thanks, Tamar."

Tamar started out of the door and then stopped. She threw a grin over her shoulder. "Now, Avery, just because you know Cade, you can't go easy on him. He has a debt to pay to Georgia Tech's athletic department." Apparently Tamar wasn't picking up on the heavy tension between us.

Avery glared at me before flashing a fake smile at Tamar. "Oh, I promise to make him earn his keep."

"Unfuckingbelievable," I muttered under my breath after the door closed.

"Excuse me?" Avery demanded.

I held up my hands. "Nothing."

Avery crossed her arms over her chest. "I never thought I'd have to see you again." She shook her head at me, which caused her ponytail to swish back and forth like a whip. "Yet here you are standing before me. I guess I must've done something epic to piss the universe off enough to put you back in my path."

Whoa, that was sure as hell not what I was expecting. "I could say the same."

Her green eyes narrowed to fury-filled slits. "Excuse me? You have some nerve to stand here in front of me and say that considering what you did."

She was right. Only an epic tool would not immediately apologize for what I did to her. It should have been the first words out of my mouth, and not just to make things run smoothly there at The Ark, but because it was the right thing to do. After all, she had truly been an innocent in the whole fucked up situation of me being an emotionally crippled bastard. I'd let her be tortured by a psychotic chick who thought she belonged to me. I'd humiliated her with my deceptive words and cruel actions, but the greatest of my crimes was that I had broken her heart.

In this instance, I was being King Epic Tool because I couldn't get those words to come out of my mouth. It wasn't something I was struggling with for the first time. I'd had three years to stay those two words. Hell, I'd started off a hundred texts, but I'd never sent them. I'd even done a few stalkerish drives by her house to say how sorry I was in person, but being an emotional pansy ass, I had never gotten out of the car.

So instead of taking the emotional high road, I went slumming. "It's been three years, Prescott. You really need to get over that."

Avery's mouth gaped open and closed like a fish gasping for its last breath. Yeah, yeah, I know what you're thinking, and I totally agree—it was a fucking heartless thing to say. I could have just said mumbled a "whatever" and asked for her to hurry up and show me around, but no, I had to go for the jugular like I was an animal or something.

I waited for her to burst into tears, but once again, I had underestimated this new Avery. The only emotion that radiated in her eyes was pure hate. I'm not gonna lie, it was a little scary.

"I see you're still an unimaginable bastard. Guess some things never change," Avery snapped.

Holding my ground, I swept my hands to my hips. "Are you going to stand here all day giving me shit, or are you going to show me around like your boss told you to?"

Avery's fists clenched at her sides. Part of me was mildly amused at the thought of her taking me on. This hellcat side of her was one I wasn't used to. "Fine. Let's go," she hissed. She then power walked out of Tamar's office, and I practically had to break into a sprint to catch up with her.

After my "sentencing", I had done a little reading about The Ark. It had been a run-down YMCA when Amad had purchased it and then renovated it. There were two stories that included an indoor basketball gym, an Olympic-sized pool, and a small outdoor playfield that had once been a parking lot.

Once we got out of the hallway, Avery motioned to an open room. "This meeting area is where we do quiet activities like art projects and tutoring." There were two cafeteria-like tables set up along with several easels.

She pointed to the right. "Over there is the theater room where we watch preapproved movies on a schedule of ten, noon, two, and four. Kids are allowed popcorn and sodas inside."

"That's a sweet setup."

Her eyes widened at my comment. I suppose she hadn't expected me to have anything nice to say about the place. "The kids really enjoy it. We do a monthly fieldtrip to the local movie theater as well since most of the kids would never have the opportunity to go."

"I see."

We walked on past the main room. I knew we were getting close to the pool when the smell of chlorine entered my nose. I peered through the glass to see a couple of kids splashing around. "Pool hours are from nine to three," Avery said.

"I'll have to remember to bring my suit."

"That won't be necessary since we have a lifeguard on duty during those hours."

"Maybe an after-hours swim?" Since I was still being a relentless tool, I added, "If memory serves me correctly, you and I enjoyed a swim together back in the day."

When Avery's body tensed, I knew she was remembering that day. What she wouldn't be able to recall was that that was the day I had the first stirrings for her above and below the waist. In a pair of cutoffs, a faded tank top, and a worn pair of cowboy boots, she was straight out of every guy's farm girl wet dream. I'd also gotten to see the usually straight-laced good girl go a little bad, but I'll get to that later on.

Avery quickly recovered and started past the pool. She swept a lanyard with a set of keys over her heard. After unlocking the door, she opened it and motioned me inside. "This is the athletic storage room."

The room was lined with wall-to-wall shelves. There were almost deflated footballs and basketballs along with some beat-up looking bats and dingy gray baseballs. "Damn, this equipment looks like it's been through the wringer."

"We do the best we can with what we have. The center is all privately funded, and with a very tight budget, we have to pay for staff, utilities, and food."

I held up my hands. "Excuse me for making an observation. I was just expecting better considering Amad Carlson is in charge of all of this."

"And what is that supposed to mean?"

"I just imagined as a baller, he would care about having good sports equipment."

"He's a busy guy who doesn't bother himself with the ins and outs of The Ark."

"Maybe he should. Maybe someone should give him a call and ask for a little more dough for new sports equipment."

"*Maybe* we should just be grateful for what we're given and not always expect to have the best handed to us," she countered.

Ah, now she was she was making it personal. Back in the day, she hadn't been a fan of the spoiled-little-rich-boy part of me. She had succeeded in making me see the world differently, at least for a little while. We'd only had four months together, so she needed more time to eradicate the eighteen years of indulgence I'd been accustomed to.

"Maybe I can check around at Tech and see if we have some extras that aren't so worn out."

Talk about shocking someone. The blown away expression on Avery's face was priceless. Of course, it also stung a little. Once upon a time, she had been able to see that deep down inside me there was a halfway decent guy. "You'd really do that?" she asked.

"Sure. Why not?"

"Just seems out of character for you."

"Yeah, well, if I remember correctly, there was a time when you didn't think I was such a heartless bastard."

Avery didn't respond. Instead, she whirled around and hustled out of the storage room. After I followed her, she locked the door back. Without another word to me, she started down the hall.

"Here are the basketball courts."

"Really? And I would have thought that was a baseball field," I quipped with a wink. I mean, the mood desperately needed some lightening.

My effort was rewarded with Avery rolling her eyes. "I see you're still a smartass."

"If you say so."

"Oh, I know so. Only a smartass would feel the need to do childish pranks."

I grimaced. "Ah, so you know about that, huh?"

"I don't know the specifics, but I do know you pulled a prank that got you in enough trouble to have you here." She gave me a pointed look. "Not to mention, I do know about your past indiscretions."

With a laugh, I countered, "I didn't hack into a laptop this time."

"If you weren't flexing your hacking skills, what exactly did you do?"

"Streaked through an alumni dinner to get back at a professor who gave me my first C."

Avery blinked at me a few times. "Please tell me you're not serious."

"Nope." I swept my right hand up. "And that's the truth, the whole truth, and nothing but the truth, so help me God."

The corners of her lips quirked as if she was fighting a smile. "Nice courtroom allusion there."

"Thank you. I thought it was a nice touch since I remember one of us wanting to be an attorney."

"I start law school in the fall."

"Holy shit. You're already through undergrad?" When Avery nodded, I said, "Now I remember that you graduated early and started college."

When a strangled cry came from Avery's lips, I instantly regretted mentioning her starting college early. Everything that had gone down between us had happened in December of senior year just before the end of the semester. I hadn't had to see her again after that until she'd stood before our class a salutatorian.

"I need to show you the gym," she said in a strained voice.

I refrained from making a smartass remark that I really didn't need to see inside because I got the basic principle. Instead, I opened the door and allowed her to brush past me. When her perfume entered my nose, I couldn't help closing my eyes. Damn, she smelled good. It was the same mixture of peaches and strawberries she'd smelled like in high school, some kind of natural shampoo she got at the local farmer's market. It was nice knowing at least one thing about her hadn't changed.

There were about twenty boys and three girls out on the court. Their ages ranged from roughly fourteen to seventeen, and they represented all colors and races. Some were just absentmindedly dribbling balls and shooting the shit with friends while others engaged in a game complete with a volunteer ref making calls.

The sound of a real whistle caused both of us to stop. When we turned around, a grinning African-American teen waved at us. "Lookin' good, Miss P," a guy said as he wagged his eyebrows. He looked around sixteen, and the fact that he was clearly jailbait didn't seem to stop him from flirting with Avery.

"Thank you, Darion."

He jerked his chin up at me. "Who's that? Your boyfriend?"

A chorus of "oohs" and kissy noises rang around us, which caused Avery's face to turn blood red. It reminded me of the old Avery I had known who always wore her embarrassment on her sleeve.

"No, he's not my boyfriend."

Darion curiously sized me up. "Then what's he doing here?"

Without missing a beat, Avery replied, "He's here to volunteer with you guys."

My brows shot up in surprise. In a low voice, I asked, "Is that what we're calling it? *Volunteering?*"

Turning her back to the guys, Avery hissed, "It's better than them thinking you have to be here with them, or that you're a spoiled, overgrown child who can't keep out of trouble."

"Watch it with the claws, Prescott."

After giving me an *eat shit and die* look, Avery whirled back around to the guys. "This is Cade Hall. You can call him Mr. Hall."

Darion motioned to my Tech shirt. "You a fan?"

"Actually, I go there, and I play football."

His dark eyes widened. "You for real?"

"Yeah."

Darion whirled around. "Marcus, Antoine, get over here!" When the two teens threw him questioning looks, he added, "This dude plays football for Tech!"

That was all it took to have the guys hustling over. "You really play for Tech?" the tallest of the two asked.

"Sure do."

Darion grinned. "Damn, I can't believe I'm meetin' a real baller!"

When I glanced at Avery about the cussing, she gave a slight shake of her head.

"I mean, Jamal Jenkins came by two years ago before I was hanging out here, but Antoine got to meet him, didn't ya?"

Antoine nodded. "He gave us signed balls, too." He gave me a look that asked where my signed balls were.

"I'll be happy bring you guys some balls next time. Maybe I can get some of the other guys on the team to sign them as well."

"That would be tight," Marcus said.

Darion's eyes grew bright. "We's just about done playin' basketball—"

"We're," Avery corrected.

After waving a hand flippantly at her, Darion replied, "Fine then. "*We're* about to go play football. You gotta come throw the ball around with us, tell us what you think of our form and shit."

"You want to play college ball?" I questioned.

Darion nodded. "I started varsity this year as a freshman. Coach says I'm sure to get recruiters after me before junior year, maybe even lock up a scholarship by then."

With Darion starting varsity, he wasn't just bullshitting me; he obviously had talent. I turned to Avery. "So, I guess I can hang out with the boys, you know, throw some balls around, something like that."

Avery shocked me by shaking her head. "No. I don't think you'll have time for that."

"Why wouldn't I? It's not like I have anything better to do."

Ignoring me, Avery said, "Boys, go ahead and go outside. I need to talk to Mr. Hall for a minute."

Although they looked bummed out, they didn't argue with Avery. "Maybe tomorrow then," Darion said hopefully.

"Maybe," Avery said tersely.

Once the boys jogged out of sight, I shook my head at Avery. "What's your problem?"

"Excuse me?"

"You heard me. I want to know what bug you have up your ass to not let me hang out with the guys."

"I'm sorry, Cade, but you're mistaken if you think that you're just going to 'hang out' for your service hours. You have a debt to pay to the athletic board at Georgia Tech."

"Well, duh, that debt could be played working with those kids."

She stared at me for a minute like the wheels in her head weren't just turning but whizzing. "I'm afraid you just won't have time to play today. We have a lot of work that needs to be done around here."

I cocked my brows rose at her. "Like what?"

"Well, for starters, the staff and kids' bathrooms need cleaning."

I jerked my chin up and smirked at her. "Hold the phone, sweetheart. You actually expect me to clean?"

"Yes, I do."

"Babe, you should know me better than that. I've never had to clean my own apartment, so I'm sure as hell not cleaning some grungy homeless kid bathrooms."

Avery's eyes flared. "Jesus, do you actually hear the bullshit you're spouting?"

"Yes, actually I do, and it's not bullshit—it's the truth."

"Other people might care about who you are, or that you play for Tech, or that your daddy is a big shot congressman, but I don't. The posh little world you're used to outside the doors of The Ark doesn't mean anything while you're in here." A truly evil smile curled on her lips, one I would have never imagined the old Avery capable of. "Inside these walls, you do exactly what I say. If I say clean the bathrooms, you'll do it, and you'll do it to my satisfaction."

"If you think I'm going to be your bitch, you have another thing coming."

"Get this straight, *sweetheart*. You *will* be my *bitch*, as you call it."

I closed the gap between us. "Just try it, and I'll rat you out to Tammy and get your ass fired."

"Is there a problem here?" a voice questioned behind us.

I whirled around to see Tammy staring curiously at us. "Yes, there is a huge problem. Miss Prescott here is confused. She thinks she is my boss, and in turn, that I'm some little bitch who is going to clean shit. I was just telling her that you would sort it out, Tammy."

"My name is Tamar, Mr. Hall," she replied coolly.

"Whatever. I'll just go throw around the football with the boys while you two get things straight."

When I started to breeze past her, Tamar grabbed my arm. "There is nothing to get straight, Mr. Hall. While I might be the head of the program here at The Ark, Miss Prescott is the day manager. That means that all employees answer to her, which includes you." She pursed her lips at me. "I'm seeing now that you are living up to the reputation in your file, and it is not one to be proud of."

"So you're actually going to let Avery boss me around and make me do menial shit?"

"Yes, Mr. Hall, I am. It is clear to me that you have more than earned a little dirty work."

"Is that right?" I challenged.

"It is. Now I will leave you to your work." She glanced at Avery. "Carry on, Miss Prescott."

"Thank you, Tamar," Avery replied. She then gave me a sickeningly sweet smile. "Now as I was saying about the bathrooms."

* * *

By the end of my first day, it was pretty clear that Avery held a grudge the size of the Grand Canyon against me and was going to make payback a real bitch. It started with having to clean the nasty-as-hell bathrooms. At first, I hadn't wanted to clean the bathrooms on principle, but then I thought, how hard could it be to swish a brush around the inside of the toilet bowl and run a mop over the floor? I mean, it sure didn't look hard when our cleaning lady did it.

What I hadn't taken the time to think about was the difference in what our bathrooms at home were like compared to public ones. I had once thought the communal bathrooms in the dorms were bad, but they didn't have jack shit on the bathrooms at the center. I realized that when I entered the first stall.

I'm not sure what could possibly get you turned on at the center, but some asshat had managed to blow his load all over one of the stalls—and we're not talking about fresh cum. I'm talking about being given some spatula looking thing to rake that shit off. The janitor, whose nametag said Bill, had gleefully handed it over to me along with a box of gloves.

"Dude, don't you have some hazmat suit or something for me to wear?"

He chuckled. "Nope. Have fun. I'll be in my office watching Sports Center if you need me."

"Thanks a hell of a lot," I grumbled.

I spent the next hour scraping cum off the walls and bleaching out the shit stains in the toilet. Once I finished in the boys' restrooms, I had to go to the girls', and I couldn't believe it when I found the girls' bathroom was way worse than the boys'. Puckered lip marks on the mirrors took forever to scrub off, not to mention the effort it took to get up all the ground-in eye shadow and blush shit on the floor. The worst was having to unclog one of the toilets where a tampon had gotten stuck. That shit caused me to gag until I eventually lost my lunch.

Once I finished something, Avery had to come check to make sure it was satisfactory, and nothing I did was satisfactory to Miss Raging Revenge Bitch. She always made me do it over. I had never been more grateful when the clock read six, meaning I could get the fuck out of there.

When I got home, I wanted nothing more than to take a scalding hot shower to wash off the gross shit I'd gotten on me, but I was way too tired, so I trudged over to the couch and collapsed face first.

When I closed my eyes, Avery's face was all I could see—but it wasn't raging revenge Avery, it was sweet, adoring Avery. The one with the shy smiles and red cheeks caused by me saying something that embarrassed her. The Avery who sucked in her bottom lip when she was really concentrating on something. The Avery who could debate world affairs and also drive a corn harvester on her family's farm. God, I missed that Avery.

I didn't know how long I'd been lying there when I awoke to Jonathan shaking me.

"Wake up. We're going to be late to the party."

Groaning, I rolled over and rubbed my eyes. "I don't think I'm going."

"Um, have you forgotten how epic Brittany's parties are?" Jonathan questioned.

Brittany was our neighbor on the fourth floor. She'd introduced herself three months before by flashing her tits at me in the elevator. She was a swimmer with a hell of a body and a trust fund that enabled serious partying.

"No, I haven't forgotten."

"Then why the hell aren't you already up off the couch?"

I yawned. "Because I'm tired as hell."

"Don't tell me a bunch of teenagers wore you out."

Brandon snorted. "He's probably exhausted from the hero worship."

"I wish," I grumbled.

Jonathan shoved my legs over before flopping down on the couch. "What happened?"

"I didn't get to throw around a football or just hang out with the kids."

"So what did you do?" Brandon asked.

"I cleaned toilets, scrubbed floors, and cleaned and rearranged two storerooms."

Brandon whistled. "Holy shit, dude. You must have the most hard-ass boss ever."

"Yeah, she is," I grumbled.

"It's a she?" Jonathan questioned.

"Unfortunately yes."

Brandon scratched his chin. "Hmm, she must be one of those bitches who have it in for jocks. Like because some baller didn't like her, she has some vendetta out against all players."

"It's something like that, except a little more personal."

Jonathan narrowed his eyes at me. "What do you mean?"

"I need a beer first."

Brandon nodded and ducked into the kitchen. When he returned, he handed it to me. I gulped down two long pulls. "So senior year there was this girl named Avery—"

"The Avery you cried about that one time?" Jonathan asked.

While I threw him a death glare, Brandon stared at me with wide eyes. "You actually cried about a girl?"

"One fucking time, and I was drunk."

He shook his head. "Damn, man, I didn't think you had it in you."

Of the three of us, Brandon was the most decent when it came to girls. He had more of a sensitive side than Jonathan or me. It probably came from being the only boy in a family with three older sisters; the estrogen just wore off on him. Of course, as insensitive assholes, Jonathan and I liked to give him shit about it.

"Finish your story," Jonathan instructed.

I downed the last of my beer. After a massive burp erupted from my lips, I said, "You could say it all started with

Shakespeare…"

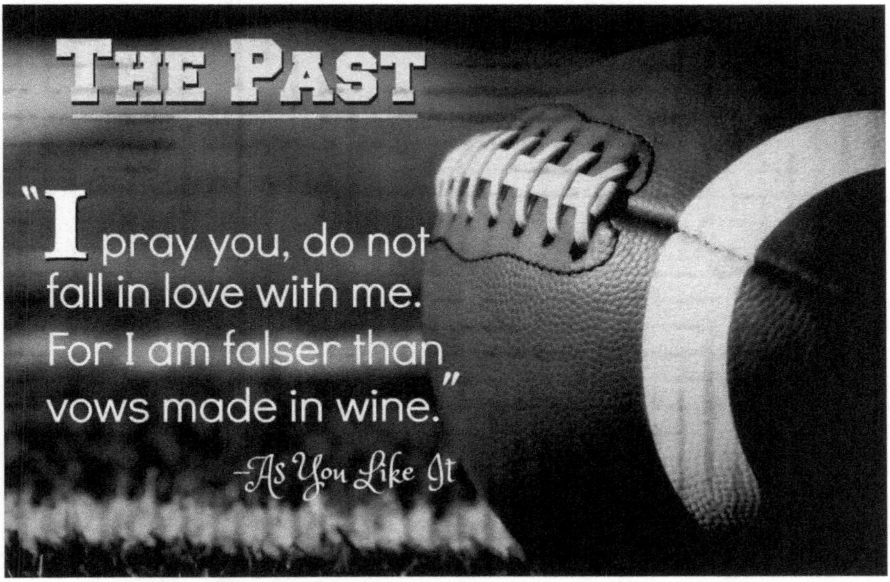
THE PAST
"I pray you, do not fall in love with me. For I am falser than vows made in wine."
-As You Like It

FOUR

AVERY

After grabbing my last period's books, I slammed my locker shut and jogged down the hall to my British literature class, ducking inside just before the warning bell rang. Keeping my head down, I made my way down the row of single file desks and slid into mine. While others chattered around me, I took out my notebook and started copying down the daily warm-up.

Once the final bell rang and several stragglers hurried inside, Dr. Paulson closed the door. She then waved her hands, signaling for us to quiet down, and the room immediately silenced. With her silver hair and grandmotherly sweaters, Dr. Paulson might've appeared to be a sweet old lady, but she ruled her class with steely reserve.

She adjusted her glasses as she stood before the lectern at the front of the classroom. "Before we get started on the reading, I will be assigning you your partners for the Shakespeare project."

Oh yeah, that was today. The Shakespeare project was legendary for seniors. You were given a particular theme that you had to explore in Shakespeare's works. Part of me was excited to start work on what would be almost like a college thesis. Since it was a persuasive paper and presentation, I would get to flex the argumentative muscles I hoped to one day use as an attorney. Of course, I had to get through law school first.

The other part of me was less than thrilled about the presentation part. It wasn't so much that I hated speaking in front of people; it was more about the fact that having to work with an assigned partner made me want to die a thousand deaths. As an introvert, I'd hated group assignments when I had attended public school, and it had become even more agonizing when I'd come to Harlington. Small talk became increasingly more difficult when you tried to make it with people who were way outside your social realm. The thirty-acre working farm I lived on was a far cry from the mansions my peers called home.

Dr. Paulson cleared her throat and began rattling off names and themes. "Avery Prescott and Cade Hall, you will be working on the theme of anti-love and anti-romance in Shakespeare's greatest love stories."

I blinked a few times. Surely I had misunderstood her. At what must've been my blank stare, Dr. Paulson gave me a disapproving look. "Avery, aren't you writing this down?"

Her admonishment caused me to fumble for my pen. "Yes ma'am," I replied as I scribbled down the information my brain refused to process.

When I wrote the name *Cade Hall*, I shuddered. Oh no. No, no, no! This couldn't be happening. Out of a class of twenty-five students, I couldn't possibly have been assigned to work with *him*. Instantly, I thought of the line from Casablanca: *"Out of all the gin joints, in all the towns, in all the world, she had to walk into mine."*

I fought to catch my breath as anxiety pricked over my body, causing me to shudder. *Cade Hall was my partner*.

When I dared to sneak a peek at him over my shoulder, I found him staring straight at me. He then winked at me. I whipped my head back around and stared at my notebook. Ugh, he was such a player. I mean, who winks at their future project partner in the middle of British lit?

I don't know why I was surprised. After all, Cade's reputation was legendary at Harlington, which was saying a lot considering he'd only enrolled the second semester of the previous year. Apparently he'd been kicked out of his last private school over the Christmas break of his junior year and Harlington was willing to overlook some of his indiscretions because of his football talent. Then there was also the fact that his dad was a state representative and had apparently given the school a sizeable donation.

Although he hadn't even been at Harlington a full year, he'd managed to screw his way through most of the A-crowd girls not just in the senior class, but in the junior and sophomore classes as well. Right then, Elspeth Manning, the Regina George of Harlington, had her hooks in him. They had just been nominated to homecoming court for the senior class, and it seemed like a no-brainer that they would be named king and queen.

Once Dr. Paulson finished assigning partners, she handed out the paper and presentation requirements. I hung on to every word and jotted down notes in the margins. When I once again looked back at Cade, he wasn't even paying attention. Instead, he was sneaking a glance at his phone, which he had hidden in his lap. Although we could have iPads and laptops out in class, phones were banned. It made perfect sense that Mr. Rule Breaker would totally disregard the policy.

I didn't know why Cade's apathy surprised me. British lit was the only class I had with him, but he always seemed to just coast along. He never volunteered in discussions, and he only participated when Dr. Paulson called on him. Surprisingly, he always had something seemingly intelligent to say in reply.

The bell rang, but none of us moved. Dr. Paulson had made it clear from day one that she dismissed class, not the bell. "That's it for today. Don't forget to read Act III in *Richard III* for tomorrow's discussion."

After sliding my book and notebook into my backpack, I felt a presence looming over me. I glanced up into Cade's smirking face. He swept a hand rather dramatically to his chest. "So, Prescott, aren't you the lucky one getting me as a partner?"

"You actually know my name?" I questioned incredulously.

"Yep."

Well, that was certainly surprising considering he was part of the A-crowd, and I was who I was. I wasn't even sure I had a crowd at Harlington. Most of my friends were from my days in public school. If I did have a crowd, it would be somewhere down the line, like D or E.

Before that day, I didn't think Cade had said two words to me unless it was to try to bum a pencil or paper. He leaned back against the desk in front of me, which caused his ample biceps to strain against his standard white button-down. "Anyway, I was thinking if you were cool with it, we should probably head over to the library for a planning session."

My mouth gaped open. I hadn't expected Cade to be so gung-ho about working on the project. After all, he'd always impressed me more as the ultimate slacker guy who waited until the night before something was due. "Um, yeah, I'd like to, but I have to be at work in half an hour."

"We could make it quick. Could you call them and ask to be a little late?"

I shook my head. "I'm the only one my mom has to relieve her." At his scrunched brows, I added, "You see, it's my mom's business. She owns an antique store with a teahouse inside. Well, it's actually a little more than just a teahouse because we serve sandwiches, soups, and desserts along with coffee."

Shut up, Avery! The guy asked a simple question. He doesn't need to hear your life's story. Next you'll be telling him about your mom having you at seventeen and how you've never met your father.

"That sounds cool," Cade mused. His tone had me wishing the floor would open up and swallow me whole.

"Yeah, it is pretty cool. She makes a lot of natural products like lotions and shampoo, too. She's really talented." *Seriously, kill me now.* What was it about Cade that made me have verbal diarrhea? Most of the time, I clammed up around guys from Harlington. The only boys I'd dated were from my public school days, and even then, I wasn't overly chatty.

"Sounds like it."

And then I did something totally out of character for me. "If you're really set on working today, you could come to the shop, and then we could get some work done between customers."

Cade's brows shot up. "Really?"

I nodded. "It's usually slow in the afternoons."

"Okay. That sounds great." He dug his phone out of his pants pocket. "What's the address?"

"2131 Main Street. It's called Rose's Garden. I always tease my mom about being narcissistic and naming it after herself since her name is Rose." I then did a very unattractive and embarrassing snort. “Well, it’s Rose Prescott, not Rose Garden.”

Amusement twinkled in Cade’s blue eyes. “I don’t think I’ve ever heard you talk so much, Prescott.”

Mortification rocketed through me. “Sorry,” I muttered.

“Nothin’ to apologize about. I’m glad to see you actually have a personality. No offense, but I kinda thought you were a social mutant who never spoke except to the teacher.”

“Um, no. I can be quite social when I want to be, thank you very much.”

Cade grinned. “I didn’t mean to insult you.”

“You didn’t.”

“Yeah, I did. That’s why you got all pissy.”

“I wasn’t pissy. I was just stating facts,” I challenged in a huff.

Instead of Cade getting “pissy” back, he merely laughed. “This is going to be fun, Prescott.”

“If you say so.”

“Oh, I know so. It’s always fun when a girl doesn’t take my shit. It so rarely happens. Most are willing to put up with anything just to hang out with me.”

“Rest assured, I’m not like other girls.”

“I’m well aware of that.” Cade was momentarily distracted by his phone vibrating in his pocket. “Listen, I’m gonna run by the dorm and change outta this get-up then I’ll head your way. How does that sound?”

“It sounds fine.”

Cade nodded. "See ya."

"See ya," I echoed as I watched him walk away.

* * *

Once Cade left, I hurried out of the building and across the parking lot to my truck. After tossing my bag in the front seat, I cranked it up and headed away from Harlington's campus. Most of the students who attended Harlington lived in the dorms, but there were a few like myself who lived off campus. It was twenty minutes to the farm where I lived with my mom and grandmother, but just ten minutes to downtown Rome, Georgia, where Rose's Garden was.

When she'd had me at seventeen, my mom's hopes and dreams of escaping small-town life with a softball scholarship to an out-of-state college were dashed. She dropped out of school and got her GED. For most of my childhood, she pinged around several different waitressing and secretarial jobs while going to school at night. She also spent time on her hobby of making soaps and lotions. After she earned her business degree, she decided what she wanted to do more than anything was open a teahouse and antique store. That's when Rose's Garden was born. So far it had been a huge success. She was even talking about expanding to a second store.

I swung around to the back parking lot and then hopped out of my truck and headed inside. Once I unlocked the door, the smell of aged furniture and brewing tea invaded my nostrils as Ella James piping in over the stereo speakers filled my ears. When it was just my mom, she played the classic crooners to give a bygone ambiance to the antique side of the shop. As soon as she left, I switched over to the local pop station.

I ducked into the employee bathroom to ditch one uniform for another. Since my mom liked a vintage feel for the store, she wanted her employees—her niece, Mae, and me—to dress vintage as well. I had a navy dress with white polka dots and a halter neck that made me appear like I stepped out of the 1950s. While I didn't hate the uniform, I would have been much more comfortable in jeans and a T-shirt, something like what they wore across town at Starbucks. Since nothing about me screamed pin-up girl hottie, I felt like a phony. My cousin, Mae, on the other hand, fit right into the persona with her long legs, push-up bras, and bubbly confidence.

After hanging up my Harlington uniform, I exited the bathroom and hurried out to the main room. Mom had taken two stores and renovated them into one enormous room. One side housed all the necessities for the teahouse. It had a vintage counter with stools, and behind it was the preparation area for the tea and goodies. Out on the main floor area were several tables and chairs along with two overstuffed sofas. As for the antique store side, it was packed with all sorts of things from large pieces of furniture to smaller lamps and china.

Gazing around the store, I couldn't help the pride that flowed through me. My mom had worked so hard to bulldoze the stereotype that a girl who got pregnant in high school couldn't make something of herself. She now sat on the board of entrepreneurs at the chamber of commerce.

Speaking of my mom, I spotted her willowy form over in the antique section where a blue-haired lady was eyeing a 19th-century sideboard. When my mother glanced over at me, I smiled and waved. She threw her hand up before motioning for me to go ahead and get behind the counter.

Although my mother was beautiful and not socially awkward like me, she struggled with men. Her story was as old as time. The man she had given her heart, soul, and body to had played her for a fool. He had whispered words of love only to get her into bed, and when he'd grown tired of her, he'd tossed her—and subsequently me—to the side. Over the years, she had dated a few guys. One guy had lasted almost two years, but she'd never found "the one".

After I sold a few soaps and a peppermint tea, Mom joined me behind the counter. "I finally nailed down Mrs. Beaufort on that sideboard," she said.

I threw my hand up for a high five. "Nice job. It's been here for a while, hasn't it?"

"Three months." After pouring herself a cup of the house tea in a to-go cup, Mom asked, "How was school?"

"Good. We got our Shakespeare project assignments today, and my partner is coming by in a little while for us to get started. I hope that's okay."

Mom nodded as she blew air into the steaming cup. "Sure. It's fine." She leaned over and planted a kiss on my cheek. "See you later, sweetie."

"Bye," I said as two ladies approached the counter.

As Mom headed out, I worked on preparing the ladies' orders. The bell over the front door tinkled, alerting me of a new customer. When I glanced up from preparing two chai teas, I saw Cade strolling in. He'd changed into a pair of khaki shorts and a *Harlington Prep Football* t-shirt that stretched tight across his muscles.

The sight of him out of uniform was jarring, and I just stood there staring. I guess it was a natural reaction considering how good-looking he was. Most of the girls in my class were always drooling over him. Before that day, I'd never really thought of him that way. Jocks had never been my type, especially the ones in the A-crowd. The guys I usually went for were the "nerdy cute" types, the ones who made good grades and gave thought-provoking responses in class discussions.

The truth was I'd never really dated that much. Even the nerdy cute guys didn't really seem interested in me. I guess it was because I never seemed to fit in. In public school, I had been the freakishly smart girl. Now at Harlington I was the outsider without a trust fund who lived on a farm. I had my hopes that once I got out of my small town and got to college, things would be different.

My finger being singed by hot tea jolted me out of my thoughts. "Ouch," I hissed before bringing my finger to my mouth. As I sucked on the afflicted tip, I met Cade's eyes. He stared at me oddly for a second before he threw up his hand.

I quickly jerked my finger out of my mouth and then waved back. While he started over to the counter, I handed over the teas to the two ladies. “Have a nice day,” I said with a smile.

Cade flopped his messenger bag onto the counter and then sat down on the stool. “This place is wild.”

“I assume that is a compliment, so I’ll say thank you.”

“Yeah, it is.” His eyes then raked over my appearance. The way he looked at me not only sent goose bumps pricking across my skin, but it made me want to cross my arms over my chest. He gave a quick shake of his head. “Damn, Prescott. I’d have to say you’re the wildest part of all of this.”

“What’s that supposed to mean?”

“Just how different you look outside of Harlington in that outfit.”

“It’s my uniform.”

Cade waggled his brows. “It’s hot.”

Embarrassment warmed my cheeks. *Did Cade Hall actually just say I was “hot”?* I was sure I must’ve stumbled into some alternate universe or something where guys *so* out of my league gave me compliments on my appearance. “Um, thanks. I mean, thank you for the compliment.”

"You’re welcome.” Caleb rubbed his hands together. “Man, I'm starving. What do you have to eat here besides tea?"

"For the record, you don't eat tea, you drink it."

Cade grinned at me. "Man, Prescott, you love to bust my balls, don't you?"

Oh God, had he actually just referred to his balls in front of me? The last thing I needed was to be thinking about his balls, even if they were just being referred to in a comical sense. Of course, the mention of his balls had me thinking about other parts of him. *Get your mind out of the gutter, Avery.* The last thing I wanted was to see Cade Hall as attractive. Nope. Not. Happening.

I then turned and raised my arm to point at the board behind me. "We have a lot of sandwich choices, and our soup of the day, which is vegetable, is pretty amazing." I cleared my throat. "What would you like?"

Cade scratched his chin as he eyed the menu board above him. "Hmm, I think I'll have two grilled cheeses with extra mayo, some BBQ chips, and a large Coke."

"I'll get right on it." I jerked my chin toward his notebook. "We can brainstorm while I work."

"If you say so, Miss Multitasker."

I set a Coke down in front of Cade and then got busy working on his sandwiches. After he took a quick swig, he dug the instruction sheet out of his notebook. "Okay, so we have to take the themes of anti-romance and anti-love and apply them to at least one tragedy, one comedy, and one sonnet." He held up one finger. "However, the more textual examples you use to prove your argument, the better your grade will be."

"Knowing Dr. Paulson, that means exhaust every possible example," I mused.

"Exactly. Course, it should be a no-brainer picking from some of the tragedies, like what idiots Romeo and Juliet were," Cade said.

I laughed. "I guess that means we're on the same page that two impetuous teenagers suffering from insta-love and hormones doesn't truly make a great love story?"

Cade nodded emphatically. "Totally. Like when peeps are going on and on about what a great love story it is, I wonder sometimes if I even read the same story. I mean, you got Romeo who is a total player who spent the first act being all emo about this Rosaline chick, and then we're to believe his heart hadn't loved until that moment and his eyes hadn't seen true beauty until that night."

I couldn't help being impressed at how well Cade remembered *Romeo and Juliet*. Oh man, there I went again; I was getting sidetracked by stereotyping Cade as an apathetic jock. He obviously packed brains along with his brawn. As much as I hated to admit it, that made him even more attractive.

"That's definitely a point we should make in the paper," I said.

"Putting it down now," Cade said as he wrote in his notebook.

Placing my palms on the countertop, I leaned in to eye the project's guidelines. "Do you think Paulson will consider *Romeo and Juliet* an easy out, or that we're challenging stereotypes?"

"Good question. I say we devote two or three paragraphs to R and J but spend more time on some of the other tragedies." Cade stroked his chin. "Which ones though?"

"How about *Othello*? It's a pretty toxic love story. You have Othello, whose obsessive and jealous love for Desdemona eventually leads him to kill her after he's been played by Iago into thinking she was cheating," I suggested.

"Good one." Cade scribbled in his notebook. "Speaking of jealousy, how about the love triangle in *King Lear* between Goneril and Regan?"

While I bobbed in agreement, I added, "Although we could probably argue that it was more of a 'lust' triangle, rather than love."

A wicked gleam burned in Cade's eyes. "Sounds like my kinda triangle. Edmund should have put his studliness to good use and just banged them both at the same time. A sisterly ménage à trois."

"Gross," I muttered as I ducked my head. I'd never had a guy talk so openly about sex in front of me. It was completely mortifying, especially considering what a noob I was when it came to those kinds of things.

"Which part? The sisters or the ménage?" Cade questioned.

"All of it, but especially the sister part."

"I hear ya."

I whipped my head up to stare at him. "You do?"

He smirked at me. "I might be into getting kinky, but being part of incest-type shit isn't part of it."

A nervous laugh bubbled from my lips. "It's good to know you at least have some morality."

"Just about the incest stuff. I would totally be down for a ménage, but only with another girl…not a dude."

For the life of me, I didn't know why I blurted out, "Why not with another guy?"

Cade's expression soured. "With another dude, there's the inevitability that his nutsack is going to brush up against me." He shuddered. "That's some sick shit."

While I silently again willed the floor to open up and swallow me whole, I turned my attention to finishing up his sandwich. "Um, we really need a subject change."

Cade chuckled. "How in the hell did we get off on this, Prescott?"

"I think the discussion took the horrifying turn somewhere at *King Lear*."

After snapping his fingers, Cade blurted out, "Hamlet."

"What about him?" I asked as I set the grilled cheese in front of Cade.

"We should totally talk about what an asshole he was to Ophelia."

"I'm glad to see that we're once again in agreement. The way he led her on and played mind games was deplorable."

With a snicker, Cade said, "Did you actually just use the word *deplorable?*"

Although heat warmed my cheeks, I countered, "What would you call a guy who played hot and cold with his amorous emotions and accused an innocent girl of being a whore just because of his"—I paused to make air quotes with my fingers—"mother issues?"

"I'd call him an epic douche."

"Exactly—not to mention, a murderer. He didn't just break Ophelia's heart; he shattered it when he killed her father."

"Well, Polonius shouldn't have been lurking around in the curtains, but that's another story. Also he was an oppressive asshole who bossed her around all the time." Cade took a huge bite of his sandwich. His eyes widened, and then he moaned in pleasure. "Holy shit. This is the best fucking grilled cheese I've ever had."

I laughed at his reaction. "I'm glad you like it."

"Seriously though. What's in this?"

"Um, cheese."

Cade rolled his eyes. "Come on. Is it like some secret recipe?"

"Not really. It's just a mixture of American, Colby, and Monterey."

"Well, it's fucking amazing. I need to do like a Yelp review or some shit."

"Thank you. That would be really nice." I tapped my finger on the instruction sheet. "Well, I think we pretty much have the plays down. Now we need to focus on the poetry."

Cade grinned. "That's an easy one. The ultimate diss in the form of a sonnet: 'My Mistress's Eyes Are Nothing Like the Sun'. The dude nails her for bad breath, brownish-gray tits, and a shitty face."

"Well, the brownish-gray…" I swallowed hard; I just couldn't bring myself to say the word *tits*. It was one of those words that felt like nails on a chalkboard.

"Tits?" Cade suggested.

"Yes, those. It's dun-colored in the text, and it isn't actually a diss because he was writing it to the Dark Lady. Her skin would be darker than snow no matter what."

"I'm pretty sure it's still a diss. You know, like how back then you could tell a person's wealth and social standing by how pasty they were? He could be dissing her social standing."

"But he goes on to say that in spite of it all, he loves her. I think that's showing true love, rather than anti-love."

Cade cocked his head at me. "Would you want some douchebag who says shitty things about you but then says he love you in spite of all that?"

Hmm, he had a point there. "No, I wouldn't, but maybe what he was trying to get across was that love transcends the physical surface to be about what's inside a person?"

With a smirk, Cade said, "If I have to put a bag over a chick's head, it's not going to be love. It's going to be that she's a butta face."

"A what?"

"You know, a butter face?" At my still blank expression, Cade added, "Everything is hot but her face. A butta face."

"That's terrible."

"Just telling it like it is. Shakespeare was a man, and men are about the physical. I highly doubt he was going to be able to get it up for some chick he didn't find attractive."

"Ugh, you're disgusting."

"For being honest?"

"No, for feeling that way. What if you were in love and got into an accident where you were disfigured? Wouldn't you hope that you would be able to find someone who would love you for what was on the inside?"

"Just how bad are we talking here? Like do I have a gnarly scar on my face like Tyrion Lannister in *Game of Thrones*, or I got so fucked up I look like Sloth from *The Goonies*?"

I rolled my eyes. "What does it matter?"

"Trust me, it matters."

"I think you're missing the point."

"Yeah, well, there really isn't a point because I've never been in love before."

"And why doesn't that surprise me?"

"Uh, maybe because I'm an eighteen-year-old dude."

"Age shouldn't have anything to do with it. My grandparents fell in love when they were fourteen."

"More power to them. It just hasn't happened like that for me."

"Even if it hasn't happened, can't you at least imagine being in love?"

Cade pinched his eyes shut and appeared to be concentrating

really hard. "I'm imagining being in love."

"Okay."

"First thing I see is monogamy, which epically blows."

I huffed out a frustrated breath. "What could possibly be so wrong with loving one person for the rest of your life?"

"Hmm…being limited to the same woman for years and years and years. More specifically, that's being limited to the same pussy for years and years and years." His eyes popped open to stare at me. "It's like a prison sentence."

I shook my head as I shot him a disgusted look. "That's a pretty negative view of love."

"Hey, you asked."

"And now I wish I hadn't."

"Sorry. Just callin' it as I see it."

"Guess your parents must've gone through a pretty bitter divorce," I remarked.

Cade smirked at me. "My parents aren't divorced. They're going on twenty-five years of marriage."

"Oh."

"But just because they're married doesn't mean they're in love."

"Then why stay together?"

"Because my father needs the seemingly perfect family to stay an elected representative, and my mother needs my father's money because she has no marketable skills besides running a household and looking pretty."

I leaned back against the counter, taking in everything he had just said. I drew in a few breaths because it had been a harsh portrait of his family, a jagged puzzle piece of what made him who he was. Cade had never experienced romantic love because he'd never been around any form of love. My heart went out to him.

He grunted. "Don't look at me like that."

"Like what?"

"Like you feel sorry for me and wanna give me a hug to make it all better."

"I wasn't thinking that at all."

"Sure you were."

I huffed out a frustrated breath. "I didn't know you were such a mind reader."

Cade laughed. "I don't have to read minds; it's written all over your face. You were staring at me like I was a lost puppy."

"I'm sorry. I just felt bad for you because of your family."

After swiping his mouth with his napkin, he tossed it onto his now empty plate. "It's okay, Prescott. Save your pity for starving children."

"It wasn't pity. I can't help having a tender heart and caring about people. It's just who I am."

"Fine. I guess you can care about me."

"As a friend," I quickly corrected.

Cade laughed. "Don't worry, Prescott. I didn't think you

meant anything more." He stroked his chin thoughtfully. "Although you did a pretty good job of staring at my bod earlier."

Rolling my eyes, I said, "Whatever."

When Cade's phone dinged, he dug it out of his pocket. "I gotta go."

"Oh. Okay." I didn't know why, but I felt a little bereft that he was leaving. If I was honest with myself, it was because I had enjoyed spending time with him. It was nice having a guy I could talk intellectually with. Of course, he had to throw some crudeness in there as well.

Cade put his notebook back into his messenger bag. "I don't know about you, but I think we have a hell of a start on blowing Paulson's mind."

I laughed. "I think so, too."

"How much for the sandwiches?"

Holding up my hands, I said, "It's on the house."

"Seriously?"

"Yes. My treat."

Cade dug a twenty out of his pocket before leaning over to toss it into the tip jar. He grinned at me as he stood up. "For your excellent service."

My heart fluttered at his extreme kindness. "Thank you."

"You're welcome. See ya back at Harlington, aka hell."

I laughed. "Yeah. See you in hell."

Cade threw up his hand before breezing out the door. Although

I should have been happy at how well we were working together, an anxious feeling pricked its way down my spine.

"This is going to be trouble. *He* is going to be trouble," I murmured.

FIVE

CADE

Two Weeks Later

On Saturday morning, I had planned to sleep in like usual, but then my phone started ringing at the ass crack of dawn. Well, it was only eight, but considering I'd been partying late into the night, it felt way earlier. I groaned at the realization that it was the *Imperial March* from Star Wars, aka my father's ringtone. Since he never just called to shoot the shit or see what was up in my life, I wasn't too stoked to answer it. "Hey Dad, what's up?"

"I need you to come home tonight. I have a photographer coming to the house tomorrow morning to do new family pictures for my campaign brochures."

I rubbed my eyes. "If the pictures aren't until tomorrow, why do you need me tonight?"

My father gave an exasperated sigh. "Because you're not exactly trustworthy when it comes to being punctual, Cade. If you're here tonight, then I know you will be ready in the morning."

"I'm supposed to be working on a school project tonight."

"So reschedule it."

Ugh, that was so like Daddy Dearest to just automatically assume the world revolved around him. "Whatever," I grunted.

"Your mother has sent your black suit out to be cleaned, so you don't have to worry about what you're going to wear."

"Peachy."

I could practically feel my father's irritation seeping through the phone. "I'll see you tonight, Cade." Then he hung up.

"And goodbye to you, too," I mumbled.

I scrolled through my contacts for Avery's number. We were supposed to meet up at Harlington's library that afternoon to start piecing our research together into an outline of what would become our research paper. I was feeling pretty stoked about the information we'd collected so far. I'm sure it's shocking that a guy like me gave two shits about Shakespeare or doing research, but don't forget that I've got beauty, brains, and brawn.

Getting Avery for a research partner was like a dream come true. Since she was a total nerd, I could count on her to take the project seriously. If I had been assigned to one of the girls in my crowd, I would've had to push for the paper to be a priority over all the social shit they were involved in.

With Avery, I didn't have to worry about her wasting study time flirting. Any other girl would be adjusting her shirt so I'd notice her tits while we read a musty tome on Shakespeare or leaning over me so her tits could rub against my shoulder while we did research on the computer. Trust me, I've experienced almost every trick in the book used by chicks trying to get my attention, and they never worked.

"Shit," I muttered when her phone went straight to voicemail. She was probably working. Throwing back the blanket, I hopped out of bed and started for the showers. If I couldn't get Avery on the phone, I would just drive into town and hook up with her there.

* * *

When I stopped in at Rose's Garden, I found Avery's cousin working instead of her. She gave me Avery's home address along with a few eye-fucks. Even though she was pushing thirty, the fact that I was jailbait didn't seem to concern her too much when it came to hitting on me.

After she offered me a free drink on the house, I quickly made a run for my car. Once I plugged the address into my phone, I headed over to Avery's. The closer I got to her house, the farther away from civilization I got. I turned off the main highway onto a gravel road and it ended at a two-story farmhouse that looked like something out of one of the reruns of *The Andy Griffith Show* our cook Sandra used to love to watch.

I parked my car, but I didn't immediately get out. Instead, I stayed in my seat looking around the farm. I tried to imagine Avery living there. It was no wonder she seemed so different from the other kids at Harlington. I doubted there was anyone there who had ever actually been on a farm, least of all lived on one.

I grabbed my phone and messenger bag. After throwing open the car door, I started across the yard. I snorted when I expected to see Aunt Bea sitting in the swing at the end of the porch. The wooden front door was open, and I could see the inside of the living room through the glass door.

My knuckles rapped against the glass, causing it to rattle loudly. After a few seconds, an older lady with white hair tucked back in a bun came down the hallway, wiping her hands on an apron. With a smile, she unlocked the door and opened it. "Yes?"

"Hello. I'm Cade Hall. I'm here to see Avery."

"Well, come on in, son. Don't want to let out any more bought air."

I squeezed past her through the doorway and into the living room. My nose perked up at the smell of what I imagined was a fresh apple pie coming from the kitchen. The woman extended her hand with the same warm smile. "I'm Margie Perkins, Avery's grandmother."

"It's nice to meet you."

"It's nice meeting you as well." She motioned to the kitchen. "Just give me a minute. I'll have to go call for Avery."

"Yeah, I already tried her but it went to voicemail."

Margie laughed. "I didn't mean on the phone. I'll have to call for her in person.

She's working on the south field today."

"Excuse me?"

She laughed. "I don't suppose you know too much about farming."

"No, ma'am. I don't."

"Avery is plowing corn in the south field."

Holy shit, I wasn't expecting that one at all. Sure, the house was out in the bumblefuck, but I'd never been on a real life farm before. Avery Prescott, who was slated to be valedictorian of Harlington, was plowing the south field…whatever the hell that meant.

"You mean, Avery's on, like, a tractor?"

"Well, it's actually called a harvester, but it's like a tractor. When she's on it, she wears a headset to protect her ears from the noise. That's why she leaves her phone behind."

I grinned. "I'm sorry, Mrs. Perkins, but Avery doesn't come across as the harvester type."

"Well, she's always done chores around the farm, but since I lost my husband this past summer, she and her mother have taken up the plowing."

My heart twisted a little at the news of Avery losing her grandfather. I'd lost mine two years ago. He was one of the few decent people in my life who had actually shown me love, and it had been hard as hell to say goodbye. "I'm sorry for your loss."

"Thank you. You're very kind."

"What does he want with Avery?" a voice questioned from the kitchen doorway. When I glanced behind Margie, I saw an adult version of Avery—well, if Avery was more of a free spirit who let her hair down and liked wearing tight shirts that showed off her rack along with short shorts. Damn, Avery's mom was a straight-up MILF.

With her arms crossed over her large chest, she glared suspiciously at me. I didn't know if she was pissed because she could read the NC17-rated thoughts in my mind or because I was there to see Avery.

"We're working on a project together for our AP British literature class," I said.

"That better be all you're working on with her. I know your kind," Avery's mother spat.

"Rose," Margie chided.

Since you could cut the tension in the air with a fucking chainsaw, I took a step back. "If this is a bad time, I can hook up with Avery later." At Rose's hiss, I quickly added, "I mean, hook up like get together. You know, to work on our project. It's about anti-love in Shakespeare's love stories."

Jesus, I was babbling now. No one ever got me rattled, but Rose sure as hell could. Maybe it was because the look in her eyes told me she would be happy to dismember my dick without a second thought.

Rose rolled her eyes. “I’ve got to go change and get to the shop.” With one final death glare, she brushed past me and headed up the stairs.

Margie gave Rose’s retreating form a disapproving look before forcing a smile to her lips. “Come on. Let’s go find Avery.”

“Sounds good.”

I followed Margie through the kitchen, out the back door, and down the porch steps into the yard. We walked in silence for a few moments before she turned to me. "I'm sorry about my daughter."

I shrugged. "It's not the first time a mom thought I was going to take advantage of her daughter."

"It's about more than that with Rose." When I glanced at her, Margie said, "I’d say you remind her of Avery's father."

"Avery's never told me anything about her dad." Actually, I didn’t know Avery well enough for her to really tell me anything. I’d put two and two together from our conversations that she didn’t have a dad around. Although I was curious, I sure as hell wasn’t going to be a nosy dickhead and ask her. He could have been some drunk abuser who had left Avery scarred emotionally, and maybe even physically.

As I processed what Margie said, I couldn’t help asking, “Do I look like him or something?"

Margie shook her head. "No. It's more about the fact that like you, Avery's father came from a wealthy background with a political father."

"You know who my family is?"

She nodded. "This is his district, is it not?"

"Yeah, it is." I guessed Margie had seen my face along with my father's on some of his campaign paraphernalia.

"I wish I could say I voted for him," Margie mused.

With a contemptuous snort, I replied, "Don't feel bad for saying that. He's an asshole."

Margie laughed. "I didn't vote for him because he's a Republican, and I'm a life-long Democrat."

"Oh, my bad."

We reached the top of a massive hill. At the bottom of the rolling grass sat a red painted barn. The sound of an engine could be heard in the distance. "Avery must be taking a break if she's bringing the harvester back to the barn."

"Okay, I'll head down there and meet up with her."

Margie nodded. "It was nice meeting you, Cade."

"Thanks. Same to you." For one of the first times in my life, I actually believed a word of praise. Margie Perkins hadn't said that to be nice or to impress me. She'd meant it. Even though I was really an asshole who didn't deserve compliments, somehow it felt good to hear one from her.

As I started down the hillside, I became enveloped in the waist-high grass. Since I wasn't a big fan of snakes, I hoped I wouldn't step on one. The last thing I needed was my man card revoked after Avery and Margie heard me scream like a little girl.

By the time I got to the bottom of the hill and made my way across the pasture, the harvester's engine had silenced, and I guessed Avery was in the barn. When I came around the side of the barn, I skidded to a stop. Avery held a bucket over her head while water cascaded over her body. "Fuck me," I muttered, but it was more like fuck *her*—at least I wanted to.

Seeing Avery in her work uniform was nothing compared to seeing her in a pair of jean shorts and a white tank top that had become see-through now that it was wet. My mouth ran dry as I watched the streams of water running over Avery's curves—the very curves that for the first time, I wanted to get my hands on. My dick jumped in my pants at the sight of her nipples hardening with the cold.

What the hell was wrong with me? I couldn't be having X-rated thoughts about my school partner. She was not one of my spank bank girls. She was way too good of a person for me to be fantasizing about banging her against the barn.

When Avery turned to put the bucket down, she caught sight of me and jumped.

I knew I needed to call attention away from the half-mast boner in my pants, so I went with the first thought that entered my mind: a Kenny Chesney song.

"She thinks my tractor's sexy. It really turns her on!" I belted.

Avery's face turned the same color of the barn. I knew she was hella mortified when the redness spilled off her face and onto her shoulders.

"W-what are you d-doing here?" Her hands flew to fluff out the skin-tight t-shirt currently molded against her body. I hid my frustration that she had cock-blocked the fantastically detailed view of her tits.

"My dad needs me home tomorrow for a 'let's pretend we're the perfect family' photo shoot. When you didn't answer your phone, I went by Rose's, and your cousin gave me your address with a side order of eye-fucking."

Avery's embarrassment turned to amusement as she picked up a towel beside the water basin. "I guess you met Mae."

"Yeah, I did."

"She's my mom's older sister's daughter, and she's a man-eater."

"I totally got that vibe."

"I'm sorry you had to be objectified because I didn't answer my phone," Avery teased as she toweled some of the water off her hair.

"Nah. It's okay. We all have our shit to do." When Avery started drying her body off, my mouth ran dry again. I fought the urge to take the towel away from her and let it be my hands on her body, not hers.

Needing a subject change, I jerked my chin at the barn. "So you're a real life farmer, huh?"

"Sort of. I just help out from time to time."

I pointed past her at the harvester. "It's pretty badass that you drive that thing."

Avery laughed. "Really, it's not that hard."

"It looks it to me."

"Maybe I can teach you how to drive it one day."

"Why not today?"

Avery's green eyes widened. "You're serious?"

"I've never been on a real farm before. Might as well see how it's done."

Avery stared at me like I'd just said I was a woman or something bat-shit crazy like that. "You actually want to go on the harvester?"

"Why does that seem so shocking?"

"Uh, maybe because you're not the farm type."

"I'm all about new experiences."

"What about our Shakespeare paper?"

"We've got the rest of the afternoon to work on it."

Avery nibbled on her bottom lip. "Okay. I was just about to put it in the barn, but I guess it wouldn't hurt to get in another half an acre."

"Awesome!"

She grinned as she shook her head at me. "You really are a man of mystery."

I laughed. "I'll take that as a compliment."

We walked over to the harvester, which looked just like your average tractor except for the funny circular things on the front and the fact that it had a small cab. "Go ahead and get in," Avery urged.

After climbing inside the cab of the harvester, I gazed around, taking everything in. "It looks like the inside of a video game," I remarked. When I glanced to my right, I saw a control pad full of buttons. "What do these do?"

"Don't touch those!" Avery commanded from her perch on the step.

I held my hands up. "Sorry. My bad."

She gave me a sheepish grin. "It's just I don't know what half of those do. I only use a few."

After she climbed inside, we both tried squeezing our asses on the small seat. "This really isn't made for a team effort."

"It's okay." I cocked my head at her. "You could always sit on my lap."

Her face colored. "I think I'll pass."

"I won't bite." After winking, I added, "Unless you ask me to."

My teasing little come-on was rewarded with a snort that made Avery seem even more real to me. The A-crowd girls would have cared too much about what people thought of them to snort.

Avery raised her brows at me. "Do girls actually like those kind of jokes?"

"Most of the time."

"That's pretty sad."

"Once again, you're busting my balls, Prescott."

"At least I'm not sitting on them."

I couldn't help busting out laughing since it so wasn't something I expected her to say. Avery grinned at me as she leaned forward to crank up the harvester. "Okay, now you're going to want to put it into gear."

"How do I do that?"

"By putting your hand on the gear with the black knob and then pulling it back toward you."

"I can do that." Of course when I reached forward, my hand accidentally brushed against the underside of her breast. When she flushed and ducked her head, I quickly said, "Sorry."

"It's okay," she murmured.

Once I pulled back on the black gear, the harvester lurched forward. "Put your hands on the wheel."

I cut my eyes over at Avery. "Wow, you don't say. I would have had no idea."

"You're such a smartass."

"Hold the phone. Did you actually just say a cuss word?" I questioned incredulously.

"Yes, I did. I'm not a total goody two-shoes."

"Could have fooled me."

After shooting me a pointed look, Avery instructed, "Now accelerate slightly."

I eased my foot down on the gas and we started picking up speed. "This is pretty cool. Kinda like driving a 5-speed car."

"I told you it was easy."

Taking one hand off the steering wheel, I motioned to the circular things on the front of the thresher. "How do you make those things go?"

"Well, first, you want to wait until you're ready to work a row of corn." Avery pointed to the left. "Pull over there to where I had stopped."

"Yes, captain," I replied with a mock salute.

Once I got in place, Avery motioned to a yellow gear that had several black buttons on it. Although I tried paying attention to all she said, I started getting lost. "Um, maybe you should just push them."

She laughed. "Okay. I can handle that." After working the buttons, a loud grinding noise filled the air before the whooshing sound of the circular things got going.

Since it was pretty loud, Avery leaned closer to me. "Basically, the harvester strips the stalks from the ground. Then the conveying system separates the ears from the stalks. The ears get dropped into the bucket down below while the stalks get blown out the fan duct to the ground."

"Ooh, I love it when you get all technical on me," I teasingly shouted.

Avery threw her head back and laughed. Although I couldn't hear the sound over the engine, I liked the way she looked when she did it. We continued down the row, and we rode along silently as corn stalks disappeared before our eyes.

"Had enough yet?" Avery called over the roar. When I nodded, she shouted, "Then just take a right and pull us out to the barn."

"Gotcha."

When we were out of the high stalks, Avery once again worked the black buttons. Thankfully, the noise died down, and I could hear myself think again. Of course, I probably needed to tune out what my mind was thinking about Avery's body pressed against mine. There was also the fact that even after toweling off, she was still pretty wet from her bucket bath.

A wet, hot body within reach of my hands just itching to do some grabbing? Oh yeah, it was time to get out of the harvester—ASAP.

"Can I hop out for some fresh air?"

"Sure."

Instead of me having to clamber over Avery to get out, she hopped down as well. Avery brought her hand to her forehead to shield her face from the sun then threw her hand up in a wave. "My mom's leaving for work."

"You know, you and your mom definitely have a *Gilmore Girls* vibe."

Avery jerked her attention from the hillside and over to me. "You actually watched that show?"

"My sister loved it back in the day. She got me hooked. I might've Netflixed it some when I was by myself too."

She shook her head. "You are full of surprises, Mr. Hall."

"Just don't tell anyone at Harlington about it. I have a reputation to protect."

"Yeah, I know all about your reputation."

"You do?"

"Yep."

"Well, a wise person once said not to believe everything you hear."

"Then tell me what's fact and what's fiction," Avery countered.

"Fine. Ask away."

"Did you get kicked out of your last prep school?"

"Fact."

She cocked her head at me. "Was it really for having an affair with the French teacher?"

I snorted. "Is that what people said?"

"It's one of the rumors I heard."

"Well, that would be a big fucking no, especially since the French teacher at my last school was not only seventy years old, but a dude."

Avery wrinkled her nose. "I guess not."

"But I did get kicked out because of a teacher."

"Oh?"

"Yeah, I stole and hacked into my history teacher's laptop to change some of my grades."

"Cade, that's horrible."

"Yeah, well, that's not all of it."

"You mean you did something else besides stealing to try to cheat?"

"While I was going through the files, I found this folder full of naked pics of Dr. Hagler. They were ones he was sending to chicks on dating sites. He had probably uploaded them to his work computer by accident. So, I decided to leak them."

Avery gasped. "You didn't?"

"I did."

"What happened?"

"Well, the IT department was eventually able to trace the leak to me. I got expelled, and Dr. Hagler got fired."

"Wow," Avery murmured.

"Yep. Pretty much."

Avery and I had been so lost in conversation I didn't realize we'd crested another hill and started toward the pasture fence.

"So this is all your grandparents' property?"

Avery nodded. "Yep. All fifty acres. Well, it's my

grandmother's now that my grandfather passed away." She motioned to the fence. "Except for that land there, that belongs to grumpy old Mr. Frost." Avery continued staring out into the woods. "It's a shame too because it has this beautiful pond with crystal clear water."

It was then that I was struck with another one of my ideas. "So let's go swimming."

Avery's eyes bulged. "W-what?"

"I said let's go swimming."

After swallowing hard, she replied, "I thought that was what you said."

"Come on. It's hot as balls out here, so let's cool off."

"But what about working on our paper?"

"Would you lighten up? It's only noon, and I don't have to be home until eight. Unless you have some pressing social engagement I don't know about, we've got all afternoon to work on the project."

"You just automatically assume I don't have anything to do," Avery huffed.

"That's not what I said at all."

"You alluded to it."

"No. I didn't. It would make sense that if you had something to do, you would have let me know earlier."

"I guess you're right."

"Of course I am." I then hoisted myself up on the fence and sat down. Turning around, I held out my hand. "Come on. Live a little,

Prescott."

Avery took a cautious step back. "But Mr. Frost is known to call the police whenever he catches someone on his property."

I rolled my eyes. "I have a feeling we can outrun Mr. Old Fart Frost before he can call the police."

From the look on her face, an epic battle was raging inside Avery's head. "Just for once would you stop worrying about what might happen *if* you get caught and instead have some fun?"

After a long sigh, she said, "All right, fine. Let's go swimming."

I grinned as I clapped my hands together. "Oh, hell yeah. It's on!"

SIX

AVERY

When Cade suggested going swimming, it felt like I had both a devil and an angel on my shoulders. The angel warned that nothing good could come of trespassing on Mr. Frost's property with Cade Hall of all people, but like Cade, the devil urged me to live a little, to throw caution to the wind and have some wild and crazy fun for once. When it came down to it, I could count on one hand the times I'd had truly spontaneous fun in my life.

So I slid my hand into Cade's and let him help me up and over the fence onto Mr. Frost's property. I hated the way my heart fluttered in my chest when our hands met. Jeez, I was starting to act like a middle school girl with her first crush. I *did* not like Cade. I *could* not like Cade.

After swatting away a mosquito, Cade asked, “How far is it to the pond?”

“It’s just around the bend. You can see it in the wintertime when the leaves fall,” I answered.

“Good. I’m fucking roasting.”

When the pond finally came into sight, Cade let out a whoop and broke into a run. Since I was in cowboy boots, it made it a little hard to keep up with him, but I finally caught him as he started out onto the dock.

“This place is awesome.”

“It is.” Considering I’d never been there before either, I was taking everything in the same as Cade. I also was keeping a watchful eye out for Mr. Frost.

“All right. Let’s strip and get in,” Cade said as he bent over to take off his shoes.

Oh shit. He couldn’t be serious. “Y-you want me to take off my c-clothes?”

“Do you know any other way to swim?”

“In a bathing suit,” I replied lamely.

Cade swept his shirt off and tossed it onto the dock. “We’re out in the middle of nowhere, so you gotta improvise, Prescott.”

I opened my mouth to argue with him, but then quickly snapped it shut. The world seemed to screech to a halt with a deafening shudder the moment Cade bent over and swept his shorts off his hips. I froze—not moving, not blinking, and only breathing because it was an involuntary reflex. I'd never seen a naked guy. Well, let me rephrase that: I'd never seen a naked guy in person. With the beauty of the Internet, coupled with my art appreciation classes, I'd seen plenty of bare, male buttocks and penises…peni…or whatever they're called.

Even so, there was something completely and totally unsettling about seeing a naked guy in person. Throw in that it was Cade Hall, and that left me pretty much gobsmacked.

Cade threw a cocky grin at me over his shoulder. "I hope you're done enjoying the view because I'm going in.

I ducked my head and stared down at the dock. "You could've left your underwear on," I countered.

"Considering I always go commando that just wasn't an option."

Oh. My. God. All the times we had been working on our paper together—not to mention when we were pressed up against each other in the harvester—he hadn't been wearing underwear. I didn't know why it got to me, but it did.

I jerked my head up at the splashing sound of Cade jumping into the water. As I peered over the edge of the dock, I was glad his lower half was now covered. It had been shocking enough to see his backside, let alone his front.

"Prescott, would you hurry up and get your ass in here?"

"Maybe I'll just sit and dangle my feet over the edge. I cooled down earlier."

"Why don't you leave your underwear on? Then you could think of it like you were in a bikini."

Hmm, he had a good point. That also meant I wouldn't have to feel guilty about skinny dipping because I hadn't actually been naked. I quickly took off my tank top and dropped it onto the dock. When my fingers came to the button of my shorts, I glanced up to see Cade staring at me. "Do you mind?"

He rolled his eyes. "Honestly, Prescott, it's not like you're the first girl I've ever seen in her underwear."

"Well, it's the first time you've seen me."

"Fine. I'll turn around. Will that make you happy?"

"Yes. Thank you."

Once Cade had flipped around, I slid off my shorts and hopped in the water. With the summer heat, the water felt a little cooler than bathwater. When I broke the surface, Cade had turned around and was grinning at me.

"You know, you really do have a nice body, Prescott."

I couldn't help being shocked by his words. It was hard imagining that someone like Cade would think someone like me had a good body. I managed to mumble a quick, "Thanks."

We swam around in silence for a few minutes, darting underwater and then back up again. When Cade would swim close to me, I couldn't help stiffening at the thought of his penis brushing against me.

Breaking the silence, I said, "So I really think our project is coming together."

"We're going to blow Paulson away with our argument."

"I hope so. I'll just be glad when it's over. Of course, that will mean I'm just one step closer to next semester, which is really scary."

Cade's brows knitted together. "But why? As a senior, you shouldn't have too much hard shit left to take."

"I'm graduating early."

Considering the appalled look Cade gave me, I might as well have said I was thinking of transitioning to a man. "Why the fuck would you want to do that?"

"So I can go ahead and start college, get a jump start on my future."

"But there's still like a half year of senior activities. You'll miss Senior Day and the trip to Atlanta."

"While it will be agonizing, I think I'll find some way to console myself," I teasingly replied.

"What about prom?"

I shrugged. "What about it?"

"Will you at least come back for it?"

"I don't think so. It's not like I have a steady boyfriend who is going to take me."

"You could by then. You never know."

"I doubt it very seriously." I wondered why he even cared

about me going to prom. With his harem of women, I was pretty sure he wasn't going to ask me. At the same time, I couldn't help being curious about who he might go with. "What about you?"

"Hell no, I don't want to graduate early. I want to put off being an adult for as long as possible."

"No, I meant, you seem so gung-ho about prom that I wondered who you would take."

"Jesus, Prescott, that's like six months away. I barely know what I'm doing next weekend, least of all this spring."

"What about Elspeth?"

"What about her?"

"You don't want to be prom king and queen as well as homecoming king and queen?"

"We could be elected that shit regardless of if we went together."

"It just seems like you two have been awfully cozy lately."

"Yeah, I took her to homecoming, but that doesn't mean I want to date her."

"Then what exactly is it that you're doing?"

"Fucking."

I wrinkled my nose in disgust. "Ew. I so didn't need to know that."

"You asked," Cade countered.

"You didn't have to be so honest."

"I never lie about sex." He flashed me a wicked grin. "It's too sacred to lie about."

"Call me cynical, but I'm pretty sure there's nothing sacred about what you're doing."

"How do you know it's not a truly religious experience?" Cade countered.

"Now you're being sacrilegious."

Cade swept his hand to his heart. "My apologies. I didn't mean to offend your spiritual sensibilities."

"I'm pretty sure sex is a sacred act done through the bonds of love."

"I think you're getting mixed up about sex and making love."

"There's a difference?"

He nodded. "Hell yeah, there's a difference. What you were talking about is making love—something you do when you actually love the person you're having sex with. Sex and fucking are pretty much interchangeable. You don't have to be in love with a person to do those things. Hell, you don't even have to like them. You can just fuck."

"Thanks for the clarification."

Cade swam closer to me. "What about you, Prescott? You ever let a guy between those creamy white thighs of yours?"

I swallowed hard. "Maybe…a little."

He snorted. "What the hell does 'a little' mean?"

"It means there's been some male action there, just not…the entire action."

Cade's blue eyes flared. "So that means you're still a virgin?"

"Yes. It does."

He slowly shook his head back and forth. "Jesus, I don't think I've ever been naked with a virgin."

"What about your first time?"

"She was my older sister's friend, and I think I was number five for her."

"How old were you?"

"Fifteen. Lost it in the pool house during Christmas break." He chuckled. "I'm pretty sure I blew my load in less than a minute, but she was so drunk she didn't seem to mind."

"How romantic," I scoffed.

He shrugged. "I didn't care. It gave me bragging rights."

"So bragging rights were all you cared about?"

"I also cared about the experience and finding out what it was like to come inside someone instead of my hand."

"For someone who can be so articulate sometimes, you sure are crude."

"Sorry. I just tell it like it is."

"Well try to tell it a little less like it is around me, okay?"

Cade grinned. "Okay, I will, but first, I have one last question."

"Of course you do." I sighed. "Fine, ask away, oh crude one."

"When do plan on cashing in your V card?"

"I don't know, and if I did, I wouldn't tell you."

"Why the hell not?"

"Because for me, sex is something special and sacred. I don't plan on having it just so I won't be a virgin any more. While I don't plan to wait for marriage, I do want to wait until I'm love."

"Then I do hope you fall in love sooner rather than later."

I laughed. "So I can get busy like everyone else?"

Cade shook his head. "No. Because someone like you deserves to have someone love them."

The shrill sound of a police siren interrupted us. As I whirled around toward the forest, blue and red lights flashed in the trees. "Oh my God! They've caught us!" I shrieked as fear ricocheted through me.

"I guess you weren't joking when you said that old fart would call the cops," Cade said with an amused lilt in his voice.

I whipped back around to stare at him. "Do you find this funny?"

Cade rolled his eyes. "We're not doing anything wrong."

"Except trespassing."

"That's not a felony, Prescott. It's barely a misdemeanor since we haven't caused any destruction of property."

"But I'm in my underwear, and you're naked."

"I'm pretty sure we won't be the first people they've caught without clothes out here."

I started to argue with him when the police car screeched to a halt on the shoreline. A middle-aged officer with a gut and a receding hairline got out of the car. After placing his cap on his head, he started to the end of the dock. "All right, you two, get out of the water. Now."

Cade didn't budge. "What's the problem, officer?"

The officer placed his hands on the gun holster on his hip. "In case you couldn't read the signs, you're trespassing on private property."

"We were just swimming. It's not like we're stealing anything or causing destruction," Cade argued.

"Quit the wisecracks and get out of the water."

White-hot mortification ran from my head to my toes at the thought of the officer seeing me in my underwear, but Cade appeared unfazed by the prospect. He practically strutted out of the water while I wrapped one arm around my chest and the other across my abdomen.

At the sight of Cade's naked form, the cop merely shook his head.

"Should I put my hands on my head?" Cade asked.

"Just shut up and get your clothes on."

I quickly threw my shirt over my head before jumping into my shorts. I had already finished getting dressed by the time Cade was pulling his shirt on.

Once we were finished, the officer walked over to the cruiser and opened the door. "Get in the back."

Cade held up his hands. "Whoa. Hold the phone. You're

arresting us?"

"If you were under arrest, I would have read you your rights. I'm removing you from the property."

"But, sir, I need to get my family's harvester back to the barn," I argued.

The officer shook his head. "I've been given an order to escort you from the property, and I will follow those instructions."

Cade snorted. "Seriously, dude. Lighten up."

The officer narrowed his eyes at Cade. "You'll shut up if you know what's good for you. I've had enough of smartass teenagers disregarding rules and thinking the whole fucking world belongs to them."

After glancing up at the sky, I squirmed at the sight of the dark clouds moving in. Considering the weather could go from slightly cloudy to pounding rain in a single moment, I would be in big trouble if the harvester were left out. "Please, officer, I'm not trying to be difficult. It looks like rain, and even the slightest moisture can damage the engine."

The officer closed the gap between us and glared into my eyes. "I don't give a fuck about some alleged machinery. I'm going to say it one last time: get your ass in the cruiser before I take you in for resisting."

"Lighten up, buddy. Let her go, and take me in. Then you've still followed your orders to an extent."

The officer turned his wrath from me to Cade. "I thought I told you to shut the fuck up."

Cade shook his head. "Dude, you really need to back off."

"Is that so?"

"One phone call to my dad, and you're finished in this county."

The officer threw Cade a murderous look. "Get. In. The. Car."

Before Cade could say another word, I put my hand on his shoulder. "Let's just do what he says."

Cade kept his gaze on the officer. "Whatever. Damage is already done."

The officer jerked open the back door of the cruiser. I slid inside first then Cade ducked in behind me. Once we were in, the door slammed shut, and a sense of panic overtook me. "If I'm arrested, I could lose my scholarships and grants. I could have my acceptance to Emory revoked." I swallowed the rising bile in my throat. "Oh God, I think I'm going to be sick."

"Easy, Prescott. It's not going to come to that," Cade replied as his fingers flew over the keys on his phone. I couldn't help marveling at how cool, calm, and collected he was considering we were in the back of a police cruiser.

"How can you be so sure?"

"Because my dad will get us off the hook. Trust me."

The officer slammed his door and cranked up the cruiser. Mr. Frost's driveway was about a mile long. It ran from the main road and snaked along his property. We had barely made it a half a mile before a crackly voice came over the radio. "Com to Charlie 59."

The officer brought his chin over to his shoulder. "This is Charlie 59. Go ahead."

"Your 10-92s need to be let out immediately, and under no circumstance should they be brought to the station."

"I'm going to need you to repeat that, Com."

"I think you heard what I said, Charlie 59."

"Yeah, I did, but I'm uncertain as to why this command is being given when I have two trespassing violators."

There was a pause before the dispatcher said, "This comes from the chief."

The officer started to argue again when another voice came across the line. "Humphrey, shut your face and put on a smile. You've got Thomas Hall's son in the back of your cruiser, and your ass in a bind."

"Ten-four," Officer Humphrey replied tersely.

"Thank God," I murmured. My body, which had been taut and tense with fear, went limp with relief. I collapsed back against the seat and exhaled in a long whoosh.

"Where is the best place to drop you two off?" Officer Humphrey asked.

"Back at the pond, please. It's the quickest way back to the harvester."

Cade shook his head at me. "You don't need to say *please* to him. He'll do exactly what we say. Won't you Humphrey?" When

Humphrey didn't reply, Cade smirked at the back of Officer Humphrey's head. "If you want him to push the harvester back instead of driving it, he'll do it, or he'll get in even more hot water."

I whipped my head around to stare in disgust at Cade. Although I was grateful to him for getting us out of trouble, I hated the way he was acting. It was like a power trip on steroids. It was obvious Cade thought the officer was beneath him. I couldn't help wondering if he thought *I* was beneath him.

Humphrey threw the cruiser into reverse then swung it around and stomped his foot on the gas pedal. When he came to the pond, he screeched to a halt. Without a word, he got out of the cruiser and opened the door. I quickly scrambled out with Cade close behind me. "Thank you, Officer Humphrey. You have a very nice day. I'm sure you'll have a lot to talk about when you get back to the station," Cade said sarcastically.

Officer Humphrey clenched his jaw and glared away from Cade. Wanting to put as much distance as I could between Cade and the officer, I started power walking toward my farm.

"Hey, where's the fire?" Cade asked when he jogged up to me.

"Nowhere. I wasn't lying to Officer Humphrey. I really do need to get back to the farm and get the harvester put into the barn."

We walked along in silence for a few more moments before Cade asked, "Avery, what's the matter?"

"Nothing."

"Then why are you so quiet?"

"I guess I'm just overwhelmed by what happened."

Cade snorted. "Yeah, I guess for a goody two-shoes like you, being in a cop car would be overwhelming."

A voice in my head told me to keep my mouth shut, but I just couldn't bring myself to do it. "I'm also confused, and kinda disgusted."

"What are you talking about?"

"It's the way you were about the officer, the way you boasted about how he had to do whatever you said or he'd be out of a job."

"Oh, excuse me for trying to get us out of trouble. Would you prefer I didn't text my dad and we were still in that cop car on the way to jail?"

"It's not that I don't appreciate your father's help."

"So what's the damn problem?" Cade demanded.

"You." I shook my head at him. "In that one moment, you became every stereotype I've ever had of rich, powerful people—everything that disgusts me about privilege."

We had reached the fence, so I hoisted myself up and over without his help. When Cade didn't drop down beside me, I glanced back at him. He stood on the other side of the fence with a strange expression on his face.

"Cade?" I questioned.

"Sorry, Prescott. I was momentarily stunned by the use of your claws." He then clambered over the fence and landed by my side.

I twisted the hem of my tank top between my fingers. "I'm

sorry if I hurt your feelings."

With a smirk, Cade replied, "You didn't hurt my feelings. You just surprised me by being somewhat bitchy with the silent treatment and white privilege judgment."

I stared incredulously at him. "Now you're deflecting and calling me out?"

"I suppose so, Dr. Phil."

"Unbelievable." I threw my hand up and motioned beyond the fence. "How you were back there? It's not the Cade I've come to know over the past few weeks. It's not a Cade I would ever like to be around, and it's certainly not the Cade I like as a person and a friend.

Cade's eyes widened at my tirade. "Wow, Prescott. You've left me kinda speechless here."

"That has to be a first."

He laughed. "Yeah, it probably is."

"So what do you have to say for yourself?"

"Is this where you want me to say I'm sorry or something like that?"

I shook my head at him. "You are a real piece of work." When he opened his mouth to protest, I added, "And I do not mean that in a good way." I then started stomping through the grass, taking giant steps like I was an irate toddler.

It didn't take long for Cade to catch up with me. For a few moments, he walked and I stomped along in silence. "Maybe we should go talk to Dr. Paulson on Monday and tell her we can't work together," I suggested.

Cade skidded to a stop, kicking up a cloud of dirt. "Why the fuck would we want to do that?"

I rubbed my hands over my eyes. "I don't know. I'm just frustrated with you right now."

"Look, I can say I'm sorry."

"No, Cade. I don't want you to say you're sorry unless you actually feel that emotion and actually give a shit about how I feel."

"But I do give a shit, Prescott."

I swept my hands to my hips. "Do you truly mean that, or are you just saying it so I won't go to Paulson?"

A low growl came from Cade's throat. "Dammit, Prescott. Why do you have to bust my balls so hard?"

"That's not the answer I was looking for."

"Yes. I'm sorry. Really fucking sorry."

"Even about the way you treated that police officer?"

"He was a total douchebag," Cade protested.

"While he could have gone a little easier on us, you didn't help matters with the way you treated him at first."

"Fine, fine. Whatever. I'm sorry for being a prick to Officer Douchebag, even though he kinda deserved it."

I shook my head but grinned in spite of myself. I guess it was going to take baby steps with Cade, and I couldn't expect too much of him too soon. I was just glad I had managed to get through to him.

As we started through the grass, Cade asked, "You know what

bothered me the most?"

"Being in the back of a police car, or having a random stranger see you naked?"

Cade laughed. "No. Neither of those."

"Then what?"

"The fact that you were disappointed in me."

The fact that I was disappointed in him? Surely he can't be serious. I stared at Cade's face and prepared to laugh at his teasing expression, but what I saw stopped me. He looked…serious…solemn, almost.

I swallowed hard. "You really cared about that?"

"Yeah, I did."

"Why?"

"Because you're one of the most decent people I know, Prescott. You're also one of the nicest and kindest. I didn't like the thought of not having someone like you in my corner." He cut his eyes over to me. "You ever see that Jack Nicholson movie where he tells Helen Hunt that she makes him want to be a better man?"

"*As Good As It Gets?*"

"That one." Cade grinned. "That's kinda like how I feel about you, so I didn't like pissing you off."

"Wow," I murmured.

"Don't tell me you're speechless now."

"Yeah, I am."

"Then we're 1-1 today, huh?"

"That's a sports reference, right?"

Cade laughed. "Yeah, it is."

"Yes, we're even."

"But are we good?"

I glanced over to Cade and his hopeful expression. "We're good."

He gave a satisfied nod of his head. "Cool. Now I have a burning question for you."

"What?"

"How do you plan on explaining what happened to your mom?"

"She's at work, remember?"

"Yeah, well, what about your grandmother?

I grimaced. While Nana probably wouldn't be too mad at me, she would spill the beans to my mom. After the day I'd had, I really didn't want to hear a lecture from her about getting in trouble because Cade was a bad influence. "Maybe I don't have to explain."

Cade's jaw dropped to his chest. "Holy shit, Prescott. I really am a bad influence if you're going to lie to your mother."

"Theoretically, is it really lying when you just don't admit what happened? I mean, if Nana asks me where we were, I can honestly say I was showing you around the farm. If she asks how I got wet, I can admit that we took a dip in Mr. Frost's pond. She can't yell at me too much since my mom was always getting caught when she was a teenager. Unless she point blank comes out and asks,

'Avery, were you almost arrested this afternoon?', then I'm not technically lying."

"I see you're already thinking like a legal eagle."

"I guess I am."

We then reached the thresher. "Do you want to drive again?" I asked Cade as we climbed inside.

"No. I think I'm good. I'll let you handle it this time."

"Okay."

As I cranked it up and we started back toward the barn, Cade couldn't help himself. He started belting more of Kenny Chesney's "She Thinks My Tractor's Sexy". I ducked my head and grinned not because the song was embarrassing, but because Cade couldn't sing. I'd finally found something he wasn't good at.

SEVEN

AVERY

Two Months Later

"In conclusion, it could be said that Shakespeare's true gift to the literary world is not just the beautiful figurative language of his poetry and prose, but furthermore, it is his uncanny ability to examine the full range of the human psyche. This is especially true when examining the repercussions of love."

Cade grinned. "And to quote the J. Geils Band, 'Love stinks.'"

Applause rang around us along with some whistles and catcalls, which were of course directed at Cade. When I dared to look at Dr. Paulson, she smiled. "Excellent job defending your argument, Miss Prescott and Mr. Hall. That was the finest presentation on anti-love in Shakespeare's works I've seen in several years. You certainly earned your A-plus."

"Heck yeah!" Cade exclaimed while throwing up a hand for me to high-five him. I couldn't help grinning when my hand slapped against his.

After eyeing the clock above the whiteboard, Dr. Paulson rose out of her chair to address us. "Thank you all for your presentations. I will have your research papers graded upon your return. Have a wonderful Thanksgiving break. Class dismissed."

As Cade and I started packing up our presentation materials, a pang of sadness and regret entered my chest. Now that the project and paper were over, there wouldn't be a reason for Cade and me to hang out any more. He would go back to his world with the A-crowd, and I would leave Harlington for an entirely different universe at Emory.

Every day I waged a silent war within myself over the growing feelings I had for him. Getting to see the real Cade, not the stereotype I had of him, had been both a blessing and a curse. The tiny little flame I'd felt those first few times we'd been alone together had now grown into an inferno that engulfed me. The day he had come to the farm had changed everything.

Cade interrupted my thoughts by exhaling an exaggerated sigh of bliss. "Ah, nine whole days without school."

"What are you doing for the break?" I asked.

Cade shrugged. "Hanging out around here, I guess."

"You're not going home?"

"Maybe for a few days. My parents are off on their usual Caribbean cruise."

"Your parents go away for Thanksgiving?"

"It's never really been a big holiday for us."

My heart ached for him. Although he was putting on a good front, I could tell that deep down it bothered him. "Wow, it's hard for me to even imagine not celebrating Thanksgiving."

With a smirk, Cade said, "Let me guess: you guys have a huge meal that your Grammy cooks, and after you eat, everyone sits around the table and tells something they're thankful for."

I playfully smacked his arm. "No, smarty-pants, we don't.

"Then what do you do?"

"Actually, my mom and I help Grammy do the cooking, along with my Aunt Lily and your favorite, Mae. And no, we don't go around the table saying something we're thankful for. It's a madhouse considering my mom's brothers bring their families. There was even a brawl one year when Mae's flavor of the month got in an argument with my mom's brother, Chris, during one of the bowl games." I gave him a pointed look. "Trust me, it isn't some Norman Rockwell painting like you're alluding to."

"I'm shocked, Prescott."

"I'm so sorry to disappoint you."

He laughed as we walked through the classroom door. "Well,

see ya after the break."

"Yeah. See you."

As Cade started down the hall, a light bulb went off in my head. Instead of pausing to maybe think the idea through, I blurted out, "Cade?

He turned around and cocked his brows at me. "Yeah?"

My heart thundered like a brass band as I power walked to catch up to him. "If you're just going to be hanging around Harlington, why don't you come have dinner at my house?"

Cade blinked a few times. "You're asking me to have Thanksgiving dinner with your family?"

His disbelief at my invitation made me feel like I'd made some huge mistake by asking him. "Sure. Why not? We'll have plenty of food since Grammy always cooks enough for a small country."

Cade's hand reached behind his head to scratch the hair at the base of his neck. It was a little thing he did whenever he was debating something—one of the many personality quirks I'd picked up on during all the time we'd spent together. "What about your mom? No offense, but she wasn't exactly welcoming when I met her before."

His hesitation was understandable. She had lectured me over and over again about the time I was spending with Cade. Whenever he stopped by Rose's Garden to work on our project, she had been icily polite to the point that Cade could've gotten frostbite. She probably wouldn't have spoken to him at all if we hadn't been in public. My mom wasn't someone who was quick to anger or hold a grudge, but with Cade, she was in extreme overprotective mother mode.

"She won't mind." When he gave me a pointed look, I held up my hands. "I'll talk to her and make it where she won't mind. I swear."

"That should be a hell of a conversation."

"Oh whatever."

"Do you guys have cornbread dressing or stuffing?"

His question momentarily took me off guard. "We're Southern, so it's always cornbread dressing," I replied.

Cade smiled. "I love cornbread dressing."

"Then you'll come and eat some?"

He remained lost in thought for a few seconds more before he finally nodded. "Yeah, why the hell not."

"Great. We eat at noon, and then everyone congregates around the TV to watch football games."

Cade's eyes widened. "Whoa, *you* actually watch football?"

I laughed. "Okay, so I usually sneak off somewhere and read."

"I thought as much."

"Maybe this year I'll stick around and watch it."

Cade's brows shot up. "You'd do that for me?"

I'd do anything for you. "Sure. Of course."

"Thanks, Prescott. It means a lot that you'd put yourself through football viewing hell just for me."

Prescott. He managed to call every other girl in school by her first name, but for some reason, he didn't with me. Of course, there was a small part of me that enjoyed it. It made me feel set apart from the others somehow, like I was special.

With a grin, I replied, "You're welcome."

After placing both of his hands on my shoulders, he bent his head and placed a lingering kiss on my cheek. His lips felt like fire against my skin, and I fought to breathe. I ended up huffing out a few breaths, and it felt like I was panting. I wanted nothing more than to press myself against him and feel the strength of his arms around me.

When Cade pulled away, the sincere look in his eyes made me feel horrible for getting so worked up about a simple gesture of kindness. *Get a grip, Avery, the guy was just thanking you for inviting him to Thanksgiving, not offering to throw you on the floor and make mad, passionate love to you.*

"Thanks, Prescott. This means a lot."

It took me a moment to find my voice. "You're welcome."

"See you next Thursday."

"See you then."

EIGHT

CADE

I stood in the middle of the floral section of Publix, trying desperately to pick out a bouquet of flowers for Avery. Well, they weren't just for her; they were for her family, to say thank you for hosting me for lunch. It was the least I could do since she wouldn't let me buy any food, and at eighteen, I couldn't buy a bottle of wine. Sure, I could've swiped one from my parents' wine cellar, but I would have come off totally wrong. After Rose's icy reception of me, the last thing I needed was to give her any more ammunition. I wanted Rose to actually like me and not just tolerate me because Avery had smoothed over her ruffled feathers. Of course, I didn't know how a bouquet of flowers was going to do that, but I was going to try.

"How about this one?" the woman behind the counter asked.

I grunted. "Don't you have anything better?"

She gave me a wounded look like I had personally insulted her, rather than her flowers. I quickly threw up my hand in apology. "I'm sorry, ma'am. It's just I need something out-of-this-world beautiful and impressive that shows I'm a nice and thoughtful guy, and something that doesn't scream cheap."

"I could put a few bouquets together, I suppose. Add in some roses."

"Yeah. That would be great."

She eyed me curiously before turning back to the cooler full of flowers. "It must be some fancy dinner you're going to," she called over her shoulder.

"Not exactly."

She paused going through flowers to turn and look at me. "Let me guess: you're meeting your girlfriend's parents for the first time, and you want to impress them while at the same time impressing her."

"Uh, no. She's not my girlfriend. Just a friend."

"Mmmhmm," was the woman's reply.

I decided then it was best to screw around on my phone until she was finished, that way she wouldn't feel like making any more commentary about my alleged *relationship* with Avery. The truth was I was fucking confused about what was going on between us.

If you'd asked me two months before, I would have said we were absolutely nothing, but then I'd gotten to know her so much better. I wasn't just talking about seeing her practically naked that day we went swimming. Avery wasn't your typical nerdy girl. For starters, she had a rocking hot body, but even though she was gorgeous, it was her personality that really made her attractive. She could give it back to me as good as I gave it, which wasn't something that usually happened in my harem of adoring women.

I had to face facts. Anything between Avery and me was complicated on so many levels. Avery was the relationship-type of girl, and I didn't do relationships. I could have if I wanted to, but I had never wanted to. I just wanted to have some good times while fucking around. At the moment, Elspeth was handling the second part of that for me. There was also the fact that Avery was leaving town to start college in six weeks. If I couldn't do a relationship with someone right in front of me, there was no way anything long distance could work.

Basically, I was screwed.

I had just answered a few texts from my buddies about a post-Turkey Day party when the woman said, "There. How's that?"

I glanced up at the newly improved bouquet that now overflowed with red and yellow roses. "Really nice."

She smiled. "I'm glad you like it." While I guessed it was nice having the woman's stamp of approval, I really only cared if Avery would like it. Jesus, what had happened to me? I was not the kind of guy that gave two shits about fruity shit like flowers. I sure as hell had never given a girl any, unless you counted the corsages my mother's personal assistant ordered for formal dances. Yet there I was in broad daylight acting like a pussy over a bouquet for Avery. I seriously needed my man card revoked.

After paying, I grabbed the bouquet and started off grumpily. The lady called out, "Good luck with the girl!"

"Whatever," I mumbled.

* * *

Although Avery had told me Thanksgiving was a mad house, it didn't quite prepare me for all the cars lining the driveway. I was beginning to wonder how the hell we would have enough food with all these people, let alone fit them in the farmhouse. After grabbing the bouquet, I started up the walkway and onto the porch.

When I reached to open the door to knock, it flew it open and I jumped in surprise.

A red-faced and beautiful Avery greeted me with a smile. "Hi," she said breathlessly.

"Hi."

She wore her long, dark hair down instead of in its usual ponytail. The sides were pulled back with those barrette thingies. Although I fully expected her to be decked out in some sorta hokey harvest outfit, she wore a simple burgundy colored dress with sexy knee-high black boots.

Damn, she was so beautiful. It felt like I was really seeing her for the first time, even though we'd spent countless days, hours, and minutes together.

Avery gave me a small smile. "Sorry if I startled you. I saw you drive up and I decided to come out to meet you."

"Are you stalking me?" I teased.

She laughed as she motioned me inside the house. "Sort of. I'd been keeping a look out so you wouldn't have to face a bunch of strangers."

Leave it to Avery to always be thoughtful. "Thanks. I appreciate it."

After she shut the door, she drew closer to me. In a hushed voice, she said, "Plus, I wanted to warn you that the men in my family are going to give you hell because they think you're my boyfriend."

Oh shit. First the nosy florist and now Avery's family. "Seriously?"

Raising her right hand, she said, "I swear on everything that is holy that I have set them straight a million times, not to mention my mom has, too."

"Ah, I guess that means she's gonna be thrilled to see me again."

"I wouldn't call it thrilled, but it's nice to see you again," Rose said from behind Avery.

"Nice seeing you, too."

"Posh flowers," she remarked with a coy smile.

"They're for all of you, but especially for Margie."

She tilted her head at me. "You're hitting on my mom?"

"Etiquette dictates that you bring a gift for your hostess. Since this is her house, she is my hostess."

"So you don't have a granny fetish?" Rose asked teasingly.

I grimaced. "Uh, no. I don't."

"Good to know. Here, let me take the flowers to the kitchen. I know a perfect vase for them."

I handed over the bouquet and Rose started into the kitchen. Once she was out of earshot, I exhaled in relief, but the feeling was short-lived because I suddenly felt about ten pairs of eyes on me. I slowly turned to the left to see the living room overflowing with the men of Avery's family. "Uh, hey," I called as I threw up my hand.

One heavyset guy rose off the couch. "You Avery's boyfriend?"

"Uncle Tim, I told you he was just a friend," Avery hissed.

"Is that because you don't have the balls to ask her to be your girlfriend?"

Oh Christ. I was *so* dead. Glancing over my shoulder, I quickly calculated if I would be able to haul ass out of there and to my car before one of them caught up to me. I knew I could beat Tim, but two of her cousins wore *Rome High School Track* hoodies.

I cleared my throat. "No, sir. It's more like Avery is too good to ever lower her standards to date me."

Silence reverberated around the room as the seconds ticked by agonizingly slowly. The next thing I knew laughter erupted around me. "Good answer, son," Tim asserted as he came over to me. After smacking me on the back, he asked in a low voice, "Wanna come out to the back porch for some beer? Mama doesn't allow it in the house."

Since I figured it was another test, I shook my head. "Thank you for asking, but I better refrain."

Tim rolled his eyes. "Lord, you sound as fancy as Avery with the way you talk."

"High praise," I murmured as I grinned at Avery.

She laughed nervously.

Margie came into the living room, and thankfully, I seemed off the hook. "Lunch is ready. Everyone come into the dining room."

All the men were off the couch in a flash before stampeding down the hall. "You handled that well," Avery mused.

"Thanks. To be perfectly honest, I pulled that one out of my ass."

She grinned. "

The bathroom door opened and a sniffling Rose stepped out. Without a word to us, she hurried on to the dining room. "Is she okay?" I asked.

"It's just today is kinda hard."

"Why's that?"

"It's the first Thanksgiving without my grandfather."

"Oh. I'm sorry."

"It's really the first time we've all been together as a family since the funeral."

"I guess your mom was pretty close to him."

Avery nodded. "She was not only the baby of the family, but she was the late-in-life baby. Nana was thirty-five when she was born, and Papa was forty. He spoiled her a lot—just like he spoiled me."

"Yeah, I had an amazing grandfather, too. He used to do all the things my parents said not to, like giving me ice cream or chocolate, just to piss them off. No matter how busy he was, he always made time for me. I used to run around his office like a hellion, and he never yelled at me."

Avery's green eyes widened in surprise. She wasn't used to me sharing stuff about my family. "Had? Has he passed away?"

"Two years ago. He had a heart attack on the golf course."

"I'm so sorry."

"Hey, he died doing what he loved, and there's no better way to go than quick."

"That's true."

"Avery, Cade, come in and sit down," Margie instructed. When she motioned to the kids' table, I couldn't help laughing.

Avery's face turned blood red. "I'm sorry that we haven't graduated to the adults' table yet."

"It's all good. The food will taste just as good no matter where we're sitting."

"I guess so."

Once everyone was seated, Margie turned to the man at the head of the table. "I know it was always Robert's place to say grace, but in his place, I think you should, Bobby, as the oldest son."

I bowed my head to the sound of Bobby saying, "Dear Heavenly Father…"

I opened my eyes and peered around the table at all the bowed heads. I felt hokey as shit, like I was having some Lifetime movie revelation, but I wondered if they knew how lucky they were to have such a loving family. It just drove home the point that while on the outside it looked like I had everything, I really didn't. I had a fragmented family who had never really gathered around a table together unless it was at some political function where we needed to make my father look good for the cameras.

Avery's family was real while mine was just a fancy knockoff.

"Amen," Bobby said.

A chorus of "Amen" rang throughout the dining room.

"Now, let's eat," Margie declared with a smile.

Avery had been right about the size of the feast. Not one but two turkeys adorned the table. Vegetables on platters overflowed the table and filled up another table in the room. Conversation flowed as freely as the food and sweet tea. Of course, everyone was curious about me, so I had to pony up some details for them. The men were especially interested in how I was set to play for Georgia Tech.

"Man, that's tight," said Blake, one of Avery's teenage

cousins.

Uncle Tim grinned down the table at me. "I'm a UGA fan myself, but I'm still impressed."

"I would have totally played for them, but their offer wasn't as good as Tech's."

"Did ya get a lot of money?" Blake asked.

"Blake, that's not polite," his mother chided.

I laughed. "It's okay. I usually get asked that question. It wasn't so much about the money, but the fact that I'd get to play college football. That doesn't happen a lot when you come from a private school."

Margie smiled at me. "Isn't it nice that you and Avery will both be attending college in the big city?"

"Yeah, it is." Damn, I hadn't even thought about that. Emory and Tech weren't that far from each other, and there was even a shuttle than ran between the two. I wondered why Avery hadn't mentioned anything about it before when we'd talked about her graduating early. I cut my eyes over to Avery, who suddenly found her sweet potatoes very interesting. "Maybe we can meet up sometime."

She glanced up at me. "Maybe."

The conversation then got heated about who was going to win between the Cowboys and the Packers in the upcoming game. While I debated with the men, Avery talked with some of her younger cousins about God knows what.

Just when I was seriously considering unbuttoning my pants, Margie stood up. "Let me go get the dessert tray."

I cocked my brows at Avery. "You guys have a dessert tray like at a restaurant?"

Avery grinned. "You seem so surprised. Doesn't this dining room reek of five-star dining?"

With a laugh, I replied, "The food is better than any five-star place I've ever eaten in."

"Nice save there with the compliment."

"I'm serious. People would pay good money for this food. I should have known how good it would be after that grilled cheese sandwich at Rose's Garden."

"If you were in heaven with the grilled cheese, wait until you get some of my Aunt Regina's cheesecake."

"I should have worn sweatpants," I moaned.

* * *

After sampling one of each of the ten—yes, ten—desserts, I expected the men to haul ass into the living room to watch football again. Instead, the women left us to clean up while they went to the den.

When I handed some of the plates to Bobby, he snickered. "What?" I asked.

"Tell me the truth, have you ever had to wash dishes in your life?"

I scratched the back of my neck and gave him a sheepish grin.

"Not exactly."

"I figured as much."

Tim slapped me on the back. "Maybe he should be the one scrubbing, Bobby. You know, to give the kid the experience."

"I'm okay."

Bobby grinned. "Like I'm going to entrust Mama's fine china to his hands."

"You know, I'm pretty good at handling precious objects," I argued.

Bobby and Tim laughed. "Then I guess I can trust you to dry," Bobby suggested.

"Okay."

I was just finishing up when Avery peeked her head in the doorway. "Are you okay?" she asked.

"Do you mean has this manual labor crushed my soul?"

"More like have my uncles been giving you a hard time and making you do all the work?"

"Nah. They've treated me just fine."

"Good."

Tim shut the fridge door after putting in the last of the leftovers. "Honestly, Avery, you act like we're out here making him plow the south field."

"He probably could since I took him out on the harvester."

Tim's brows shot up. "Oh, you did?"

I nodded. "Since I'd never been on a farm, Avery showed me

around." I met her gaze and gave her a knowing look as I thought about us almost getting arrested.

Tim glanced between us before crossing his arms over his broad chest. "I hope the south field was all she showed you."

Avery's face reddened like an overripe tomato. "Uncle Tim!" she shrieked.

I couldn't help laughing at both her reaction and the irony of the situation. Little did he know I'd seen *a lot* of Avery that afternoon when we went skinny dipping.

Tim chuckled before throwing an arm around my shoulder. "Come on, kid. Let's go warch the Packers clobber the Cowboys."

"Actually, I think it's going to be the Cowboys doing the clobbering."

"Bullshit."

I crooked my finger at Avery. "What?" she questioned.

"You told me if I came you'd watch football with me."

She grimaced. "I was hoping you wouldn't remember that."

"Oh, I totally remembered."

"Okay, okay. A promise is a promise."

As I led Avery to the living room, it felt like I was leading a prisoner to their doom. Since the couches were taken, we sat on the floor as the last strains of the national anthem were sung. After kickoff, I pointed to one of the guys. "That's the running back. That's what I play."

"Really?" She sounded generally interested, and that was the difference between Avery and any other girl I knew. When she sounded genuinely interested, it was because she actually was. There was not one fake bone in her body.

"Yep."

"Since I didn't come to any of Harlington's games this year, I'll have to come see you play next year."

"I'd like that. Maybe I can swing you some tickets." When it looked like she might protest out of embarrassment at the insinuation that she would need free tickets, I said, "So I can get you in the VIP section or something like that."

She smiled. "I've never seen myself as a VIP."

"Oh, you're total VIP material."

A grunt came from behind us. "Would you two shut up? We're trying to watch the game."

While Avery turned red, I just laughed. We watched the rest of the game in silence, except for during halftime when Avery listened intently as I rehashed some of the game highlights with the guys. For someone who hated football, Avery was a really good sport about watching with me. Of course, I had to explain some of the fundamentals to her so it was more than just a bunch of guys smacking into each other over an oblong ball.

When the game was over, I turned to her. "I guess I better get going."

She opened her mouth, but Bobby interrupted her. "You sure you don't want to stay for the eight thirty game?"

"I appreciate the offer, but I really need to get back to the dorms."

After I stood up, I held out my hand to help Avery up out of the floor. "I'll walk you out."

I threw up my hand at Avery's remaining family members. "Thanks again for letting me hang out."

"You're welcome. You can come back any time. We'll be looking for you on TV next year at Tech," Tim said.

I laughed. "I don't know how much play I'll get as a freshman, but you can try."

After hugging and thanking Margie, I walked out onto the front porch with Avery close behind me. "I had a really good time today," I said as we started down the steps.

Avery smiled. "I'm glad to hear that. I was afraid my family might have you running for the hills."

I shook my head. "No. They're great. You're really lucky to have them."

"I'll try to remember that the next time they're teasing me relentlessly about something."

"They're just doing it because they love you."

"I know."

"It's funny how different you act around them than you do at school."

Avery's brows shot up. "How do I act differently?"

"You just seem more comfortable, more like yourself.

Harlington seems to make you uptight."

"Or maybe it's the people who make me uptight," she murmured.

I could see her point with that one. "Well, whatever it is, I'm just glad I got to see it."

"Me too."

"I guess I'll see you next week at school." *Smooth, Hall. It's pretty much a given you will see her at school. If you're going to miss hanging out to work on the project, maybe you should ask her to do something outside of school, but then that would be a date, right? That wouldn't be good because I don't date.*

"For just a few more weeks," Avery said, a hint of sadness in her voice.

"Well, thanks again," I said. I didn't know why I leaned in to give her a hug. Being platonically touchy with a girl was so not my usual style. With the talk about her leaving soon, I wanted to be as close to her as I could.

"You're welcome," Avery murmured against my neck. Her breath scorched my skin, and in that instant, I wanted nothing more than to feel her soft, delicate lips against mine.

Slowly, I pulled my head back to stare into Avery's eyes. The expression in them seemed to mirror every emotion I was experiencing: confusion, lust, sadness. Although I knew it was the last thing in the world I should do, I dipped my head and brought my lips to Avery's.

Fuck. They were everything I thought they would be, everything I knew I'd been missing out on when I had been more concerned with second and third base action than first.

At the sound of the front door opening, Avery jerked away. Panic now replaced the other emotions in her eyes. I knew I needed to get the hell out of there, both for her sake and mine. "Bye, Avery," I muttered.

I barely gave her time to move out of the way before I threw open the car door. I hopped inside and started the engine. After I turned the car around, I gunned it down the driveway. When I glanced back in the rearview mirror, I saw Avery standing with her arms wrapped around her, watching me go.

That's exactly what I should have been doing: driving away, leaving her. Avery Prescott was everything soft, sweet, and beautiful. She was…real. The last thing in the world she needed was someone like me in her life.

But like the ultimate asshole, I had gone and kissed her. Even as I drove farther away, I could still feel her lips against mine as the sweet smell of her perfume clung to my clothes.

I had kissed Avery, and she had kissed me back.

And I hadn't wanted to stop.

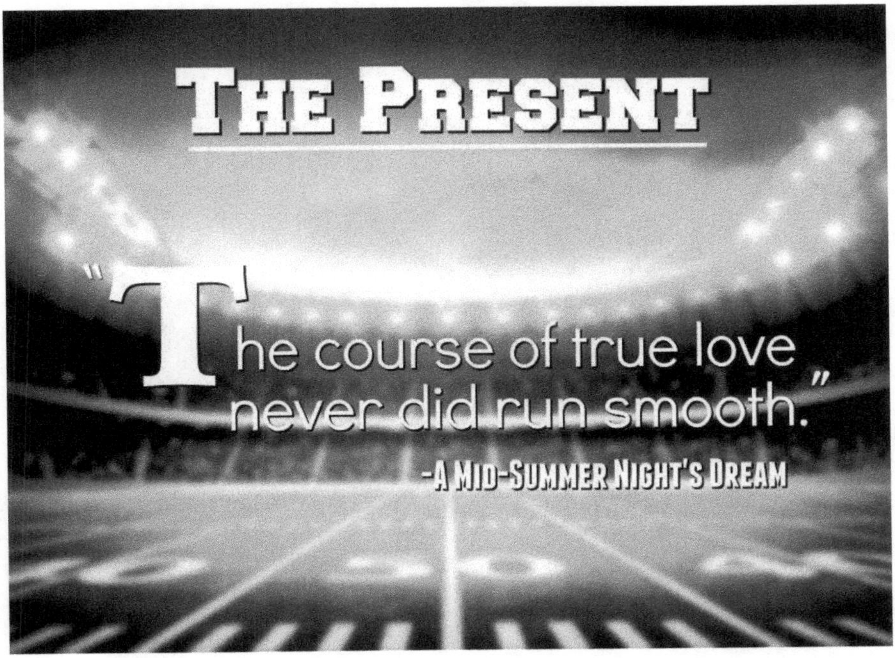
The Present
"The course of true love never did run smooth."
-A Mid-Summer Night's Dream

NINE

AVERY

Usually whenever our closing manager Jason arrived at five, I hung around and gave him the rundown on how the day had gone. That day I merely threw up my hand in greeting as I breezed past him on the way out the door. There was no way in hell I could stay one minute more at The Ark. I had to get away from there.

More specifically, I had to get away from Cade.

The stifling summer heat smacked me in the face as I made my way to my car. In the four years since I had last seen Cade, I had traded in my grandfather's old pickup for a more reliable Honda Civic. As I unlocked the door and slid inside, I couldn't help grunting in frustration that I was once again thinking of Mr. Asshole.

After showing Cade around, I deserved an Academy Award for the performance I had pulled off. For the remainder of the day, I had somehow managed to keep a smile plastered to my face. Inwardly, I was crumbling, but no one would have thought a thing was wrong. I didn't want to take out my shit on the kids; it wasn't their fault that the guy who'd shattered my teenage heart had shown up.

My reserve momentarily faltered when Tamar dragged me into her office after I finished Cade's tour. "Okay, girl, dish it. How do you know Cade Hall?"

Groaning, I put my head in my hands. "It's bad, T."

"I can tell that. I just need to know *how* bad."

I drew in a deep breath before giving Tamar the quick lowdown on Cade's and my relationship. When I finished, she let out a low whistle. "Oh honey, I'm so sorry."

"Thanks."

"Look, I can totally call the dean back and ask for Cade to be sent somewhere else."

"You don't have to do that."

"And you don't have to force yourself to be part of a hostile work environment." Tamar placed a hand on my shoulder. "The last thing I want is having you feeling miserable here."

I shook my head in firm resolve. "But the last thing I want is to give Cade the satisfaction of thinking that after four years, he still holds any power over me or my happiness."

Tamar sighed. "If you're sure."

"I am." *That's right, I am sure. I mean, I have to be sure. I want to be sure…*

She cupped my chin. "You are one amazing woman Avery Prescott."

"While I appreciate the compliments, you might want to hold them back."

"What do you mean?"

I grinned slyly at her. "I was thinking that one way to make things easier for me would be to make Cade's life here at the center a living hell."

She laughed. "Honey, he deserves every bit of it."

So, with Tamar's blessing, I had come up with a quick list of hellish tasks for Cade to complete. I have to give him credit for not vocally bitching about anything. I was sure inwardly he was cussing me out., and while it was a slight victory to punish Cade, it certainly did nothing to quell the emotions raging within me. There was too much history, too much pain, and so much unresolved between us to simply forget and go on.

Before I could make the turn that would lead me to my apartment, I veered off onto the I-75 North interstate ramp. It didn't matter that it was almost an hour and a half to get home—I just knew I had to go there. I had to see my mom.

As I drove along the long stretch of highway dotted with trees and rolling green grass, I thought about the happy times I'd shared with Cade. When the memories of that first deep love swept over me, I couldn't fight the tears. The emotional dam that had been holding back my emotions imploded. I began crying around Cartersville, and I didn't stop until I rolled into downtown Rome.

Instead of pulling around back to the employee entrance, I wheeled into an empty spot at the front of Rose's Garden. When I threw a quick glance at myself in the rearview mirror, I grimaced; my cheeks were stained black from my mascara. I was suddenly grateful for being OCD and carrying wet wipes in my console. I did a quick cleanup of my face before grabbing my purse and heading out of the car.

The bell tinkled over my head as I entered the store. I had forgotten that during the busy summer months, Mom had a guitar player singing. Because the guy happened to be hot, he had a gaggle of female admirers littering the café side of the store. So much for being alone with my mom.

She had just finished up an order when she glanced up. "Be right—" She froze on her usual greeting and her brows instantly creased in worry. "Avery? What are you doing here?"

I forced a smile to my lips while I walked up to the register. "Can't a girl just come home to see her mother?"

Mom shook her head. "Not without calling and not on a Monday night."

With my back to the crowd, my resolve started to wane. "Oh Mama," I murmured as my lip quivered.

Mom held up one finger before calling out, “Emily?”

My sixteen-year-old cousin came bounding out of the back. “Yeah, Aunt Rose?”

“I need you to man the counter.”

Emily’s brown eyes widened. “But I’m just training. I can’t make a panini without burning it,” she protested fearfully.

Mom placed both her palms on Emily’s shoulders. “I know that you can do this, and if shit gets crazy, come get me. Okay?”

“Uh, okay.”

I walked down the length of the counter as Mom did on the other side. When she came out on the end, she threw an arm around my shoulder and drew me close to her. We barely made it down the narrow hallway to her office. Once we got inside, Mom closed the door.

“Are you sick?” she asked.

“No,” I murmured as I sank down onto the couch.

She paced in front of me. “Are you pregnant?”

My eyes bulged. “Of course not. You know Hal and I broke up onths ago.”

“Just because you’re not in a committed relationship doesn’t mean you can’t get pregnant.” She gave a rueful smile. “I should be the best example of that one.”

“Okay, let me rephrase: I’m not pregnant because I’m not having sex—period.”

Mom exhaled a relieved breath as she sat down beside me. “If you're not sick and not pregnant, what's going on?"

My chin trembled as I fought to not cry again. "The universe hates me…"

I then proceeded to tell Mom all about Cade showing up at The Ark. When I finished, she sat so dumbfounded before me that she couldn't speak. She blinked a few times.

"Well?" I prompted.

"The universe does hate you," she finally said.

Picking up one of the throw pillows, I then whacked her with it. "I just drove an hour and a half for words of wisdom, and you give me that bullshit?" I teased.

Mom smiled. "You're going to have to give me a minute. Honestly, I think I would know more of what to say if you were pregnant."

"I don't think I know how to respond to that."

"Now you feel my pain."

I groaned as I put my head in my hands. "I just can't believe it. I mean, all day I just kept pinching myself in the hopes I would wake up and find it had all been some horrible nightmare."

"Can't you have him sent somewhere else? There has to be another volunteer opportunity in the city."

"Tamar offered, but I said no."

Mom jerked my hands away from my face. "What do you mean you said no?"

"I didn't want to give him the satisfaction of thinking he still got to me."

"Sweetheart, he *does* still get to you. If he didn't, you wouldn't have come home on a Monday night."

"I'm well aware of what he does to me, but he doesn't have to know that."

Mom's brows furrowed. "It isn't too late to have him transferred, is it?"

"Why?"

"Because I think it would be for the best."

"Nice vote of confidence there."

With a shake of her head, Mom said, "You just lost it over one day with him, Aves. What's going to happen when you have to see him day in and day out?"

"This is just a momentary flake out after seeing him. I'm sure it will lessen the more I'm around him."

Mom sighed. "I don't like you being around him. I don't want a resurrection of what happened four years ago."

I knew Mom was referring to what happened after my run-in with Cade and Elspeth's assault. With only three weeks remaining until winter break, I hadn't returned to school. Thankfully, Mom didn't push me to go back. Instead, she allowed me to finish up my senior year at home.

Since I started at Emory in January, I didn't have to see Cade again…until graduation. As salutatorian, I had to be at the ceremony—I even had to speak. Although almost six months had passed since I had seen Cade, I was still just as much in love with him. I was also just as devastated and wounded by how I'd been treated. Time heals all wounds, but some are so deep it would almost take an eternity to truly repair them.

The first day I saw him at graduation practice, I had to bolt away to find a bathroom so I could throw up. By the time the actual ceremony rolled around, my family doctor had prescribed me some anti-anxiety medication. Once I got through graduation, I never had to take it again, mainly because I didn't have to see Cade again.

"Man, I was a wreck," I murmured.

"Do you know how hard it was for me to see you like that? To see my perfect, poised daughter broken like that?" Tears glimmered in Mom's eyes.

"I'm sorry."

She wagged a finger at me. "You have nothing to apologize for. It's all that prick's fault."

"True."

"You should have let me castrate him when I had the chance."

"While I appreciate your thinking, whether or not he had a penis has nothing to do with him showing up at The Ark."

"I think the odds of an egomaniac like Cade going streaking with no dick would have been a lot slimmer. Therefore, he wouldn't have been sentenced to charity work at The Ark."

I laughed. I could always count on my mom to not only be there for me, but to make me feel better. That day, more than anything, I needed her comfort, but I also needed her to make things lighter and make me laugh.

Mom grinned and patted my leg. “Why don’t you stay the night? We can pig out and stay up late watching movies. A total girls’ night in.”

I could’ve argued that making the drive back in the morning would be hell with traffic, or that I had a million things to do at my apartment, but I didn’t. I knew more than anything I needed to be with Mom right then. “That sounds amazing.”

“Great.” She rose off the couch. “I better get back to the front before Emily burns the place down.”

“Okay.”

“Will you be all right?”

“I’ll be fine. In fact, I’ll wash my face and come out and help you.”

“Great. Closing up will go so much faster, and then we can get home.” She started for the door, but then stopped. Whirling around, she asked, “You know what movie I’d love to see and haven’t watched in forever?”

“What?”

“*Sixteen Candles*. Gah, Jake Ryan still makes my panties wet.”

Instead of groaning about her grossing me out, I stood frozen at the mention of the movie. There was no way Mom could have known the connection I had between *Sixteen Candles* and Cade, or what had happened the night we’d watched the movie right there in the store.

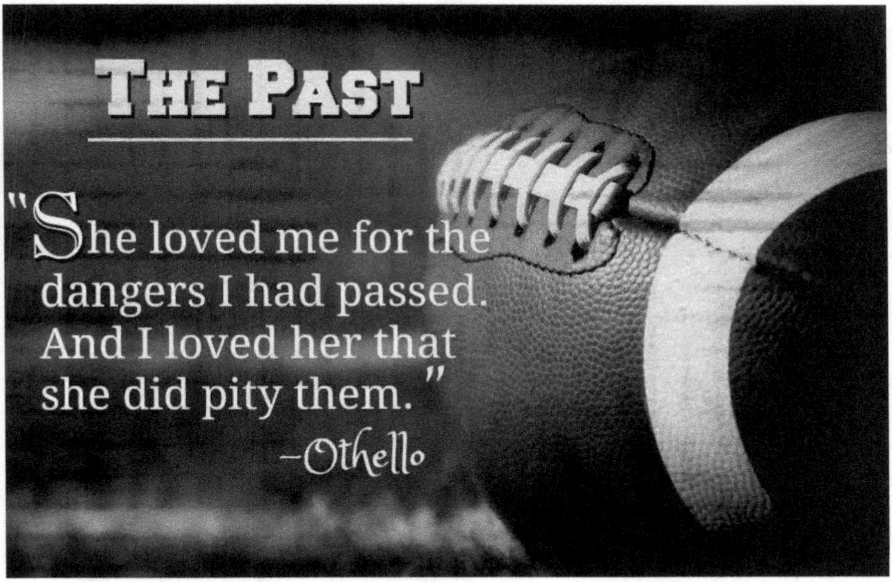
THE PAST
"She loved me for the dangers I had passed. And I loved her that she did pity them."
–Othello

TEN

CADE

"Mmm, I want to suck you off so bad."

I cut my eyes over to Elspeth. While she looked like she had stepped off the cover of Cosmo in her designer dress, she sounded like a bimbo out of a cheesy porno. It seemed really out of place standing under the white Christmas lights that were supposed to transform Harlington's cafeteria into a winter wonderland. I'm not sure why she was suddenly so horny considering the other decorations of snowmen and frosted trees didn't exactly scream *fuck me now*.

When I didn't respond, she ran her hand down the front of my jacket, letting it rest at the top of my fly. "You look so hot in your tux, Cade. I can't wait to get you out of it."

I clenched my jaw and tried to fight the irritation I felt at her comments. Normally, I would have been rock hard at Elspeth's dirty talk—after all, I was an eighteen-year-old dude with a dick so just the wind blowing could get me hard—but that night, it got under my skin, and not in a good way.

Fuck. Nothing about the night felt right. If I manned up and faced the music, I knew nothing had felt right since I'd kissed Avery on Thanksgiving night. I couldn't do anything but think about her—her lips, her eyes, her body. The more I thought of Avery, the more frustrated I got, and not just in a sexual way.

It all came down to the fact that I didn't do feelings with girls, least of all relationships. When you got your ass tangled up in a relationship, it meant it was more than just the physical. It meant you had found a deep, emotional connection with someone, that you were willing to give over not only your heart, but your dick as well. Relationships meant monogamy, a term I understood but had yet to practice.

Of course, Elspeth knew the score. She wasn't the only girl I fucked. Why should she expect to be? All the girls at Harlington made it clear they wanted me. I sure as hell didn't need a relationship to get laid, so what would be the point?

Avery was one hundred percent a relationship kind of girl—the long term—and there was no way I could give her what she needed...what she deserved.

Because of that fact, I'd been avoiding her the past few days. I'd even lowered myself to skipping English a few times. I'd somehow managed to convince the nurse I had a stomach virus, and she'd written me a note. Since I felt nauseous any time I thought of Avery, it wasn't stretching the truth too much.

The blaring song the band was playing screeched to a halt. My best friend, Renly, strolled up to us. He swept his sweat-soaked hair out of his eyes. "You guys ready to blow this joint and then get blown?"

His flavor of the week, Emily, threw his arm off her shoulder. "Ew, Renly. Why do you have to be so crude?"

The crew usually spent an hour or two at the Harlington functions and then went back to someone's house or hotel room to party. "Where are we going?" I asked.

"My house," Gemma Worthington piped up. I didn't bother asking if her parents were home—they usually flew their private plane to South Carolina to stay at their beach house on Hilton Head.

"Gotcha."

Elspeth pressed herself against me. "You coming with us in the limo?"

The thought of being trapped in a confined space with Elspeth wasn't appealing at all. "Uh, no. I better drive myself."

Her lips turned down in a pout. "But I wanted to snuggle on the way."

"Sorry. You'll just have to go without me."

"You're such a party pooper tonight, Cade," she whined.

Renly grinned. "It's just because he's sober. Wait'll we get a little booze in him. He'll be his old self then."

That misguided hope perked Elspeth right up. "Then I'll see you there." As she leaned in for a kiss, she threw one hand around my neck and the other went to squeeze my junk.

Once again, it didn't rise to the occasion, which kinda worried me. Maybe instead of going to the party, I needed to go back to my dorm and watch some porn, you know, to make sure the equipment was still working and this was just a fluke thing.

Then an image of water cascading over Avery's curves entered my mind and caused my dick to jump. Elspeth jerked back and flashed me a triumphant look like she was the Dick Whisperer or something. "I'll take care of that when we get to the party."

"Whatever," I muttered.

She gave me one last smacking kiss on the lips before pulling away. Her fellow mean girls crowded around her, and they walked away, giggling like loons. I followed behind the others as they made their way out the side door of the cafeteria to the parking lot. "See you in a few, Hall," Renly said before he ducked inside the waiting stretch limo.

"Yeah. See ya." When I arrived at my convertible, I took my tux jacket off before getting inside. By the time I cranked the car up, the limo's lights were fading in the distance.

Before I knew it, I was cruising down Main Street and almost past Rose's Garden. Just the sight of the storefront caused an ache to burn through my chest. Wanting to get away from it and the feeling, I gunned the engine.

I couldn't stop myself from throwing a quick glance in the rearview mirror. As I found myself driving farther away from Rose Garden and from Avery, my chest clenched again. It was starting to become unbearably tight, so much so that I debated loosening my tie and unbuttoning my shirt to see if it would lessen the pressure.

Deep down, I knew from my psychology class that the pain was psychosomatic. Nothing but seeing Avery was going to make it better. I had to stop running from her. I knew she had to be clueless as hell about what was going on between us. I'd kissed her and bailed. She wasn't the kind of girl to text or call; she fully expected me to make the move, and I was failing miserably.

After surveying the nonexistent traffic in my rearview mirror, I cut the steering wheel hard. The tires screeched as I made a U-turn in the middle of the abandoned two-way street.

Almost on autopilot, I eased my car into one of the parking spaces in front of the store. Peering through the windshield, I searched for any sight of Avery. For all I knew, she wasn't working that night. The last thing I needed was to run into Mae again—my ass wasn't safe around her.

Then I caught a glimpse of Avery. I felt like the biggest pussy when my heart thundered in my chest. As I watched her wipe the counter, I gripped the steering wheel tighter. Considering the weird way I was feeling, there was no way in hell I should be around her. It was inevitable I was going to say or do something I would regret.

While the voice in my head continued telling me to get the hell out of there, my hand fumbled on the door handle. Almost in a trance, I stepped out of the car and started toward the store. It was like Avery had some magnetic pull on me that no matter how hard I tried, I was incapable of resisting.

The sound of my knuckles rapping against the glass door caused Avery to jump. With her back to me, she called over her shoulder, "Sorry. We're closed."

"It's me. Cade."

Avery's hand froze mid-swipe. Slowly, she turned around. "Cade?"

"Yeah."

She stared at me for a few seconds like she was wondering if I was some sort of ghost. Finally, she tossed the rag on the counter and started over to me. After flipping the locks, she threw open the door. She did a quick head-to-toe sweep of me before shaking her head. The corners of her lips twitched. "I think you're a tad bit overdressed for a Friday night around Rome."

"I just came from the winter formal."

Disappointment momentarily swelled in her eyes. "Oh yeah. That was tonight." She waved me inside. "Come on in. It's freezing."

After I entered the store, she locked the door behind me. When she turned back around, she crossed her arms over her chest like she was cold. I held out my tux jacket to her. "Need this?"

She shook her head. "I'm fine. It's not so much the cold."

"Then what is it?"

"I gotta say I'm a little surprised to see you, and the tux isn't part of it."

My hand snaked behind my neck to tug at my hair. "Yeah, I guess things have been a little weird lately."

Avery jerked her chin up. "Maybe that's because you've been avoiding me."

"No. It's not like that. You see, I've had this pukey stomach thing, and then I…" When Avery pursed her lips at me, I knew there was no point in going on. She deserved the truth. "Yeah, you're right. I've been avoiding you."

"Why?" she questioned softly.

"Because I'm an asshole," I answered honestly.

Her brows shot up. "That's not exactly the response I was expecting."

"It's just, things got a little complicated at Thanksgiving."

"I'm sorry if my family came on too strong. That's just the way they are."

I shook my head. "It's not your family that was the problem."

"Then what is it?"

"You."

She gasped. "Me?"

"Yeah, you. In case you missed it, I kissed you Thanksgiving night."

"I'm aware of that, Cade."

"I don't go around kissing just anybody."

"Are you sure? I'm pretty sure you've built a reputation on that."

I rolled my eyes. "I built a reputation on fucking, not kissing."

"Excuse me for being naïve, but aren't the two related?

"I kiss girls before I fuck them. It's because I'm feeling something here—" I motioned to my dick, which caused Avery's cheeks to redden. "I don't kiss a girl because I feel something here." I placed a hand above my heart.

Avery blinked a few times as if she was fighting hard to process what I had just said. "So you're feeling something for me?"

"Yeah, I am."

The corners of Avery's lips twitched. "I'm glad to hear it."

"Oh, you are?"

She bobbed her head. "I'm feeling something for you, too."

My chest puffed out with pride. "I figured you were."

"Excuse me?"

"Girls always end up feeling shit for me."

Avery gave me a disgusted look. "Seriously, Cade? Way to ruin a moment." She whirled around and stomped over to the counter.

"Wait. Shit. Don't go."

"I need to finish closing up."

"Fuck," I growled as I jerked a frustrated hand through my hair. After taking a few deep breaths, I walked over to stand in front of her. "Look, I'm sorry, okay? This is all new to me—uncharted territory. I'm bound to screw it up epically, but will you at least give me a chance?" *A chance? Am I seriously asking her that? And holy shit, Avery feels something for me?*

Avery studied me intently, her green eyes boring into mine as if she was searching their depths for an ancient mystery. After what seemed like an eternity, Avery said, "Okay."

I cocked my brows at her. "Really?"

With a small smile, she replied, "Yes, Cade. Really."

"Fuck yeah." Inwardly, I was doing a victory dance like a quarterback in the end zone.

She motioned to one of the antique barstools. "Why don't you have a seat?"

"Thanks."

After I eased down onto one of the stools, Avery asked, "Hungry?"

"Yeah. I didn't eat much at the dance."

She smiled. "Your usual?"

"Sure. Thanks."

As Avery started working on my sandwiches, I leaned my elbows on the counter. "I thought I might see you there. I mean, I hoped I would."

"You did?"

"Yeah."

She cocked her head at me. "And what would you have done if I had been there?"

"I would have asked you to dance."

She rolled her eyes. "Yeah, right."

"I'm serious."

Avery's hands stilled. "You would have really paraded me around in front of your A-crowd friends?"

"Why wouldn't I?"

"Maybe because they would give you shit for dancing with someone like me?"

"Fuck that. I make my own rules." It was the truth. Because I was Cade Hall, no one would have talked shit to my face about being with Avery. Sure, they probably would have run their mouths behind my back, but no one would dare challenge me to my face.

Avery shook her head as she poured me a Coke. "What? You don't believe me?"

She laughed. "Oh, I believe you. It's more like I have trouble comprehending what an egomaniac you are."

I grinned. "I'll take that as a compliment."

"Of course you will." She set the Coke down in front of me.

"Why didn't you go to the dance?" I asked.

"Like anyone from Harlington would ask me."

I shrugged. "You could have brought someone from around

here."

"There wasn't anyone I wanted to go with." Avery held my gaze for a moment before she whirled around to go over to the sink.

"All I know is it would have been a lot better if you had been there."

"Then why didn't you ask me?" Avery questioned, her back still to me.

"I thought we already established why." When she threw a curious glance at me over her shoulder, I replied, "Because I'm an asshole."

"You *were* an asshole. You're working on that, right?"

"Yes, ma'am. I intend to be fully rehabilitated under your tutelage."

Avery laughed. "Did you actually just use the word *tutelage?*"

I bobbed my head. "Yup. You're rubbing off on me."

"I'm glad to hear it."

"You'll probably be the only one to hear it. If the guys heard me, they would revoke my man card," I joked.

Avery set my sandwiches down in front of me. "Speaking of your A-crowd, where are they right now?"

"Getting wasted at Gemma Worthington's."

"Is that where you were going?"

"Yeah, I was on my way there, but then I saw the Rose Garden. and you know…"

"You decided instead of being with your partying friends you wanted to be with me?"

Holding her gaze, I said, "Yeah, I did. Just the idea of the same old party with drunk idiots and casual hookups made me wanna puke." I chewed thoughtfully on my sandwich. "I've never felt like that about my friends before, like I was above their maturity level or something."

"Wow," Avery murmured.

I laughed at how incredulous her expression was. "I know. I'm thinking I should head to the ER to have an MRI or something."

"Sounds like you're having a Jake Ryan epiphany."

I swiped my mouth with the back of my hand, which caused Avery to pass me a napkin. "Who is Jake Ryan?"

Avery choked on the tea she was sipping. "You're joking, right?"

"Nope."

"The hunk with a heart from the movie *Sixteen Candles*." When I shook my head, she demanded, "You mean you're not fluent in Hughes?"

"Um, considering I barely passed French, that would be a negative."

"John Hughes is a filmmaking genius from the '80s and '90s. Besides *Sixteen Candles*, he did *Pretty in Pink, The Breakfast Club...*" At what must've been my continued blank stare, Avery added, "What about *Ferris Bueller's Day Off*?"

"Nope."

"Wow, I find that shocking since you and Ferris have a lot in common."

"Ah, so he's a badass who makes women's panties wet?"

Avery wrinkled her nose. "No. It's more about him being a popular jackass who always manages to talk his way out of trouble."

"Whatever."

"Okay, there's only one way to remedy this urgent situation."

"And what's that?"

"We're just going to have to watch *Sixteen Candles*."

"Here?"

"Yes, here. Right now." She swept her hands to her hips and said in a pretentious tone, "That is unless you have a more pressing social engagement to get to."

"No, smartass, I don't, but what about you?"

She rolled her eyes like I had just said the dumbest thing in the world. "You should know I have nowhere else to be but the farm."

"What about your mom and grandma? Won't they be expecting you home?"

"I'll tell them I'm going to stay here and watch a movie with you."

"Are you sure that's such a good idea? You're mom warmed up to me at Thanksgiving, but I'm not sure how she would feel about us having alone time." Considering how close Avery and her mom were, I wondered if she had told her about our kiss. If she had, there was no way in hell Rose would want us hanging out together.

"Fine. I'll just tell her I'm going to hang out at Mae's and maybe spend the night."

I made a choking noise. "You mean Miss Goody Two-Shoes is going to lie to her mother?"

Avery giggled. "It's just a little white lie about a movie, Cade. It's not like we're eloping in Vegas."

"Fuck no! No marriage for me."

With a roll of her eyes, Avery said, "Thanks for clarifying." She grabbed her phone from beneath the counter and fired off a text to her mom. After a few seconds passed, her phone dinged. "We're good to go."

I grinned. "Let my education begin."

Eleven

AVERY

“Nice tits,” Cade mused.

I groaned and tossed a piece of popcorn at him. We had come to the shower scene in *Sixteen Candles* where Samantha and her friend do the creepy stare down of Jake’s girlfriend, Caroline, in the gym shower.

His response was to flash me a wicked grin. “I can’t believe you held out on me about the nudity. This is awesome.”

With a roll of my eyes, I replied, “Enjoy it while it lasts because this is it.”

“Bummer.” He took a long swig of his Coke. “I gotta say I’m a little surprised to see a teen movie flashing tits and dropping the Fbomb that isn't rated R or something."

"The rating system was a little wacked in the '80s. This came out just before PG-13."

I readjusted the pillow behind my head. Cade and I were sprawled out on a rug from the 1920s in front of a giant armoire from the '40s watching Netflix on a TV from 2014. A while back, my mom had decided to keep a TV in one of the armoires for times when business was slow. She had made sure it was hidden away from prying eyes by other pieces of furniture so anyone who walked by couldn't see that she was just chilling watching TV.

"I can't imagine my mom ever forgetting my birthday," I mused about Samantha's plight.

Cade snorted. "I sure as hell can. I'm sure if my dad's secretary didn't send them reminders, they would totally forget."

"Seriously?"

"Yep."

His parents' callousness caused my heart to hurt. "I'm sorry," I murmured.

Cade kept his eyes on the screen "Not your fault, Prescott, so don't be apologizing."

"I know it's not my fault, but I can still hate the way they treat you. That happens when you care about someone."

He flicked his gaze over to mine. "Okay. Apology accepted."

I smiled. "I'm glad."

By the time the movie ended, we had polished off a six-pack

of Coke, four bowls of popcorn, and some of the leftover banana bread we'd served in the store that day. As I started cleaning up, Cade stretched his arms over his head. "That was a pretty cool movie, Prescott."

"I'm glad you liked it."

"And I agree that I'm totally Jake Ryan."

I laughed. "I didn't say you *were* Jake Ryan; I said you were having a Jake Ryan moment when you realized you didn't want to hang out with your immature friends."

"Um, I think I have all the qualifications of being Jake Ryan. I'm rich, handsome, popular"—he swept his hand to his chest—"and I have a deeper, sensitive side."

"Which you don't really show that much."

Cade waved his hand dismissively. "Whatever. I'm a work in progress." He started helping me dry the dishes. "There's only one problem I have with the movie."

"The fact that there weren't graphic sex scenes?" I suggested.

He chuckled. "While that was certainly a bummer, that's not what I meant."

"Then what?"

"The happy ending."

I frowned at him. "What kind of person hates a happy ending?"

"It's not so much that I hate the happy ending—I'm glad Jake wised up and got with Samantha—it's more about the fact that it leaves you hanging. Like how does everyone at school take Samantha and Jake as a couple? Does Caroline get shit when she shows up at school with part of her hair chopped off? Does she start speaking to the nerd guy when she sees him in the hallway since they spent the night together in that car?"

I blinked at him. "Wow, I never thought about any of that."

"Guess I'm too much of a realist."

"While I was too caught up in the happy-ending aspect." I bent over to put the popcorn bowls up when I knocked a bottle out of the cabinet. "Crap," I muttered as it rolled to a stop at Cade's feet.

"Is that wine?"

"Yeah. It's homemade muscadine. My mom used to keep it displayed because of the antique bottle it's in, but then everyone kept wanting to buy it, so she put it away."

Cade's brows popped. "Homemade? For real?"

"Yep. My grandfather used to make it from the muscadine vines that grew along the pasture. Want to try some?"

A teasing gleam burned in Cade's eyes. "Are you trying to get me drunk and take advantage of me, Prescott?"

As if I would even have a clue as to how to do that. "Were my motives that obvious?"

Cade grinned. "Fine, I'll have some—on one condition."

"You have a condition?"

He nodded. "You have to drink with me."

Oh man. I hadn't expected that one. Sure, I'd had a sip or two of wine during the holidays and at church during communion, but I'd never sat down and actually had a glass. "Um, okay."

With a snort, Cade said, "Prescott, you disappoint me with how easily you cave to peer pressure."

"I've had wine before." At his pointed look, I added, "Just not a lot."

"Have you ever been drunk?"

I shook my head.

"I can't say I'm surprised by that." He jerked his chin at the bottle. "Pour it up."

Since we didn't have any wine glasses on hand, I had to use some of the teacups. After pouring them almost full, I handed one to Cade and then took one myself. Cade clinked his to mine. "Here's to us."

As I brought the cup to my lips, the beat of my heart thrummed wildly. Was that a generic toast like to us as people, or did it mean more like us as a couple? The giant question mark hanging over us was so frustrating. Although I knew I should be cautious, I still couldn't help the feelings I had for Cade. They had been growing stronger and stronger over the last few months, and after Thanksgiving, I knew he felt something for me.

After taking a few sips, Cade said, "It's good."

"I've always liked it, but it's not like I would really know the difference."

"Well, it really is good, and my opinion means something

since I have extensive wine knowledge."

I grinned. "I should have known you would be a wine connoisseur among your other talents."

"It was my parents who started me off. They took my sister and me to Paris with them when I was seven. The wine is kind of free flowing there, so I made sure to have my fill." At what must've been my horrified look, he added, "I didn't get drunk, Prescott."

"Oh, good," I replied in relief. I couldn't help judging Cade's parents a little for letting him have wine at seven years old.

Cade refilled our cups before walking over to the antique side of the store. He stopped in front of one of the marble-top tables then threw a glance over his shoulder at me. "Is this one of those old-timey record players?"

"A Victrola," I answered as I joined him.

Cade snapped his fingers. "That's right. There was one of these at my grandparents' house." He eyed the contraption curiously. "Does it work?"

"Sure." I set my cup down before winding up the crank. Then I placed the needle on the record, and a slow instrumental tune came out of the Victrola's horn. At Cade's groan, I grinned. "Not a fan of classical music?"

"No. It's more about the fact that it's one of Strauss's waltzes."

Cocking my brows at him, I asked, "You know Strauss?"

With a snort, Cade said, "Don't look so surprised, and no, I didn't learn about him in Harlington's music appreciation class either."

I held up my hands. "I wasn't alluding to anything."

"Yes, you were alluding, as you say, to the stereotype of me being an uncivilized jock," Cade teased in a snooty-sounding voice.

"I'm sorry. I've got to stop doing that. You really are so much more than a jock."

He swept his hand to his heart. "Why, thank you."

"So tell me how you know Strauss."

"I have waltzed at ten cotillions and three debutante balls."

"Wow. That's quite impressive."

"What about you?"

"I've never been to a cotillion or deb ball."

"No, I mean, haven't you ever waltzed before?"

I laughed. "Oh yeah, I often practice my dance skills out in the corn."

"Every lady should know how to dance."

"But I'm not a lady."

Cade smiled. "Yeah. You are." When I started to protest, he said, "Money and position aren't what make a lady. It's what's inside you that counts."

His words and his tone caused the breath to wheeze out of my lungs. Just when I thought he couldn't surprise me any more with the things he said, he went and said something like that. "Thank you," I finally mumbled.

"You're welcome." The world seemed to slow to a crawl around us as we stood there staring at each other. The sound of Cade clapping his hands together caused me to jump. "Okay. One waltz lesson coming up."

"I'm going to warn you that you're probably going to regret this. I'm the worst dancer ever."

"How can anyone who plays the piano suck at dancing?"

"I'm not sure how it's possible, but trust me, it is."

Cade laughed. "We'll see."

A tingling jolt of electricity shot through me when Cade took one of my hands in his. After he put his other hand on the small of my back, he drew me closer to him. Even with all the times I had sat next to him while we worked on our project, I hadn't been this close.

"Now you put your other hand on my shoulder."

"Okay."

"Step back with your left foot and then bring your right to the side." After I followed Cade's lead, he said, "Now bring your left foot to your right, and then step forward with your right."

My mind spun as I frantically tried processing Cade's instructions. Somehow it managed to click together, and I followed his lead. "Hey, you've got it," he remarked with a smile.

"It's not because of me—it must be the teacher." I glanced up at him and smiled. "Sports, brains, and dancing; you're really a true triple threat."

"You forgot devastating good looks and charm."

I grinned. "Does that make you a quintuple threat?"

"Make it a sextuple threat if you throw in the money."

"I should have known you'd find a way to have 'sex' in your title."

Cade threw his head back and laughed. "Always busting my balls, Prescott."

"Yep. Just consider me your Little Ball Buster like Judith in *Walking Dead* was called Little Ass Kicker."

Cade's brows rose in surprise. "You watch *Walking Dead*?"

"Sure I do."

"That surprises me."

"Why?"

"I guess I just figured you only watched pretentious stuff like *Downton Abbey*."

"*Downton Abbey* is not pretentious."

Cade grinned. "I'll take that as a yes that you watch it."

"I certainly do."

"At least I'm 1 and 1 on picking the TV shows you like."

"While you know me pretty well, you have a lot more to learn, Mr. Hall," I teased.

"I look forward to you educating me."

As I stared into his face, Cade's expression grew serious. The idea of educating him suddenly seemed to take on a deeper meaning—one of both mental and physical knowledge.

Cade dipped his head to where our mouths were just inches apart. His breath fanned across my cheek, causing me to shiver. I stared into his eyes, silently pleading with him to go ahead and kiss me. We'd already been down this road before. Since Thanksgiving night, I'd wanted nothing more than to feel his lips on mine again.

When he finally kissed me, it sent energy humming all over my body. I'd kissed other boys, but it had never felt the way it did with Cade. It was all-consuming of my mind, body, and spirit.

Considering his experience, it shouldn't have been too surprising that Cade was a good kisser. What surprised me the most was the emotion behind his kiss. It ran so much deeper than just a physical act, as if he was putting his heart and soul into kissing *me*.

Cade deepened the kiss by plunging his tongue into my mouth. It tangled along with mine in a waltz of its own composing. My hand snaked up his back to capture the hair at the base of his neck, and I ran my fingers through the silky strands, marveling at how much softer it was than I had imagined.

The Victrola ran out of steam, and the only sound filling the room was heavy breathing. At the loss of music, Cade stopped leading me around the floor, and his hands slid underneath my buttocks. He gripped the globes of my ass before hoisting me up to wrap my legs around his, and I molded myself tighter against him. I couldn't seem to get enough of him—the way his strong arms felt around me, his thick waist against my legs, his broad, muscular back underneath my hands. Even though I knew I shouldn't, I wanted all of him.

When we crashed into a chest of drawers, Cade momentarily released my lips to breathlessly ask, “Are you okay?”

“Mmhmm.” I gazed into his hooded eyes. “Don’t stop. Please don’t stop.”

I rubbed myself against the ridge in Cade’s pants, causing him to groan against my throat. “Jesus, Prescott, if you keep doing that, I won’t be able to stop.” When I did it again, my action was rewarded with a growl.

Cade’s wild eyes glanced around the room before leading us over to the wide red settee in the back corner. We collapsed onto the smooth velvet material. I widened my legs to allow Cade’s hips between them and his mouth sought out mine in a frantic kiss.

As our tongues battled against each other, Cade’s hand came to my breast. He kneaded and cupped it over the fabric of my uniform, my nipples hardening under his touch. When he began undoing the buttons of my dress, he broke the kiss to glance at me as if asking my permission. At my nod, he practically ripped the remaining buttons open.

He gave me a sheepish grin as he pulled me into a sitting position. “Sorry about that.”

“It’s okay,” I said as I slid my arms out of the sleeves.

My breath hitched when Cade’s arms snaked around my back to undo my bra. Once it was unhooked, I couldn’t help bringing my arms to cover my chest and keep the bra in place. I hated that in this moment I couldn't seem to get past my modesty, or my fear that my average-sized chest would turn him off.

Cade tilted my chin with his fingers, forcing me to look him in the eye. "You sure you're okay with this, Prescott?"

"I am, I promise."

"Then what's wrong?"

"I'm just a little scared," I whispered.

"That I'll hurt you?" Cade questioned with a wounded look.

I gave a quick jerk of my head. "That you won't like what you see."

"Huh?"

"You've been with so many other girls. I'm afraid I won't measure up."

His expression darkened. "That's the stupidest fucking thing I've ever heard."

I ducked my head. "I'm sorry, but I can't help the way I feel."

Cade cupped my face in his hands. "There's only right here and right now, and there's no one else but you and me. None of the past, just us and this moment."

My heartbeat thrummed wildly at his sentiment. "Okay," I murmured as I stared deeply into his eyes.

"And you could never not be beautiful to me. I like everything about you, both inside and out." At what must've been my incredulous look, Cade grinned. "And I'm not just saying that so you'll let me in your pants."

"I know you wouldn't." Deep down, I knew it to be the truth. If Cade had really wanted to just screw me, he would have attempted it over the past two months.

"I wouldn't be here tonight if I didn't want to be with you for the long haul."

Once again, my heart began to beat so erratically that I felt a little dizzy. "Really?"

He nodded. "You're all I need, Avery."

I was so overcome by his words that I lunged at him, practically tackling him down on the other end of the settee. I kissed him with everything I had in me, like a dying woman trying to experience every last moment of feeling left.

My body came alive as Cade raked his hands over me and goose bumps rose on my skin under his fingertips. All my senses became incredibly heightened, from the woodsy smell of his cologne permeating my nose to the way the stubble on his face felt as it brushed against my neck and the slick feel of his tux pants as they rubbed against the tender skin of my inner thighs.

With one hand on my breast, Cade slid the other up my thigh to come between my legs. He stroked me there, his fingers dancing along my clit, sending moisture pooling. He certainly knew exactly where to touch me to make me feel the most pleasure. Just like with the kissing, it hadn't been this way with the other guy I'd been with. It had felt good and I had liked it, but it was nothing like with Cade, who had me writhing beneath his touch.

Cade pushed my panties aside and slid one finger into my wet core. One finger became two, and then he began pumping them in and out of me. I moaned into his mouth as I started to build toward coming. My hips began to buck against his hand, desperately seeking more friction.

Sensing I needed more, Cade tore his mouth from mine and kissed a trail over my chin, down my neck, and across my chest to one of my breasts. When his lips closed over the nipple and sucked it deep into his mouth, I pinched my eyes shut and cried out his name. He pumped his fingers a few more times, and then I saw stars behind my closed eyes as I came. I have no idea what I said or did in those moments of bliss; all I could do was focus on the sweet pulsing between my legs.

When I came back to myself, I flicked my eyes open and stared into Cade's face. After withdrawing his fingers from me, he brought them to his lips. He sucked them deep inside his mouth. I was unable to look away as I watched him taste me on his fingers. More than anything, I wanted his mouth on me.

As if he read my mind, Cade unbuttoned the rest of my dress and opened it to where I was naked except for my panties, but that was short-lived as he made quick work of whisking them away. "God, you're so beautiful."

With my insecurities once again working in overdrive, I teasingly replied, "I'm sure you say that to all the girls."

"No, I don't, and I mean it when I say it to you."

His hands came to my thighs, and he ran his fingers up and down my sensitive skin. He then gripped my knees and pushed my thighs apart. I'd never felt as vulnerable in all my life as I did having Cade staring down at me, especially between my legs. He licked his lips before dipping his head. At the feel of his tongue sliding along my clit, I sucked in a harsh breath. He licked and kissed me before sucking my clit into his mouth. "Oh God!" I shrieked as I clawed the settee.

As he continued sucking, his tongue swept inside me, sending me shooting straight up into a sitting position. My hips began to rock in sync with him thrusting his tongue inside me. One of my hands came to grip the settee while the other went to his head. I entangled my fingers in the strands of his hair, tugging it when the pleasure grew greater and greater. Sweat broke out along my forehead, and my thighs shook.

"Oh God!" I shrieked as I once again saw stars. For the second time that night, I found myself floating back down from the stratosphere after coming. Staring up at the ceiling, I swept my hand to my forehead. "Wow," I murmured.

Cade chuckled. "You're welcome."

I flicked my gazed to his. "I'm sorry. Should I have said thank you?"

"Feeling you come around my tongue while screaming my name was thanks enough."

Mortification rocketed through me, and it warmed my face and neck. “Don’t be embarrassed. You were so fucking hot when you came,” Cade argued.

“I was?”

“Oh yeah, and I love the way you tugged my hair.”

Feeling bolstered by his compliment and what he had done, I glanced down at his crotch. “So I guess I should…”

“Repay the favor?” When I nodded, he replied, “I don’t know about that, Prescott.”

“Don’t you want me to touch you?”

Cade groaned. “Of course I want you to touch me.”

“Then what’s wrong?”

“I’ve been rock hard since we were dancing. The feel of your hand or your mouth…” Cade’s rolled his eyes shut. “Fuck. I don’t want to come before I get inside you.”

“I don’t mind.”

Cade brought his lips to mine. When I tasted myself on them, I fought the urge to pull away in disgust. This was all so new to me. As I experienced the emotion behind the kiss, I realized the intimacy of the connection. I couldn’t possibly refuse him.

Cade stared down into my face, his eyes searching mine. “Are you sure about this, Avery?”

I knew how serious he was since it was one of the first times he’d ever questioned me and not called me Prescott.

“Somewhere in the back of my head, there’s a voice screaming at me to slow down, saying this is all happening at warp speed. It’s too much too fast and too soon." I brought my hand up to brush against his cheek. "But in spite of all that, I want nothing more than to be with you."

He nodded. "I want to be with you, too."

I gave him a small smile. "Then let's be together."

Cade's reply came in the form of sweeping off his pants. After taking his wallet out of his back pocket, he produced a condom. It didn't surprise me that he was prepared; guys like him always carried condoms. The thought of Cade being one of "those guys" caused a tug of discomfort in my chest. *He said to ignore the past and only think about the here and now, so that's what I'll do.*

When Cade started to put the condom on, I looked away. Something about the act made me feel shy and slightly embarrassed. Once he finished, he dropped back down onto the settee before climbing on top of me. We lay there for a moment, skin on skin, while the rush of our breaths of anticipation were the only sounds in the room.

Cade pushed his hips between my legs. At the feel of the head of his shaft against my opening, I bit down on my lip and sucked in a breath. I tried to steady my emotions for what was about to happen to me physically. It was a big moment—one of the biggest in a woman's life. I was ready—well, as ready as I could ever be.

Sensing my apprehension, Cade kissed me tenderly. When he slid inside me, I whimpered at the burning, stretching pain. Cade immediately froze. His frantic gaze met mine. "Are you okay?"

For a moment, I couldn't find my breath. Finally, I replied, "Yeah."

He then pulled out and eased back into me again. I could tell the restraint he was showing by not slamming into me like he clearly wanted—needed to. After a few more slow and steady movements, I swept my hand down his back to cup one of his butt cheeks. "I'm good, Cade. Show me how you like it."

He grinned. "We'll need to work up to that, babe." He did increase his pace. I grew to like the way he felt as he moved inside me, the way we felt so connected, two bodies merged into one.

While it felt okay, it certainly didn't feel good like when he was touching me with his fingers and tongue. When I felt Cade straining to keep going for me, I whispered, "It's all right. Go ahead."

My words were all he needed. With a satisfied groan, he came. A smile lit up my lips when he called out my name. We lay entwined in each other's arms for several minutes. I made slow sweeps along his back with my fingertips. With my eyes closed, I floated along in a dreamlike world, and I couldn't help thinking about *A Midsummer Night's Dream* and Prince Oberon's magical flower that blossomed the unlikely romances in the play. Cade and I were certainly an unlikely romance. On the surface, we had so many differences, but in the end, they just seemed to bring us together.

Cade finally broke the silence by asking, "You okay, Prescott?"

"I'm more than fine."

"That's good to hear."

I exhaled a satisfied sigh. "I think I could stay like this forever."

"At least until one of us has to pee," Cade quipped.

I smacked his arm playfully. "Way to ruin a moment."

Cade chuckled. "My bad, but you should know I'm not one to do the mushy emotions."

I pulled my head up off his chest to pin him with a stare. "Maybe you didn't do all that before, but I'm going to expect more from you in the emotions department."

He smiled. "For you, I'll try."

Returning his smile, I replied, "Thank you."

"You're welcome."

Before I could lay my head back down on his chest, Cade said, "One second."

He then eased himself off me and got off the settee. "If you're going to the bathroom, you better cover up. It might be late, but someone could still see you once you step out of the nook."

When Cade tossed the condom in the trashcan, I made a mental note to take the can to the dumpster before I left. He glanced back at me over his shoulder. "I'm not going to the bathroom."

"Then what are you doing?"

"Getting us a blanket so my balls don't freeze."

I laughed. "Sorry about that, but the heater cuts off at

midnight."

Cade picked up the TV remote along with one of the antique quilts we'd been laying on earlier before returning to the settee. "It's all good." He winked at me. "We were doing a good job keeping each other warm."

"Yeah, we were." After he curled back up on the settee, he covered us up and turned on the TV. I nibbled my lip before I finally asked the question that was gnawing at me. "You're planning on staying the night?"

Cade flicked his gaze from the TV over to me. "Are you trying to get rid of me?"

I shook my head wildly back and forth. "No, that's not what I meant."

"Then what is it?"

I momentarily stalled by running my fingers over the flowers etched on the quilt.

"Avery?" Cade prompted.

"This is all new territory for me. I just assumed you would want to leave because we were done…" I swallowed hard. "Well, you know."

"Having sex?"

"Yes."

Cade snorted. "You're not a booty call, Aves."

"I know."

"I'll only leave if you want me to."

"I don't want you to. I promise."

"I don't want to go either."

I smiled. "Good."

"Okay then, I'm staying."

"You're staying."

"And I'm watching ESPN."

I groaned. "You can't be serious."

"Oh, I am."

"What if I told you there was another John Hughes movie we could watch?"

Cade's brows rose in curiosity. "Then I might turn on Netflix."

"Thank God."

"We're really going to have to work on how you hate on sports."

"Yeah, I know."

As he worked the remote, Cade asked, "Is it the one with the cool Ferris guy?"

"No. It's called *Pretty in Pink*."

"Whoa, whoa, whoa. I'm *so* not watching something with the word *pink* in the title."

"It's not like that."

"Yeah, well, it sounds awfully fruity."

"I think you'll like it."

"Does it have gratuitous sex scenes?"

Wrinkling my nose, I replied, "No."

"Lots of action with badass CGI sequences?"

"Um, no."

"Then what could I possibly like?"

"It's a story kind of like us."

"What do you mean?"

"Well, it's the cliché of the poor girl from the other side of the tracks who falls for the rich guy."

"Hmm, it sounds sorta interesting."

"We could give it a try. If you hate it, we can turn on ESPN."

Cade grinned. "Look at us already working the compromise."

I laughed. "We're pretty good together."

"Yeah. We are."

As the jazzy strains of *Pretty In Pink's* opening music played, I snuggled closer to Cade. Although my eyes started getting heavy, I didn't want to close them. If I went to sleep, then the night would end, and everything had been so perfect.

Despite my efforts, it wasn't long before I drifted away feeling happier than I ever had.

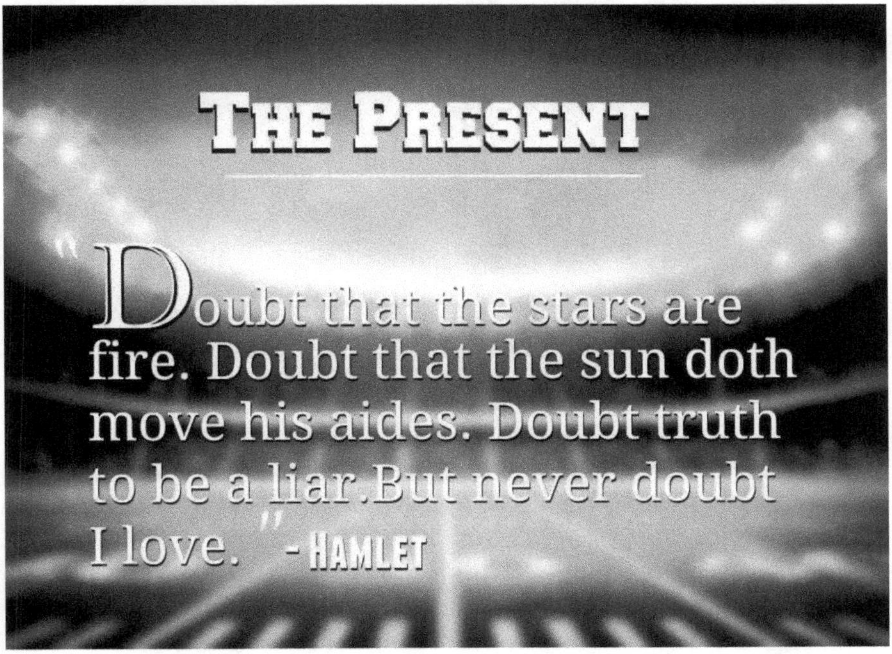
THE PRESENT
"Doubt that the stars are fire. Doubt that the sun doth move his aides. Doubt truth to be a liar.But never doubt I love." - HAMLET

TWELVE

CADE

By the time Friday rolled around, I had made it a week at The Ark, but I was so dead-ass tired it felt more like a month. Between practice and Avery making my life hell, I could have passed for a Walker from *The Walking Dead* with my glassy eyes and lifeless shuffle. Because of spending a week as a zombie, I was forcing myself to connect with the living by going to a party with Jonathan and Brandon when I left The Ark. I needed to be around people who could legally consume large quantities of alcohol.

As for Avery and me, we were barely speaking. After she gave me my daily task list, we went our separate ways. To anyone who didn't know better, it was like we were complete and total strangers.

I was sure none of the kids would have ever imagined we'd liked each other once upon a time.

Okay, so it had been more than just us *liking* each other.

Whenever Avery was dishing out my work schedule for the day, I wanted to say, "Before I scrape the shit stains out of the toilet, I wanted to let you know how epically sorry I am for treating you like a douche." I guess *douche* didn't quite cover it. *Heartless bastard with a blackened soul* was probably more accurate.

But the words never came. I didn't know what the block was about. Yeah, I wasn't real big on having to say I was wrong about something, but normally I wasn't too paralyzed to say two simple words. Part of me wanted to make an appointment with my mom's shrink to ask what my deal was. What was it about Avery that made me want to be a better person yet behave like a total bastard at the same time?

The one bright spot in the shit-storm of a job was Darion. The kid had become my shadow on Wednesday. When his buddies were shooting hoops or watching movies, he was tagging along on trash detail with me. I'd never really been idolized in person. I knew it wasn't about me personally, but more about the fact that I played for Tech.

Although I could have told him to get lost, I kinda liked having him around. It was nice having someone to talk to while cleaning up. We rehashed old Super Bowl games and the latest NFL player stats.

On Friday, Darion's mom cleared it with the center that I

could sign him in and out to come to morning practice with me. When I came to pick him up, Avery was at the desk chatting with Vicki, the sweet, white-haired secretary.

Avery's brows rose in confusion at the sight of me coming in so early. "Did practice get canceled?"

I shook my head at her as I reached for a pen. "No. I'm here to sign Darion out."

Avery's mouth opened and closed a few times like a fish out of water. "Why are you doing that?"

"He's coming to morning practice with me."

"He is?"

"Yep."

Vicki smiled at Avery. "Denise came in this morning with the paperwork. Isn't it sweet of Cade to give Darion this opportunity?"

Avery still stared at me in surprise. "Yes. It is."

Darion came bounding out of the gym area. "Yo. I'm ready!"

"Cool. Let's get going."

"Darion, will you wait here just a moment? I need to have a word with Cade."

I groaned. "Seriously, Prescott? It's going to have to be a fast word since I still gotta get back over to Tech, and I can't be late."

"I promise it'll be quick." Avery then pulled me into a corner out of earshot of the others. "What are you doing?"

"Um, I'm taking a kid to practice with me."

"Yes, I realize that. I'm more concerned with your motives."

I snorted. "Motives? You sound like you're interrogating me on the witness stand or something."

"I'm serious, Cade."

"Look, there are no *motives* behind what I'm doing. Darion has college scouts already eyeing him. I thought it might be cool for him to come watch a collegiate practice. If it's okay with his mom and with Tech, what's your problem?"

"I just don't want Darion getting hurt."

"Uh, I wasn't gonna let him suit up and play today, but thanks for telling me what to do anyway, *Mom.*"

Avery narrowed her eyes at me. "That's not what I meant. He's a very trusting and sweet young man."

"I know he is. That's why I want to hang out with him." Suddenly, it hit me what she was talking about. "Jesus, Prescott. You think I'm going to be a dick to Darion, don't you?"

Jerking her chin up at me, she countered, "You do seem to have that pattern."

I rolled my eyes. "Do us both a favor and get over yourself. It's been four years. Let it go. What happened between us has nothing to do with Darion and me."

When Avery sucked in a breath like my words had sucker-punched her in the gut, I instantly regretted saying them. Even though I was angry at her for questioning my motives, I shouldn't have gone for the jugular by mentioning our past.

After a quick recovery, Avery snapped, "Just so you know,

I'm not putting any of this time toward your hours."

"That's fine. I hadn't expected you to anyway."

"I find that very hard to believe."

"Yeah, I'm sure you do." With that, I stormed away from her and over to Darion. "Come on. Let's go."

Darion glanced over his shoulder. "Dude, what did you say to Miss P?"

"Nothing," I grumbled.

"Yeah, I call bullshit since she looks like she's about to cry."

I ignored his comment as we breezed through The Ark's doors and out into the already scorching heat of the early morning. I had parked on the curb in one of the metered spots and when I started for my car, Darion forgot all about Avery, letting out a low whistle and saying, "Damn, bro, a Mercedes convertible? You're sportin' one hell of a ride!"

I laughed as I hit the unlock button on the key fob. Instead of getting in, Darion did a slow walk around my car. "Is this baby brand new?"

"About a year old." It had been a twenty-first birthday present from my parents.

"Can we put the top down?"

"Sure."

"Hell yeah," Darion replied with a fist pump.

I grinned as I slid across the leather seat. After cranking the car up, I hit the button to put the top down. Darion hopped in the passenger seat and tilted his head back to watch the roof disappear. "So cool," he murmured. Turning his gaze to mine, he remarked, "I've never ridden in a convertible before."

His comment caused an unfamiliar pang of sadness to enter my chest. I didn't want to pity Darion, but I hated that he hadn't been able to experience something as simple as riding in a convertible. I wondered if what I was feeling was what that asshat MacKensie wanted me to experience.

We drove along the busy streets which were crowded with morning traffic. Thankfully, The Ark was only five minutes from the stadium. My ass really would be in a bind if I were late. We only had a few weeks of May practice, and then we got off the month of June. In late July, we started up our fall practice outside the city; I wasn't sure how I was going to work my hours around that.

"So what's the story with you and Miss P?"

I grunted as I shifted lanes. "Jesus, you're not letting that go, are you?"

"My spidey senses say there's something between you guys."

Damn, this kid was good. "We knew each other before I came to The Ark." I threw a quick glance at Darion, whose expression told me I wasn't getting off so easily. "We went to high school together."

With a snort, Darion said, "That ain't all of it, bro."

"Fine. Since you seem to know everything, you tell me."

"You guys know each other really well, like you dated." Darion stroked his chin thoughtfully. "I'm guessing you pulled some sort of douche move and broke her heart."

I almost ran into the back of the truck in front of me. "Wow. You do know everything."

Darion grimaced. "Aw, man, Miss P is a good lady. Why you have to go break her heart?"

"Let's put it this way: I was young and stupid."

"And you ain't ever apologized, right?"

"Nope. I'm a giant dick."

"You are."

I laughed as I pulled into the parking lot. "One day, I swear."

Darion's eyes narrowed. "You better."

Taking one hand off the steering wheel, I said, "I will."

"Good."

"Until then, will you try not to hold it against me?"

Darion didn't answer me. He was too busy taking in the players streaming into the stadium. "Are we good?" I asked again.

"Yeah, yeah, we're good," he murmured as he fumbled for the door handle. After he got out of the car, I had to hustle to catch up to him as he made a break for the stadium entrance. As soon as I got inside, all thoughts of Avery were pushed from my mind, and the only thing I focused on was football.

* * *

When practice was over, I headed to the showers while I left Darion shooting the shit with some of the defensive line coaches. "That's pretty cool you brought one of the strays to practice,"

Jonathan remarked as he shampooed his hair.

"Strays?" I questioned.

"You know, he's homeless, so it's kinda like a stray dog or cat."

His comment sent rage boiling inside me. I glanced down at the bar of soap in my hand before I lobbed it at the back of Jonathan's head.

He whirled around. "Jesus, dude, what's the problem?"

I jabbed a finger at him. "You're the problem. Darion isn't some stray dog. He's a human being."

As Jonathan's eyes widened, I couldn't help also feeling a little surprised by my words. Was it possible that after only a week at The Ark, I was already starting to see things differently, just like Dr. Mackensie had wanted? Or was it more about the fact that even being in the vicinity of Avery brought what little goodness I had out? Oh Jesus, what the hell was wrong with me? I desperately needed to man up and stop overanalyzing everything.

Holding up a hand, Jonathan said, "I'm sorry. I didn't mean it the way it came out. I swear."

"I sure as hell hope not. I didn't take you for such a douchebag."

"No. That's usually your job," Brandon piped up from behind us.

Jonathan chuckled. "He has a point, man. You kinda are the king of us douchebags."

"Whatever," I muttered. I then threw Jonathan an apologetic look. "Sorry about hitting you with the soap."

"You can make it up to me by paying for the Uber to get us to tonight's party."

"Fine. It's a deal."

Once I was done in the showers, I made quick work of drying off and getting dressed. When I exited the locker room, Darion was waiting on me. He waved a pass on a lanyard in front of my face. "I'm a motherfucking VIP!"

I grinned at him. "Where did you get that?"

"Coach Baines hooked me up. He said it gets me into any game. I can even sit in one of the air-conditioned boxes." Darion shook his head. "Can you believe that shit?"

I was impressed by Coach Baines's kindness. Getting to come to Tech's games was like winning the lottery to Darion. I needed to see about getting some tickets for Antoine and Marcus, or they would give me hell about being left out.

As we started to the car, Darion talked a mile a minute, giving me a replay of practice like I hadn't been there myself. I couldn't help grinning at his enthusiasm. The kid was like a freakin' ray of sunshine. For someone who had been through some rough shit, he had the best attitude. I didn't understand why, to be honest. Maybe because I had come from a life of privilege, nothing got me as excited as Darion was.

Throwing the car in reverse, I asked, "Wanna grab something

from The Varsity on the way back to the center?" Darion's happy expression momentarily darkened. "Hold up—don't tell me you don't like The Varsity?" I asked.

"Hell yeah I like it."

"Then what's the problem?"

"I'd just feel bad if I went back to the center with kick-ass food when the other guys didn't have any, especially after getting this VIP pass to the games."

Jesus, did this kid have a kind heart. When I was his age, I wouldn't have given two shits about whether my friends got a treat or not, as long as I did. If I was honest with myself, I still felt that way now.

"We could get enough for the guys."

Darion's eyes widened. "Are you serious?"

"Sure."

"But that'll cost a fortune."

"Although I haven't seen you and the guys eat, I'm thinking it probably won't put me back more than a hundred fifty bucks."

Darion shook his head. "Hey man, to me, a Franklin is a fortune."

"I'm good for it, so don't worry. Okay?"

"That's tight, man."

I grinned at him. "Now things might get a little dicey if you're wanting me to cater in for the whole Ark."

"Nah, just Marcus and Antoine. Maybe Shemar and Pete. We

can have them sneak out to your car and eat it where the other kids won't see."

I laughed as I turned into The Varsity's parking lot. "Sounds like a pretty good plan."

After I eased into one of the carhop spots, an attendant jogged over to me. With his notepad poised to write on, he uttered the legendary Varsity phrase: "Whatta ya have?"

I then proceeded to rattle off an order of a dozen chili dogs and cheeseburgers along with fries and onion rings. The attendant glanced between Darion and me before repeating the order. "That's right."

"Be back in ten."

As we waited on the food, I checked my phone while Darion played with the radio, trying to find the best jams. When the attendant returned, I gave him the money along with a nice tip.

Darion leaned over the boxes on his lap and inhaled heartily. "Damn, that smells good."

"Go ahead. Crack yours open."

Darion's brows creased. "What if I drop something?"

"Then I'll vacuum it up."

"If you say so." When he still looked hesitant, I said, "Hand me a chili dog."

Once he saw me start scarfing down the dog, Darion decided it was safe to start eating too. We both polished off our food by the time we got back to The Ark and with a loud, satisfying belch, I pulled into a space in the staff parking lot.

After turning off the car, I handed my keys to Darion. "Bring these back to me after the guys eat."

"Okay."

We got out and started inside the building. After we made it down the long hallway with employee offices and the break room, I noticed Vicki wasn't sitting at her desk in the rotunda like she usually did. Instead, she stood as she spoke animatedly with a buff dude across from her. She was all red-faced and flustered while the man looked like he was going to Hulk out on her.

"Oh shit. This ain't good," Darion remarked.

"You know that guy?"

He nodded. "That's D'Andre's dad, Ron. He's bad news, like prison bad. He did time for gang shit and drugs."

"Damn. That is bad news."

"I'm pretty sure there's a restrain' order out on him that he ain't supposed to be around D'Andre."

Vicki's voice rose a few octaves. "I'm sorry I can't do anything for you personally. If you'll wait just a moment, The Ark's supervisor is on her way out."

Avery came hustling out from the gym area. The hem of her dress kicked up, and I couldn't look away from the view of her thighs. Jesus, I needed help.

"I'm Avery Prescott. What seems to be the problem?" she asked.

Ron turned his wrath from Vicki to her. "I came for my son, but this bitch is wastin' my fuckin' time by sayin' I can't have him."

Avery's gaze bounced from Ron's to Vicki's. "There's a red flag on D'Andre's checkout list that Mr. Carnes is not to take him," Vicki explained.

"Fuck your lists. He's my son!"

"Sir, I'm going to ask you to lower your voice and refrain from using profanity," Avery chided. I wanted to roll my eyes at her being all uptight and pretentious, but at the same time, I couldn't help being impressed at how she wasn't cowering back from this asshole.

Ron's hand smacked against the counter, causing Vicki to jump. "Bitch, don't you be tellin' me how to talk. I'll come across this desk and pop you in the mouth."

Instantly, my fists clenched at my sides at his threat against Avery. Who the hell did he think he was to talk to her that way? And Vicki for that matter. They were just doing their jobs; it wasn't their fault he was a gangbanger who wasn't supposed to be around his kid.

"Mr. Carnes, I'm not sure how to make it clearer for you. Just as Mrs. Laramie previously explained, you are not authorized to check your son out of this facility. Since there is no way we can allow you to have him, I'm going to ask that you leave."

"I ain't leavin' without my son," Ron growled.

Avery shook her head. "Since you're unable to speak rationally about this, I will just let the authorities handle it." She nodded at Vicki who then hit the panic button hidden under the table.

"Daddy?" a voice questioned from behind us. I turned around to see a ten-year-old kid looking scared as hell. Although he resembled Ron in the face, he was small for his age. From the way he shrank back, I could tell he had been on the receiving end of some of Ron's rage in the past.

Ron's face momentarily softened. "Yo, son. Get your stuff. I'm bustin' you outta here."

D'Andre's eyes widened. "B-but M-Mama said I-I'm n-not supposed to go with you."

"Bullshit. I'm your daddy and I'm telling you to come on."

"I can't," D'Andre replied with shake of his head.

When Ron started toward D'Andre, Avery bolted out from behind the counter. She rushed ahead of Ron and past me to put herself in front of D'Andre like a human shield. "Mr. Carnes, the police are on the way and—"

"You called the cops on me, bitch?" Ron demanded.

"You are unauthorized to take your son, and you refused to leave the premises. I think the situation will be best handled by the police."

Ron reached into his pants' pocket and yanked out a pistol. At the sight of the gun, Vicki screamed and dropped under the desk while the other kids who had come to see what the yelling was about scattered across the room with shrieks and cries of panic. Avery's face paled considerably, but she didn't move away from D'Andre.

In a cold voice, Ron said, "Bitch, you got five seconds to get the fuck out of the way before I end you."

When he raised the gun and pointed it at Avery, every molecule in my body shuddered to a stop. The world began to crawl by in slow motion. It felt like I was standing outside of myself and watching the situation unfold.

In that moment, I heard Avery's girly giggle. I tasted her strawberry lip gloss from our kisses. I felt the soft curves of her body beneath mine when we had had sex. I knew I had to do something to save her—not because I should, not because it was the right thing to do.

Because I still loved her.

Doing what I did best, I broke into a sprint. I barreled into Avery, tackling her to the ground like she was my opponent on the field. As soon as we were down, I covered her body with mine, shielding her from Ron's wrath. While I hated that I had left D'Andre exposed and vulnerable, I knew Ron wouldn't shoot him. In his own warped and toxic way, he loved him too much to kill him.

"All right, freeze! Drop your weapon!" an officer shouted.

I exhaled the breath I'd been holding while I thanked God that The Ark was close to one of the downtown precincts. There was a flurry of movement behind me, and I glanced back to see Ron drop his gun and sink to his knees. Two police officers rushed over to him and handcuffed him while a female officer put her arm around

D'Andre and got him away from his father.

After rolling Avery onto her back, I stared down into her face, which remained paralyzed with fear. "Are you okay?"

She was so shocked she couldn't speak. Her body trembled as the shakes went through her, and I reached my hand up to tenderly touch her face. "Prescott, I need you to tell me you're all right."

Finally, she murmured, "Mmhmm." Tears pooled in her eyes, and from the way she was biting on her lip, I could tell she was trying hard not to cry. Typical Avery to try to be strong no matter what.

Since I knew she needed more room to try to catch her breath, I eased off her and onto my knees. Her wild gaze spun around the room. "D'Andre?" she questioned.

"He's fine. An officer took him over to Vicki."

Once she knew D'Andre was safe, the dam that had been keeping her emotions in check broke and she began to weep uncontrollably. "Hey now. It's okay," I said as I drew her into my arms. I knew the best thing I could do was let her get it out of her system, so I just let her cry.

"Miss Prescott?" one of the officers questioned.

"Y-yes," Avery replied in between her sobs.

"I'm Officer Beasley. I have a few questions for you. Do you think you can answer them?"

Avery eased herself out of my arms and then swiped her eyes. "I-I can try."

I rose to my feet and then reached down to help her up. I winced at the sight of her knees, which were busted and bleeding. Putting my arm around her waist, I guided Avery over to one of the chairs. After I got her seated, I remained at her side as Officer Beasley went through a barrage of questions about what had happened. Although I could tell she was close to losing it again, she somehow managed to keep it all together. She really was amazing.

When he was finished with Avery, he glanced at me. "All right, hero, I'm going to need to get your statement as well."

Shifting on my feet, I protested, "I'm not a hero."

He grinned. "I don't know what your definition of a hero is, buddy, but for me, I consider anyone willing to take a bullet for someone else a hero."

Part of me wanted to puff my chest out with pride and gloat about what I had done. I knew my father would piss his pants with excitement if the story got out about me doing something heroic, but another part of me felt uncomfortable taking credit for saving Avery. What kind of asshole would have left her in the firing range of some idiot? Fuck, he'd threatened to kill her. *Kill. Avery.*

I had just finished relating what I had seen and heard when Vicki came over to us. "Avery, I called Jason, and he's on his way in to cover for you. After talking with Tamar, we both feel it's best you go on home."

Avery shook her head. "No, no. I'm fine, I swear."

"Prescott, you're so *not* fine." I motioned to her knees.

"You're bleeding for Christ's sake, not to mention you're emotionally spent."

Vicki patted Avery's shoulder. "Cade is right, sweetheart. You need to get out of here and get some rest."

Avery nibbled her lip. "But the kids need me, especially the ones who just witnessed that."

"Don't you worry one bit about the kids. They're resilient, and Tamar is leaving her conference meeting to be here for them."

After weighing Vicki's words, Avery finally nodded her head in agreement. "Okay. I'll go on home."

"Good. Since you're in no shape to drive, how about Cade drives you home?" Vicki suggested.

Avery's face paled slightly. "Uh, I don't think—"

"I'd be happy to do it," I piped up.

After snapping her gaze to mine, Avery said, "I appreciate the offer, Cade, but you've already done enough."

While on the surface her statement was positive, it also went back to our past. I had certainly done enough to her by breaking her heart and causing her so much grief and pain. I might've saved her life, but in the vast scheme of things, I still owed her. Hell, it would probably take a lifetime of good deeds to repay her. "I really don't mind."

"If you insist," Avery replied while forcing a smile to her lips.

From her tone and expression, I could tell it was going to be an interesting ride home.

THIRTEEN

AVERY

Just when I thought things with Cade couldn't get any more complicated, it reached a whole new level when he saved my life. *Oh God, I could've been killed.* I swallowed the rising bile in my throat when I was assaulted with a flashback of Ron pointing his gun at me.

After Vicki left us to go back to the front desk, Cade and I stood in an awkward silence. With a wave of his hand, Cade said, "Come on. We need to go get you cleaned up before I take you home."

I was still too shaken to argue with him that there was no *we*. Instead, I trailed behind him as he started for the employee hallway.

“Where’s a first aid kit?” Cade questioned.

“The break room.”

He opened the door and then held it open for me. Cade patted the counter. “Have a seat, and I’ll get you patched up.”

While he got the first aid kit out of the cabinet, I tried hopping up on the counter, but no matter how hard I tried, I couldn’t seem to do it. Without a word, Cade put down the materials he had dug out, slid his hands around my waist, and hoisted me up like I weighed nothing at all. “Thank you,” I murmured. I tried ignoring the warmth of his hands through the flimsy material of my sundress. Even after four years, I could still remember what his hands felt like on me. The illicit reminder caused me to shiver.

Staring intently at me, Cade replied, “No problem.”

I ducked my head from his intense expression. When I did, I noticed blood staining my dress above my thigh. I furrowed my brows in confusion as I lifted the hem of my dress. A long gash ran midway down my thigh. “How did that happen?” I questioned curiously.

“It had to be something sharp and pointy.”

“I had my keychain in my hands from unlocking the storeroom.”

Cade nodded. “The keys must’ve cut you when I knocked you down.” Remorse flooded his face. “I’m sorry I was so rough.”

“You don’t need to apologize. You did what you had to do.”

“I blame the adrenaline. The minute I saw that gun it went into overdrive."

"I can only imagine."

After we stared at each other for a moment, Cade gave a slight shake of his head before going back over to the first aid kit. Realizing I was exposing too much skin to him, I quickly dropped my dress back down.

Cade came back to me with gauze and antiseptic then worked it over the broken skin on my knees. It didn't hurt as bad as I thought it would considering how rough the wounds looked. After putting a large bandage on both knees, I thought he was finished and started to get down, but Cade stopped me.

When he started pushing my sundress up my thighs to clean the gash, I froze. There shouldn't have been any difference between him attending to a cut on my thigh after he had done the same thing on my knees, but it felt very different.

Inwardly, I was slapping his hands away before busting him in the mouth for even assuming he could touch me again with such familiarity…such intimacy. After all, I wasn't the same Avery from years ago who had yearned for the feel of his fingers on my skin. While inwardly I boiled with rage, on the outside, I remained a perfect statue—a rigid, marbleized Avery Prescott.

My reaction caught Cade's attention because his hands stilled. Of course, that meant his fists were precariously close to my vagina. A heat began to coil below my waist, causing my vagina to thaw—if a vagina could actually thaw.

As if we felt the same pull, Cade jerked his hands away, leaving my thighs exposed with the material of my sundress bunched at the top of my legs. His brows knitted together in concern. “Are you all right?”

I narrowed my eyes at him. “Peachy, except for the fact that I’m not used to being manhandled.”

With his nostrils flaring, Cade countered, “Well, excuse me, princess. I was just trying to help you. It’s not like—” He then abruptly snapped his mouth shut.

“It’s not like what?” When Cade refused to answer me, I spat, “It’s not like you haven’t seen it all before, right?”

Surprise flooded me as a regretful grimace spread across Cade’s face. He raked his hands through his hair. “Fuck, I’m sorry. That was a totally douche thing for me to allude to.’”

His apology took me so off guard that I was once again rendered frozen. “Thanks,” I finally mumbled.

Cade nodded before dabbing more antiseptic on the cotton ball. When he touched it to my skin, I sucked in a breath.

He glanced up at me. “Sorry about that.”

“It’s okay. Not like you can help it.” I laughed. “I guess it’s more about me being a wuss.”

Cade grinned. “I’d hardly call you a wuss. This cut is pretty bad.”

“Think I need stitches?”

“I don’t think it went that deep.”

Silence then enveloped us as he continued cleaning my cut. As I studied him with his head bent in deep concentration, it was clear what I had to do. I had to thank him. Although it was just two little words, for some reason I was having a really hard time forming them on my lips.

Maybe it was because, based on his usual cockiness, I imagined he was waiting for me to make a big deal out of him saving me. Maybe it was more about our prior history and how he had cut me so deep emotionally that it was hard to imagine thanking him for anything. Then again, maybe it was the fact that I could be a stubborn, hardheaded ass, as Grandpa always said.

I exhaled a long breath. "Cade?"

"Yeah," he replied, making one final sweep along my cut.

"I haven't thanked you yet." When he jerked his gaze up to meet mine, I said, "You know, for what you did out there."

He shrugged. "It was nothing."

Well hello, Mr. Modest. That was certainly a surprise. "You're wrong. It wasn't 'nothing'. Ron had a gun…" I shuddered. "He could have shot Vicki or D'Andre."

"Or you."

I swallowed hard at both that thought as well as the intensity in Cade's eyes. "Or me," I whispered. The thought of how close I had come to being shot or *killed* caused a shiver to run through me. "You saved my life, Cade, and for that, I'm very, very grateful."

"Then I guess you're welcome."

Cocking my head curiously at him, I asked, "Why are you being so modest about all this?"

"I'm not," he replied as he stuck a bandage on my thigh.

"Uh, yeah, you are. The Cade I knew would be outside seeing if he could be interviewed by the media to brag about what he had done."

Cade's growl of frustration took me off guard and he jerked one of his hands through his hair. "Maybe I'm not that douchebag guy any more. Maybe I realized that while I might've saved your life today, it doesn't erase what I did to you. Maybe I feel like a fucking mess as I'm trying to process what the hell just happened out there."

I stared open-mouthed at him. "Maybe," I finally murmured.

Cade started putting the materials back into the first aid kit then glanced at me over his shoulder. "You need a drink."

I snorted. "Is that the usual next step after almost being shot?"

"Come on, Prescott. You're pale as a fucking sheet."

"Seriously, I'm fine."

With a shake of his head, Cade countered, "You've been holding it all together pretty well. You're going to bottom out soon, so you need something to settle your nerves."

Although I hated to admit it, Cade was right. Considering how jangled my emotions felt, I did need something to take the edge off. "Fine. We can stop by a bar on the way to my house."

"Glad you could see it my way, Miss Stubborn."

"I'm not that stubborn," I protested.

Cade grinned. “Do you get the irony that you’re being stubborn about being stubborn?”

“Whatever.”

When Cade’s hands once again came to my waist, I reached up to grip his bulging biceps. Gently, he eased me back down onto my feet. “Thank you,” I murmured.

“You’re welcome.”

Neither Cade nor I let go of each other. “Will you do something for me, Prescott?”

“Yes. What?” I questioned breathlessly.

“Will you not put up a fight when I buy you a drink?”

Although it wasn’t the question I expected, I still laughed. “Okay. Deal.”

Cade winked. “Good.”

* * *

Cade hovered over me on the way out to his car. Although it was slightly irritating, I didn’t yell at him. Instead, I let him feel like he was what I needed.

“I see you’re still a Benz fan,” I remarked when he opened the door for me.

“I am, but I have a Hummer now, too.”

“What could a single guy possibly need with a vehicle that big?”

“To pile all my buddies in,” he replied with a grin.

“I should have known.”

After putting me in the car, Cade hustled over to his side. Once we were out of The Ark's parking lot, he made a few turns before pulling in at an Irish pub. The orange and green sign read *O'Malley's*. "Ever been here before?" Cade asked as we got out of the car.

"No, I haven't."

"It's a cool place. They have a back room filled with big screens. The guys and I come here sometimes to watch the NBA games."

"I guess you're too busy during football season to come down here for the NFL games."

"Pretty much. Sometimes we catch a few on the plane or in hotel rooms."

I smiled at him. "It must be so cool to get to travel like that."

"It is. Even though we don't get a lot of time while we're in different cities, I try to soak up some of the culture."

"Really? Not just the night life?" I teasingly asked.

He held the front door open for me. "Ha, ha."

Since it was almost one, the bar was pretty packed with the lunchtime crowd. A waiter approached our table. "Hey guys, I'm Blane. What can I start you off with?"

My gaze snapped to Cade's at the name Blane. In my mind, I could hear John Cryer's voice disdainfully saying, "Blane? That's a major appliance, that's not a name!" Of course, the thought of the movie immediately took me back to *Pretty in Pink* and the night

Cade and I made love.

I ducked my head. “I’ll have a vodka and cranberry as well as a water.”

“Shot of Crown Royal.”

She nodded and left to fill our orders. Glancing around, I said sheepishly, “I can’t believe I just ordered alcohol this early. I never drink in the daytime during the week.”

Cade grinned. “That doesn’t surprise me, Prescott. I just hope that statement means that you do drink in the evening.”

“Yes. I do.”

“Good. You need to go wild every once in a while.”

“I’m not so sure having a glass of wine at night while I’m studying law cases really constitutes as going wild.”

Cade leaned in on the table with his elbows. “Please tell me that in the last three years, you’ve at least attended one college party.”

“For your information, I’ve attended several.”

Tilting his head at me, Cade said, “Parties still aren’t you’re thing, are they?”

Apparently he remembered how antisocial I could be. “Nope.”

“I guess some things never change.”

The waitress returned to deposit our drinks on the table. When I took a hearty gulp of my cranberry and vodka, it burned a trail all the way down to my stomach. After I set the drink down, I eyed Cade curiously. I realized that even though we’d seen each other for a week, we had yet to really catch up. "So what have you been up to besides streaking through alumni dinners?"

Cade laughed. "Doing my premed thing. Mostly As, a few Bs, and the one C that led to the previously mentioned streaking."

"No special lady?" I blurted out, regretting it instantly.

Cade pinned me with an intense stare. "No one lady and no one special."

I shook my head. "I see you haven't changed in that area."

"No. I guess I haven't. What about you?"

"Do I have a special lady?"

Cade grinned. "I'm not going to lie that the idea of you with a chick gets me a little hard, but I meant do you have someone in your life?"

"Not right now."

"So there was someone recently?"

"Yes, there was."

"And?"

"He was a nice, decent someone that I had for a year." I traced the rim of my glass with my finger. "But I realized it wasn't fair to him because I didn't love him like he loved me."

A low whistle came from Cade's mouth. "Jesus, Prescott, who knew a sweetheart like you would be breaking hearts?"

"I have to say it's a hell of a lot easier than having your heart broken."

Cade grimaced. "Touché." He then waved his hand for Blane.

"On that note, I think I need another drink. Want something else?"

"I'll take another cranberry and vodka."

"What about something to eat?"

I wrinkled my nose. "I'm not sure I can."

Cade's brow creased with worry. "You probably need to. Why don't I order the appetizer platter and you can see if you find something you like?"

My heart fluttered at his thoughtfulness. Wanting to ignore the surge of emotions in my chest, I jokingly said, "Okay, Mom."

Ignoring me, Cade said, "We'll take another cranberry and vodka for the lady, a Bud for me, and the appetizer platter. In the meantime, can you bring us out some rolls?"

"Sure thing," the waitress replied.

Cade rolled his eyes in exaggerated bliss. "Wait until you try one of their rolls. They are seriously to die for. They kinda remind me of the ones your Nana made at Thanksgiving."

I blinked at him in surprise. How was it possible that after all these years, Cade remembered what Nana's homemade rolls tasted like?

"Speaking of your Nana, how is she?"

"Good." Cade appeared relieved that nothing bad had happened to Nana. "She's still working on the farm like she was my age. We can't get her to slow down. She still insists on cooking a big meal every Sunday and having all the family in."

"She's an amazing woman."

"She really is."

"And your mom? How's she?"

"She's been dating a guy for the last two years. He's proposed twice, but she still refuses. I'm hoping the third time will be the charm."

"You must like him."

I nodded. "Bryan is a really nice guy. He has sole custody of his two teenage sons."

Cade waggled his eyebrows. "Are they hot? The whole stepbrother thing could be some kinky fun."

"Um, ew. Jace and Jeremy are thirteen and fifteen."

"Hmm, you might want to wait a few years before making your move, you know, when they're legal."

I laughed. "I don't want to hook up with them, pervert. I like hanging out with them in a brother/sister way. That's it."

"Do you go home much?"

Yeah, I actually went home Monday because I was so emotionally crippled by seeing you. "Not as much as I'd like. Two weekends a month, maybe three. Sometimes I pick up shifts at the Piedmont women's shelter on the weekends."

Cade smiled at me. "Always trying to make the world a better place."

"Since it's a paying job, I don't know how noble it is."

"It's noble."

"Thank you."

The waiter returned with our new drinks and rolls. Before I could protest that I really didn't think I could eat one, Cade had already started buttering one for me. "Come on. Just a few bites," he urged.

"Okay, okay." The moment I bit into the roll, I moaned. "Wow, these really are good."

"See, I told you," Cade replied as he began buttering a roll of his own.

"How are your parents?"

"The same. My dad narrowly got reelected a year ago, so he's even more hypersensitive about his family's image than usual. You can imagine how thrilled he was when he got the call about me streaking."

I winced. "I'm sure that wasn't a fun conversation."

"Nope, it wasn't. He did work pretty hard to get me out of working at The Ark."

"That doesn't surprise me."

Cade grinned as he took another swig of his beer. "I forgot you had firsthand knowledge of my dad's ability to get me and my friends out of trouble."

I couldn't help smiling a little at the memory of the day we'd almost gotten arrested for trespassing on Mr. Frost's farm. "I am grateful he helped out that day."

Cade's brows popped up. "You are?"

"Of course I am."

"See the way I remember it, you told me off that day."

"Not because of your dad—for the way you treated that officer," I argued.

"Yeah. I was a real jerk to that guy."

"I'm glad you can see that. Of course, I would imagine the same could be said for the professor whose dinner you ruined with your streaking."

An uncomfortable look came over Cade as he shifted in his seat. "What can I say? I'm just an asshole."

"You were."

"What?"

"You *were* an asshole." I shook my head. "But not any more."

The corners of Cade's lips quirked. "That's right. It's in the past, and I guess it was meant to be; otherwise I wouldn't have met back up with you."

I couldn't speak for a moment. Instead, all I could think of was how if Cade hadn't been at The Ark, I could have been shot. I could have been dead. The thought caused a shudder to ripple through me. Those feelings were also compounded by the fact that things would have been so different emotionally if I hadn't met back up with Cade.

He sat a little straighter in his seat before clearing his throat a few times. "Listen, there's something I need to say—something I've needed to say for a long, long time."

Oh my God. Was this really happening? After all this time was

Cade really about to apologize to me? My fingers gripped the edge of the table as I held on for dear life. Truthfully, I wasn't sure I could cope with any more emotional trauma at that point though. I had nearly been shot just an hour before and I didn't think I had yet processed that completely, but the way Cade was looking at me was so intense, I didn't feel I could escape it.

Cade's expression turned agonized. "I'm sorry, Avery. I'm really fucking sorry for the way I treated you."

The breath I'd been holding whooshed out of me, and I felt like a deflated balloon. I'd waited three long years for an apology from Cade. I'd resigned myself to the fact that I would never get one, especially after how he had treated me the past week.

When I continued sitting in a stunned stupor, Cade kept on talking. "I wouldn't blame you for not forgiving me, but believe me when I say that while it might not have seemed like it bothered me, I've been haunted about what happened between us."

"You have?" I whispered.

He yanked a hand through his hair. "Yeah, I have. When I think about what I said to you that day at school…" He closed his eyes as if he were in pain. "Jesus, Prescott, it was so horrible I don't even have words."

Pinching my eyes shut, I said, "I can't believe we're doing this right now. Wasn't it enough that I was almost shot an hour ago?"

"I know the timing is fucked, but if I've learned anything in the last hour, it's that you can't take one minute for granted. You have to make things right—I had to make things right."

Regardless of all the reasons not to ask, I couldn't ignore the question burning inside me. "Why?" Tears stung my eyes, and I fought with everything within me to not start sobbing hysterically in the middle of the bar. "After everything we had been through together, after everything that had happened at Mom's store, how could you toss me aside like that?"

Cade downed the rest of his beer. "I guess after all this time, you deserve the truth."

"I sure as hell do."

"What I did had everything to do with how much I cared for you."

"I find that very hard to believe."

"Just hear me out, and once you do, you can tell me if you still think that."

I eased back against the padded back of the booth. "Okay. I will."

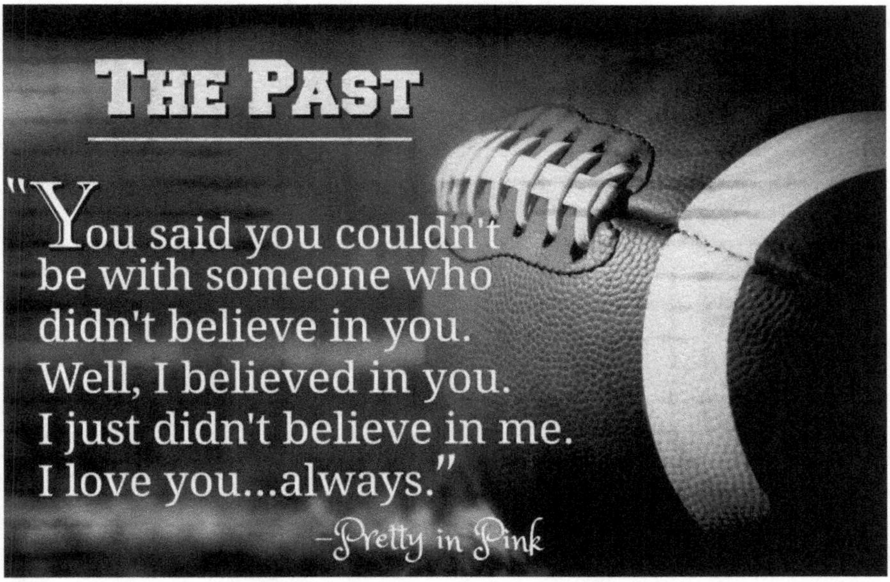
THE PAST
"You said you couldn't be with someone who didn't believe in you. Well, I believed in you. I just didn't believe in me. I love you...always."
–Pretty in Pink

FOURTEEN

CADE

As I came out of a deep sleep, I blinked my eyes a few times. Gazing around at the unfamiliar surroundings, I had the usual *oh shit* moment people tend to have when they wake up somewhere other than their bed. It was then that my mind quickly processed that my surroundings weren't actually unfamiliar. I knew exactly where I was—I was sprawled out on a red velvet couch in Rose's Garden.

I was naked.

And I wasn't alone.

As I dipped my gaze, I took in Avery's exposed curves. Her beautiful face was hidden by her long dark hair and her cheek was pressed into my chest. Her labored breaths tickled across my skin, causing goose bumps to rise on my arms.

I got a swift kick in the junk at the sight of her nakedness. Somehow during the night, she had slid out from the quilt that covered us. As my morning wood bucked against Avery's thigh, I silently cursed it. I'd never been with a virgin before, but I was pretty sure Avery wouldn't be feeling like another round this morning. The last thing I wanted was for her to think I was some sex fiend, although she probably already did.

At the thought of us having sex, regret thundered through my chest. While I had enjoyed every single second of us being together, I hated myself for letting things go too far. I should have told her no and made her wait. Hell, we really hadn't even had an actual date before. I might've been an asshole to women before, but I was a special kind of unimaginable bastard for fucking her—taking her virginity—without taking her out first. Isn't that what guys in relationships do? *Fuck,* it was no different than how I normally got laid.

There was also the fact that I hadn't told her I loved her. Wait, did I love Avery? The idea of love was such a foreign concept to me that I had to really consider it. It wasn't like I was Avery, who went around freely saying the words to her mother and grandmother, and her clan of relatives. The words had rarely come from my lips, and they'd only been directed at my grandfather and my nanny. I might've said them to my parents when I was young and didn't understand the weight of the words. I'd sure as hell never told a girl I loved her, not even to get one in bed.

Maybe I did love Avery. Maybe the feeling of warmth I got in my chest whenever I was around Avery was love. The way the world seemed a little brighter with her around. The way I missed her when she wasn't around. The way I wanted to be a better man for her. The way I wanted to make her life better. If that was love, I wanted that.

While it was great that I was having this epiphany about my feelings, it still didn't erase the shadiness of what had happened. What if Avery woke up and regretted giving her virginity to me? What if that regret turned to hatred, and she told me she never wanted to see me again because I was a heartless bastard?

Lying there staring up at the ceiling, the walls began to close in on me. I had to fight to catch my breath. Anxiety like I had never experienced before pricked its way over my skin like tiny needles.

"Hey," Avery whispered.

I flicked my gaze from the ceiling to her. "Hey."

Her brows creased in worry. "Are you okay?"

"Fine." I forced a smile to my lips. "I think I should be one the asking you that."

She pulled the quilt around her before easing up into a sitting position. "It was the expression on your face that worried me." She once again played with the flowers on the quilt. "Like you were regretting being here with me."

"I was." At Avery's gasp of horror, I quickly pulled her against me and pressed a kiss to the top of her head. "It's not what you're thinking."

Jerking her chin up defiantly, she countered, "Oh really? You just said you regretted being here with me."

"But not how you're thinking."

"Then how?" she demanded.

I sighed. "If I looked regretful, it was because I was feeling like a bastard for taking your virginity."

Avery shook her head. "You didn't take my virginity, Cade. I gave it to you willingly."

"While that might be true, I could have turned you down, asked you to wait. I mean, Jesus, Aves, I didn't even buy you dinner last night. We've never even been out together." I groaned and rubbed my hand over my eyes. "I'm a fucking hack."

"No, you're not."

"Yeah, I am."

"Would it make you feel better if I made you pay for the sandwiches, popcorn, and Cokes we had last night?" Avery asked with a teasing smile.

I chuckled. "Maybe."

"I'd be happy to do it if it would make you stop beating yourself up."

Peering curiously at her, I asked, "You don't have any regrets about last night?"

She shook her head. "It was everything I hoped it would be."

"On a junky piece of furniture in your mother's store?"

"No, because it was with someone I loved. Sure, I had romantic fantasies of having sex in front of a fire or on the beach." She cupped my face in her hands. "But this was just as beautiful as anything I had ever imagined."

"It certainly beat my first time," I quipped.

Avery wrinkled her nose. "I would say so."

Realizing she needed something remotely romantic from me, I said, "It was pretty amazing for me, Prescott."

Her brows shot up into her hairline. "Really?"

"Yeah, really. You shouldn't be surprised by your sex appeal."

Her cheeks flushed. "I just didn't think I knew the right things to do."

"Trust me. You did everything right."

"Except a blow job," she teased.

The air wheezed out of my lungs as I quickly shot down any ideas my dick had about volunteering as tribute. "There's always next time."

A shy smile curved on Avery's lips. "Sooner than later, right?"

I laughed. "Don't tell me having sex one time has turned you into a nympho?"

She giggled. "No. I just want to be with you again."

For the first time in my life, I felt the same. I wanted to be with Avery. I wanted her back in my arms, my body wrapped around hers, our souls and bodies making love.

"And you will." I hope to fuck it was going to be soon. Now

that I had had Avery, there was no way I could not have her again.

A playful smile curved on Avery's lips. "What about now?"

"Uh, well, I didn't think you'd be ready to go again."

When her hand came between my legs to grab my cock, I almost jumped out of my skin. "I think I could try."

"You do?" I questioned hopefully.

"Mmhmm."

Her hand stroked up and down my growing length. Considering it was already at half-mast, it didn't take long to have it at full attention. Although her hand felt fabulous, I wanted to be inside her. Since I knew she needed some prepping time, I took her hand away.

At her questioning look, I said, "I'm good to go, babe. Now I need to get you ready."

Her face flushed. "Okay," she said softly.

I pulled her up to straddle my lap. When my cock touched her core, we both sucked in a breath. I lay back against the settee. With my hands gripping her hips, I started sliding her up my body. Avery's expression became panicked. "Cade, what are—"

"Just trust me."

After nibbling on her full bottom lip, she nodded. I then pushed her up to where her thighs were on either side of my face. I began to lick and nip at her pussy. Avery gasped before throwing her head back. I worked her over with my tongue, sucking her clit into my mouth. For someone without a lot of experience, she was so damn responsive. I brought my thumb up to rub her clit while I pumped my tongue in and out of her like I soon hoped to do with my dick.

"Cade!" Avery cried. Her thighs started to shake, and I felt her walls convulsing around my tongue. God, she was beautiful when she came.

Now that I felt she could take me again, I slid Avery back down my chest. I kinda liked the idea that I would be smelling like her all day. After fumbling in my wallet for another condom, I slid it down my length. Then I took Avery by the hips and eased her down on my cock. "Fuck…you feel amazing," I grunted.

"You feel good, too," she panted.

I kept my hands on her hips and worked her on and off my cock. After a few thrusts, Avery began to move in time with me. As smart as she was, I should have known she'd be a fast learner when it came to sex. Her bouncing tits were too inviting, and I slid my hands up her ribcage to squeeze them. As Avery rode me hard, I pinched and rolled her nipples into hardened points. "Oh, Cade," she murmured.

Although I wanted to pound into her, I restrained myself. It was sexy as hell thinking of her being sore because of me, but at the same time, I didn't want to hurt her. Closing my eyes, I tensed and began to come inside her. I shouted her name as I clutched her hips tight with my hands.

When I came back to myself, she was smiling down at me.

"That was amazing," she said.

I grinned. "I thought so too. Fucking amazing."

Avery dipped her head and brought her lips to mine. When she pulled away, she threw a glance at one of the clocks. Her eyes widened and she groaned. "We better get going."

"Are you throwing me out? 'Cause I'm kinda still inside you."

"Yes, I'm aware of that, but unless you want my mom to find us when she opens the store at nine, we need to go."

That was all I needed to get moving. Since I imagined Rose would cut off my dick if she found out I had de-virginized Avery, I knew I needed to get the hell out of there. While Avery, who was wrapped tight in the quilt, went to the staff bathroom in the back, I went to the public bathroom. After disposing of the condom and washing up as best I could, I hopped into my pants and threw on my shirt.

I had just located my tux jacket when Avery reappeared in a Harlington hoodie and a pair of jeans. I couldn't help stopping to admire her form in the fitted jeans. I'd probably seen them on her before, but there was something different about seeing them on her now. Maybe it had to do with the fact that I had touched every inch of the body beneath the jeans.

We stood there, just staring at each other. After a few moments passed, Avery smiled. "Thanks again for last night."

I grinned. "Ditto."

Avery laughed. "That is *so* something you would say."

"You know me well."

"I'm glad I know you—the real you."

I closed the gap between us and drew her into my arms. Since I didn't have the words I needed to express how I felt, I just dipped my head and brought my lips to hers. After a few breathless moments of kissing, I pulled away before things got too crazy. "Bye, Prescott."

"Bye, Cade."

I tossed my jacket over my shoulder and then unlocked the door. With a goofy smile on my face, I made my way over to my car. After cranking the car up, I turned the radio on and sang along like a lovesick fool.

When I made it back to Harlington, I eased into a parking spot in front of my dorm. When I started to get out of the car, a flash of red caught my eye. "Oh fuck," I grumbled as Elspeth started stalking over to me. She was still in her dress from the night before. From her hair and smeared makeup, she looked like she had only crashed for a few hours—maybe not even at all.

"How could you do this to me?" she demanded as I opened the car door.

"If you've come here to give me shit about ditching the party, you're wasting your time and mine."

"You didn't just ditch the party. You ditched *me*."

"Get real, Elspeth. I asked you to the dance, so I fulfilled any commitment to you. I didn't sign on for anything that happened afterward. I didn't owe you anything."

When I started past her, Elspeth grabbed my arm, her acrylic nails digging into my skin. Instead of slinging her arm away, I gently took it off of me. I almost smiled because it was like a small sign of Avery rubbing off on me to be a kinder Cade. "Go back to your dorm and get some sleep."

I then brushed past her and started for the door, but Elspeth wasn't finished with me.

"Dammit, Cade, I'm not here just because you ditched me. I'm here because you fucked Avery Prescott!"

The world shuddered to a slow crawl around me and my ears felt like I was underwater. "I don't know what you're talking about," I replied lamely.

"I saw you."

Whirling around, I demanded, "What's the fuck? Were you spying on me?"

"When I was on the way home from the party this morning, I saw you leaving her mother's store."

"Fine. I was with Avery. Are you happy now?"

"I thought we were together."

I shook my head. "You knew the score with me. Don't make it into more than it was. If you're honest with yourself, you don't give two shits about me. You wanted me because I was a prize—something to make you look cool to your friends."

"That's not true. I really liked you."

"I call bullshit on that. I bet if I asked you what my favorite song or movie was, you'd have no fucking clue."

Elspeth's brows creased. "What does that have to do with anything?"

"Because little shit like that—it's everything when it comes to a relationship. When you really care for someone, you find out what they like and don't like. Face it: all you know about me is that doggy style is my favorite position."

A volatile mixture of anger and hurt swept over Elspeth's face. The next thing I knew she had hauled off and slapped the hell out of me. My face stung as her nails scraped across my cheek. "Very classy," I muttered as I rubbed my jaw.

Elspeth huffed dramatically as she swept her hands to her chest. "Oh that's rich. You're accusing me of not being classy when you're the one fucking some low-rent scholarship case."

I jabbed my finger at her. "Do not talk shit about Avery."

"I'm speaking the truth." Her head shook wildly. "Jesus, Cade, how could you embarrass me like this?"

"Shockingly enough, everything isn't about you. This is about Avery and me."

"You should be thinking about you. Fucking someone like her…" Elspeth made a horrible face. "It's like social suicide."

"I couldn't give a shit less what anyone has to say about who I'm fucking." I started to turn to go, but then I stopped. "For the record, we aren't just fucking. We're together."

Elspeth's head flew back like I'd slapped her. While she could barely believe I would have slept with Avery, it seemed incomprehensible to her that I could actually want more. "You're *dating* her?"

"Yeah, I am."

Her mouth dropped open in horror. "What has happened to you?"

"Something you couldn't possibly understand." With that, I unlocked the door and slammed it in her face.

* * *

After falling into a deep sleep, I woke to the sound of someone pounding on my door. When I glanced at the clock on my nightstand, I saw it was after one in the afternoon. Shit. I hadn't meant to sleep so long.

I trudged across the carpet to the door. Thinking it was one of my buddies, I threw it open without questioning who it was. Immediately, I regretted it. Standing before me with his usual sour expression was my father.

"Dad, hey. What are you doing here?"

"I need to talk to you." Without an invitation, he swept past me into my bedroom.

"Normally, we talk with a phone call."

"You haven't been answering your phone."

"I'm sorry. I had it on vibrate so I could get some sleep."

"Sit down, Cade."

His tone and mannerisms told me something epically shitty had happened. “Is everyone okay? Nothing’s happened to Mom or Catherine has it?”

“No. It’s nothing like that.”

A relieved breath whooshed out of me. “So what’s up?”

“I received a disturbing phone call about you this morning.”

“Yeah, well, I find that a little hard to believe considering I’ve been towing the line lately. Besides, I can’t imagine any of my teachers are so dedicated that they make student calls on Sunday mornings.”

“It’s about who you have been seen with.”

“Elspeth?”

Dad shook his head. “The scholarship girl.”

I raised my brows in surprise. “Avery?”

“Yes. Avery Prescott.”

“Wow, I guess Elspeth called you.”

“She has nothing to do with this. It is Miss Prescott I am concerned with.”

“Just what are you concerned with?”

Dad’s expression darkened. “You’re not to see her any more.”

“Excuse me?”

“I believe you heard me correctly.”

“Yeah, I did. I guess it’s more that I couldn’t believe I actually heard you say that.”

“I know you’re young, Cade, but you have responsibilities to yourself and to your family. I can understand wanting to sow your oats with young girls below your social standing, but apparently it is more than a fling with this girl."

Crossing my arms across my chest, I firmly replied, "Yeah, it is."

Dad tilted his head. "You don't actually think you love this girl, do you?" The sneer on his face made me even angrier.

"Yeah, I do."

He grunted. "Jesus Christ, Cade, sometimes I wonder how you can possibly be my son."

"Maybe you should have Mom do a paternity test," I snapped.

Dad jabbed a finger at me. "Watch your tongue with me."

With a roll of my eyes, I said, "Whatever."

In a flash, Dad was before me. He cuffed the back of my neck and jerked my head back to where I had to stare up at him. "You are not to see Avery Prescott again."

I jerked away from his grip. "Get serious, Dad. I'm eighteen. I can do whatever the hell I want, and thanks to the stipulations of my trust from Grandfather, you can't threaten me with my inheritance."

An almost evil smile curved on my father's lips. "There are other ways to make your life hell."

"Like what? You'll go off like Neil's dad in *Dead Poets Society* and send me to military school?"

"While I could pull strings to do that, I won't. Instead, I'll hit you where it truly hurts: with football."

My world came to a jarring stop. Had he actually said that? "What?"

"If you insist on staying with this girl, you will *never* play collegiate football."

I shook my head furiously from side to side. "You seriously think you're God, don't you? Have you forgotten I have a scholarship to Tech?"

Dad narrowed his eyes at me. "Schools can rescind scholarships and offers, Cade. Regardless of what your inflated ego thinks, you are replaceable."

In that moment, I could barely process his words. I felt like I was in a horror movie where the monster had tracked me down and backed me into a corner from which there was nowhere else to turn. I had to resign myself to my dark fate.

My father had given me lots of ultimatums in my life, but this one was gut-wrenching. How could I possibly choose? Football was my life, my great escape from all the unending bullshit surrounding me. There was no greater feeling in my life than when I was sprinting down the green. The roar of the crowd echoed not just through your ears, but your whole body.

Then Avery's sweet and caring face appeared before me. How could I give up the best thing I'd ever found with a member of the opposite sex? I couldn't help thinking of what me ending things would do to Avery. I hated the thought that I would be hurting her. She deserved to be loved and worshipped—not tossed aside.

In the end, it came down to what I had known for just four months versus what I had known my entire life. Even though it would kill me, I would have to give Avery up.

Dad crossed his arms over his chest. "What's it going to be, Cade? Your football career or this piece of white trash?"

Trying to put as much space as I could between Dad and myself, I eased back against the headboard of my bed. "You don't even know her," I murmured.

"I don't need to know her. The little I know of her is enough."

"She has a scholarship to law school—she's going to make something of herself," I feebly protested.

"While that's all well and good, she can do it without you and your money and connections."

"She doesn't care about my money and connections."

Dad gave a bark of a laugh. "Am I supposed to believe she actually cares about *you?*"

What. The. Fuck.

His words bruised me harder than if he had hit me with his fists. In a way, I wished he had beaten me rather than destroying my life. The pain would have been intense, but it would have faded. This was much worse. He was not only forbidding me to be with the girl I loved, but he didn't even believe I was loveable.

I pulled my knees to my chest and wrapped my arms around my legs. "Just go."

"Not until you assure me that you will stop seeing Avery."

Glaring at him, I bit out, “You have my word, you bastard.”

Dad nodded. “I’m glad you decided to see it my way.”

“Fuck you,” I muttered.

Dad walked over to the door. After he opened it, he paused. Turning around, he said, “I know you gave me your word, but just so you know, I have eyes all over this campus and town. If you try to sneak around behind my back, I will know.”

Then he slammed the door behind him.

If I had it in me to cry, that would have been the moment I started sobbing uncontrollably—but men aren’t supposed to cry. We’re supposed to bury our feelings and suppress our emotions. *Fuck my life.* I decided to handle the situation the best way I could: to get roaring drunk. The best place to start that process was the secret stash I had hidden under my bed.

After I unscrewed the cap on the Crown Royal, I held the bottle up. “To my father, thanks for ruining the best thing that’s ever happened to me, you fucker.”

With the toast finished, I began guzzling down the burning liquid and continued binging until, thankfully, I passed out.

FIFTEEN

AVERY

When Cade finished explaining what had happened with his father, silent tears streamed down my cheeks. Hearing the story had been positively gut-wrenching, bringing back everything I had experienced those final days we were together—both the good and the bad. All the shattered pieces of myself that I had fought so hard to put back in place three years before had come unglued, and I was once again that emotionally battered and broken teenage girl.

Hearing the truth was a tremendous shock. I had never in my wildest dreams imagined that something like that had transpired between Cade and his father. From the way Cade talked about him, I knew Representative Hall was an asshole, but I never could have fathomed him capable of something so cruel. With one prejudiced ultimatum, he had ruined the happiness of two people.

After sitting in silence for a few minutes, Cade handed me his paper napkin. “I’m sorry, Avery. I’m so fucking sorry,” he repeated for the millionth time.

I dabbed my cheeks. “It’s okay. I mean, I’m glad you told me the truth now.”

“From your reaction, it doesn’t seem like you’re glad.”

“No. I needed to hear it, regardless of how painful it was.” I placed the napkin down on the table and then looked at Cade. “Why didn’t you tell me this then?”

“I knew I was going to hurt you, but I didn’t want to hurt you as a person.”

I narrowed my eyes at him. “Newsflash, Cade. You didn’t hurt me—you *destroyed* me.”

Jerking a hand through his hair, Cade said, “I know that, but back then, all I could think about was what would hurt you less. If I had told you that my father was forbidding me to see you, then that would have made you feel bad about yourself as a person and about your family, like you weren’t good enough because you didn’t come from money.”

“But don’t you get it? I still felt bad about myself. Do you know how many nights I lay awake wondering what had I done to drive you away? What it was about me that was so horribly wrong that you couldn’t be with me?”

"Look, I know it sounds fucked up, but I just wanted all the blame to be on me. I wanted you to just hate me."

"Trust me, I did."

"And I'm glad."

"Is that why you didn't call me?"

Cade nodded. "I thought the best way to make you hate me was to just cut you off. No explanation, no reason. Just a clean break."

I laughed at the absurdity of his words. "A *clean break?* Trust me, I was a *mess*."

"I know. I think you're forgetting the part where I also went through something horrible. I mean, I…I really cared for you, Avery. I could've even loved you."

Sweet, Jesus, no. *He could have loved me?* That statement was like a blade piercing my chest, and the agonizing pain seemed to go on and on. Cade had never told me exactly how deeply he felt for me. Everything had been implied. Hearing it now made everything that had transpired even harder, especially the fact that he had walked away.

I quickly masked my pain with anger. "If this is where I'm supposed to feel sorry for you, I don't."

"I didn't ask you to. I was just stating facts." Cade leaned his elbows in on the table. "Can't you see—even in the smallest way possible—why I did what I did?"

I stared at him for a moment before trying to imagine myself as a teenage Cade. He was someone who had never really experienced love before, least of all with a member of the opposite sex; I remembered that much from the time we'd spent together.

Finally, I shook my head. "I'm sorry. I need to get out of here." When Cade started to protest, I held up my hand. "Just please take me home."

Although he looked pained, Cade replied, "If that's what you want."

"Yes. It is."

As I stood up, Cade reached into his back pocket for his wallet. Without calling the waiter over, he tossed a hundred onto the table, which I was sure more than covered our bill. He rose out of the booth and then motioned for me to go on ahead.

My knees had grown stiff from sitting, and when I put weight down on my right one, I winced in pain as I staggered to the side. When Cade rushed forward to give me a hand, I swatted it away. "I've got it."

While he nodded in agreement, he stayed close beside me on the way out to the car, just in case I needed him. As he held open the door, Cade asked, "Where do you live?"

I furrowed my brows at him. "Why do you need to know that?"

"Because I'm going to take you home."

"You don't need to do that. I'm fully capable of driving home."

"I'm aware of that, I just wanted to make sure you were okay."

Pinching my eyes shut, I said, "Just stop."

"Stop what?"

"Stop trying to be the hero to make up for everything you did in the past."

"I wasn't trying to be a hero." At the feel of Cade's hand on my cheek, my eyes popped open. "I care about you, Avery, and I want to make sure you're okay."

"I'm fine, or at least I will be once I get home."

A resigned look took over Cade's face. He removed his hand before turning and walking around the front of the car. I eased down onto the seat and then closed the door.

The drive back to The Ark was one of pained silence. It was hard being in such a confined place with Cade. I wanted nothing more than to be out of his presence. Part of me thought I was being overdramatic and holding a grudge. He had apologized to me: why should the reasons behind why he'd left me matter?

We had barely gotten into The Ark's parking lot when I reached for the door handle. "You're that ready to be rid of me, huh?" Cade said.

"I just need to be alone. With what happened with…"—I couldn't bring myself to say his name again—"…and with what you told me…" I swallowed hard. "It's all just too much." I was struggling to hold it all together.

"If you need anything, just call me."

I finally turned to look at him. The sincere expression on his face along with the sadness in his eyes almost broke me. "I appreciate that." I opened the car door and hopped out. Just before I closed the door, I stopped. Leaning my head in, I said, "For what you did today—"

"You don't ever need to thank me for that. The fact that you're still here is enough and all the thanks I'll ever need."

Of course he would have to go and say something like that. "Bye," I said quickly before I slammed the door. Cade waited until I was in my car and had pulled away before he left.

Once I was one the road, I called Mom to let her know what had happened at The Ark. Since Cade and I had passed a TV news van when we were leaving, I didn't want her to hear it that way. After assuring her a million times that I was okay and didn't need to be seen by a doctor, I told her it was Cade who had saved me.

I didn't give her time to react before relating what had happened at O'Malley's. When I finally finished, the line was so silent I thought the call had been dropped. "Mom?"

"I'm here," she replied.

"Why didn't you say anything?"

"Because your story rendered me speechless. I mean, I was already trying to recover from hearing you were almost shot, then you spring the news on me that the ultimate soulless bastard saved your life *and* that he then proceeded to apologize for what happened and told you he wouldn't have broken up with you if his father hadn't made him."

"Yeah, that pretty much sums it up."

"Where are you?"

"On the way to my apartment."

"Turn around. I want you to come home."

"Mom, I was just home on Monday. Besides, I have shifts this weekend at the shelter. I really can't afford to miss work."

"I'll pay you whatever you were supposed to make."

Her offer brought tears to my eyes. More than anything in that moment, I wanted my mother. It didn't matter that I was allegedly a poised and self-reliant twenty-one-year-old woman. I'd been through not one but two traumas that day.

"Okay. I'll be there in a little while."

"Good. I'll call Nana and have her make dumplings for you."

"That would be awesome, Mom. Thanks."

"Don't thank me. I'm not the one who is cooking."

I laughed. "Okay, then thank Nana for me."

"I will."

"See you soon."

"Bye, baby. Love you."

"Love you, too."

The Present
"Love's a bitch. "
Duck. Love's a bitch.
- Pretty in Prink

SIXTEEN

AVERY

Even though I went to sleep in my childhood bed, I didn't have a restful sleep. Most of the night was spent in fitful nightmares about being tortured and killed by Ron after he came after me for vengeance. The other part was spent in dreams about Cade. Most of them were of our happy days together while a truly disturbing one was a vivid sex dream.

I finally abandoned my bed around seven and went downstairs to help Nana make breakfast. After eating a mammoth stack of homemade pancakes and washing it down with freshly squeezed orange juice, I went back to bed. With Nana off at a church function and Mom working, I had the house to myself. I had been asleep for a few hours when a pounding at the door had me bolting upright in bed. After fumbling to get out from underneath the covers, I staggered out of the bed and then pounded down the stairs.

"Who is it?" I called.

Life in the city had changed me. Growing up, I would have thought nothing about throwing open the front door without knowing who was behind it. Of course, it was most likely one of Nana's friends or some of my family.

"It's Cade."

What. The. Hell. I turned the locks and threw open the door. I had half expected not to see him—to instead realize that I had hallucinated his voice—but there he was in a polo shirt and khaki shorts looking like he had the first time he'd shown up there all those years ago. "What are you doing here?" I demanded.

"I wanted to check on you, so I got your address from Tamar."

"Did you ever hear of a phone?"

Cade smirked at me. "I figured if I called, you might hang up on me, and then where would we be?"

"Good point," I muttered.

"Anyway, when I went by your apartment, your roommate told me you'd gone home for the night. She also called me a cocksucker who deserved to die a horrible death from my dick rotting off, but that's another story."

I snorted a laugh. Only Tori would think of saying something like that. As not just my roommate but my friend, she knew the full story of what had happened between Cade and me. "I see."

"Since it was a nice day out, I decided to put the top down and take a little drive."

"A little drive? It's an hour and a half."

Cade shrugged. "It's a good stretch of road to drive, and I enjoy being out of the city." He gave me a pointed look. "But even if the drive had sucked, I would have still come to make sure you were all right."

Holy shit. Suddenly it felt like I'd stumbled into a romantic movie, like the part where Jake Ryan shows up outside Samantha's sister's wedding. It was seriously overwhelming. "That's really sweet of you to want to check on me."

"I didn't just come to check on you."

I furrowed my brows at him. "You didn't?"

He held out a shopping bag I hadn't previously noticed. "I brought you lunch."

After I took the bag from him, I peeked inside. "Chinese?"

"Yeah, from Mui Lan."

"Mui Lan is my favorite," I murmured.

"I know. I remembered when we were working on our Shakespeare project, you always loved their Mongolian chicken and hot and sour soup."

Cade had not only driven an hour and a half to check on me, but he'd brought me my favorite Chinese takeout. The enormity of it all made me feel a little lightheaded, and I staggered back.

"Whoa. Are you okay?"

"Just a little dizzy."

"Come on, let's get you inside."

Instead of arguing with Cade, I let him lead me inside the house. Although it had been three years since he had been there, he seemed to remember the floor plan very well, taking a left off the foyer to get us to the living room. Once he helped me sit down on the couch, he took a step back. "Are you sure you're okay now?"

"Yeah. I'm fine."

Cade nodded. "Okay then. I guess I better go and let you rest."

Wait, after the two grand gestures, he was just going to leave? I couldn't let him go—not yet. "Wait. You don't need to go."

"I don't?"

"No. Stay and have Chinese with me."

"Are you sure?"

"Yes, I'm sure."

Cade gave me a sheepish grin. "I was hoping you would say that. Otherwise, I was going to have to dig my lunch out of the bag and take it with me."

I threw my head back and laughed. "I should have known you weren't just going to say hello and then bail."

"I didn't want to stay if it was going to upset you, like if you couldn't stand to be around me after what I told you yesterday."

"Oh that," I said as I took the soup from Cade. While he got his food out, my finger traced the label on the soup container.

"Cade?"

"Yeah?" he asked, his head buried in the shopping bag.

"I do forgive you."

He jerked his head up to look at me. "You do?"

I nodded. "It's time I let the past go. You did what you did at the time because you thought it was for the best, and you thought it would cause me the least amount of pain. I guess I can't really fault you for that."

"Or for choosing football over you?"

"At first, I let that bother me too much, but then I realized football wasn't just your world, it was your future. You had a scholarship to think about along with your love of the game."

"That's true."

"And when I really think about it, I'm not sure what I would have done if I had been put into a similar position."

Cade's brows popped up into his hairline. "Really?"

"Yeah."

"Although you've forgiven me, I'll always regret what happened. It's one of the worst things that's ever happened to me."

"Me too," I replied.

Cade then went back to rummaging around in the food bag. "Want an eggroll?" he asked.

"Sure," I replied.

Since he remembered where the kitchen was, Cade went to get us some plates and something to drink. When he returned, we poured our food out of the boxes and started eating.

We ate in silence for a few minutes. Cade swiped his mouth with his napkin then asked, "So how are you really doing with what happened at The Ark?"

"I didn't sleep very well last night. Lots of nightmares." At the thought of Ron, my appetite suddenly waned. I dropped my fork onto my plate. "Some of the nightmares were about Ron coming after me, you know, in retaliation for what happened."

"I don't think that's going to be possible. The fact that he was carrying a gun is a parole violation. He's going back to prison."

"Really?"

Cade nodded. "I did a little investigating to see what was going to happen."

I exhaled a relieved breath. "You don't know how much better that makes me feel."

"I thought it might help."

"I appreciate it."

After taking a few more bites, Cade put his plate down on the coffee table. "Man, that was good."

"It really was. Thanks again for bringing it."

"You're welcome."

Cade didn't appear like he was ready to leave, and I wasn't ready for him to go. "Wanna watch a movie?"

Cade smiled. "Sure."

When I bent over to retrieve the remote control, he said, "How about a repeat of *Sixteen Candles*?"

My hand momentarily froze as it hovered over the remote. I had managed to talk Mom into something else on Monday night. I couldn't imagine watching that movie again considering all the memories it held, but so much had changed since Monday night. After the past couple days, I felt like I could watch it.

I picked up the remote and smiled at Cade. Then I said something I never thought I would ever get to say again: "I would love to watch *Sixteen Candles* with you."

SEVENTEEN

AVERY

The weeks following Cade's apology seemed to fly by. With the air cleared between us, it was so much easier getting up for work. It was nice not feeling the urge to pull over and throw up on my morning drive into the city, and I also didn't have a feeling of dread hanging over me while I was at work. I could see Cade in the hallway without wanting to simultaneously cry and beat the shit out of him.

I had peace about more than just work. I finally had closure about the question that had been haunting me for three years—why Cade had thrown me aside. Knowing the reason why he'd done what he'd done also made me hate him less. Sure, there was still a tiny part of me that resented that he had chosen football over me, but I could understand why he had. He'd been put into a horrible position by his father, and although it had been misguided, he had tried to save me more pain and humiliation about my humble roots. There was also the fact that he was just eighteen.

When I returned to work on Monday after the incident with Ron, I was really glad to have Cade at my side. He gave me both the physical and emotional strength I needed to be back in a place where something so traumatic had happened. He stayed within my sight most of the day except for when Darion and the guys wanted him to play football. Ron Carnes was back in jail, so I felt safer in that aspect, too. Vicki had worked at The Ark for quite a few years, so sadly, it hadn't been her first brush with frightening parents. I also got a big hug from D'Andre, who was also back that day.

Even though everyone fawned over Cade for being a hero, he didn't let it go to his head. For the first time ever, he was being asked for his autograph not because of football. He was even going to turn down an interview with the Atlanta Journal until I insisted he do it. Not only was it an opportunity to raise awareness for The Ark, it gave people the chance to see that he did have goodness inside him.

The day the article about Cade came out, Tamar and I sat in her office reading it. "'In that moment, I couldn't think about anything but saving Avery's life. It didn't even cross my mind that I should probably take Carnes down. I just wanted to make sure she was okay,'" Tamar read aloud. She took off her glasses. "Girl, sounds like someone still has a fire burning for you."

I ducked my head at her comment. "I don't think so. It was just a reflex since I was the one with a gun pointed at me."

"Do you actually believe the bullshit you're spouting?"

With a groan, I met her intense stare. "Yes and no."

"What is that supposed to mean?"

"It means I don't know what to believe."

"I think you should believe me when I say that Cade still cares for you. He might not realize it now, but deep down, he does."

I opened my mouth to argue when I was interrupted by the sound of music blaring from the cafeteria. Tamar and I exchanged questioning looks. "Are they playing Nicky Minaj?" Tamar asked.

"Sounds like *Superbass*."

When a roar of shouts and whistling began, Tamar and I hopped to our feet. We hustled out of her office and up the hallway toward the cafeteria. Nothing could have quite prepared me for what I saw when I got there.

"Oh. My. God," I muttered.

Cade stood on one of the tables in the center of cafeteria with most of The Ark's older kids population encircling him. Cade wasn't just standing on the table, and oh no, he wasn't just dancing. He was lip-syncing to the words while acting out the song.

I walked up to Kevin, one of the other day counselors. "What's all this about?"

He grinned. "Cade lost a bet to Darion."

“He was gambling?” I questioned in horror.

“Nah, it was nothing like that. More like a ‘I bet I can throw this football so many yards’ kinda thing. Darion beat him, so he picked one of the most humiliating songs possible for a guy to lip-sync.”

“I would have to agree.” Standing on my tiptoes, I peered through the crowd for Darion. He was doubled over laughing at Cade’s performance, which at the moment included twerking his ass to the *boom, boom, boom* part of the song.

Tamar joined us. “I just realized Cade’s performance is just like when Joseph Gordon Levitt did that lip-sync battle on Jimmy Fallon’s show."

I laughed. "It is. He’s certainly giving Joseph a run for his money."

When he saw me on the fringes of the crowd, Cade’s face lit up in a beaming grin as he crooked his finger at me. I furiously shook my head. "Come on, Prescott. Live a little!" he shouted over the music.

"Oh no. I didn’t lose a bet!" I called back.

A wicked look flashed on Cade's face, which caused anxiety to prick over my body. I knew that look. It was the kind of look he’d had when suggesting we go skinny dipping. I was in serious trouble.

"I'll bet you a hundred dollars toward new sports equipment that you won't get up here with me."

Damn him. He was hitting me where he knew it would hurt

me. "No."

"Fine then. Two fifty."

"Forget it, Cade."

"Five hundred."

Double damn him! When I glanced around at the kids' excited faces, I knew I was screwed. Five hundred dollars would buy a hell of a lot of equipment, but we could also use new art supplies as well.

"One thousand," I countered.

Cade threw his head back with a laugh. "Done."

Part of me had hoped he wouldn't go that high, but I should have known Cade better than that. I started making my way through the crowd and cheering rang all around me. "Go Miss P!" the kids cried.

When I got to the edge of the table, Cade held out his hand for me. I placed both my hands on his and let him drag me up. It had come to the bridge in the song, so I drew in a deep breath and fake belted the line, "See I need you in my life for me to stay."

Knowing I would shock the hell out of them, I did my own version of twerking when it came to the *boom, boom, boom* part. My reward came not in the screams and whistles from the kids, but the wide-eyed look of extreme shock on Cade's face. He managed to quickly recover, and we finished out the song together.

When the music ended, Cade drew me into his arms for a bear hug. "That was fucking awesome, Prescott."

"I'm glad you enjoyed it so much."

He pulled away and winked at me. “I enjoy any time I get to see you outside your comfort level.”

“Yeah, well, I think I should be a little concerned about just how comfortable you seemed being Nicky Minaj.”

Cade and Darion did the guy hand clasp and then a quick chest bump. “That was epic, man,” Darion said.

With a dramatic bow, Cade mimicked Elvis by saying, “Thank you, thank you very much.”

Darion turned his attention from Cade to me. “And Miss P, I didn’t think you had it in you.”

Cade and I both laughed. “For your information, I’m a woman of many hidden talents.”

At their disbelieving looks, Cade said, “Hey guys, she’s serious. She can drive a tractor like nobody’s business.”

Darion and the others stared at me in surprise. “You’s a farmer, Miss P?” Antoine asked.

“Are you,” I quickly corrected, which earned me an eye roll. “And yes, my family are farmers. While I have driven a tractor, I’m more familiar with the corn harvester.”

“So, do you like booty dance out in the cornfields and scare away the crows?” Darion asked with a grin.

I smacked his arm playfully. “Whatever. You’re just jealous of my mad dancing skills.”

Antoine smiled. “Don’t let him fool ya, Miss P. You looked hot up there.”

"While I appreciate the compliment, I seriously doubt that."

He nodded his head emphatically. "She did look hot, didn't she Cade?"

My gaze bounced from Antoine over to Cade as the corners of his lips quirked up. "Yeah, she did."

"See, I told ya."

As hard as I fought it, I could feel my cheeks flushing from their attention. "Um, thanks, guys."

Marcus smacked Darion's chest. "Come on. Let's see if you can beat me like you did Cade."

"Even if I don't, I ain't gettin' up and makin' a fool outta myself like Cade did," Darion replied.

Cade laughed. "Don't be hatin' on my dancing."

Darion grinned. "You comin' with us?"

"Nah, I think I better rest my arm for a while."

"Okay. See ya later."

I drew in a breath when I realized Cade and I were alone together—well, as alone as you could be with fifteen children milling around. "I've never been in here before," Cade remarked as he looked around. He then gave me a pointed look. "Except to scrape the gum off the bottoms of the tables."

I grimaced. "Sorry about that."

"It's all good. I deserved it. I'm sure Dr. Higgins and Dr. MacKensie would have totally agreed with your punishment"

"That's all in the past. You don't have to worry about doing all that menial labor any more."

"You mean, no more scraping cum in the boys' bathroom?"

I widened my eyes. "Excuse me?"

Cade laughed. "Trust me, you don't want to know."

Since I could only imagine what he was talking about, I decided I didn't want any more clarification. "Anyway, I think your time would be better used hanging out with the kids."

"I'd like that a lot."

We spent our time weaving our way through the tables, surveying the art projects. He even sat down with some of the younger teens and me to color. Although I was enjoying our time together, the more I eyed the clock, the more anxious I became. I couldn't concentrate on the kids' conversations and kept having to ask them to repeat themselves.

When I abandoned my coloring and resorted to nervously wringing my hands, Cade asked, "What's the matter with you?"

"Nothing."

"You're acting all weird."

"I'm socially awkward. I always act weird."

"Bullshit."

With a sigh, I leaned back against one of the tables. "If you must know, I'm acting weird because this afternoon I have to perform in front of a lot of people, and I'm scared to death—like pee-my-pants kind of scared."

"What kind of performance?"

"Playing the piano. Well, actually it's an organ, which I have very little experience with." As a wave of nausea overcame me, I swept my hand to my mouth. "I'm going to screw up and ruin Jamal's solo."

Cade's brows popped up in surprise. "Jamal sings?"

I knew he was a little surprised since Jamal seemed to be sports obsessed. At twelve, he hung around Darion and his group whenever he could. Usually they made him their errand boy, but he was happy to do it.

"He has an amazing voice and sings in the Atlanta Innercity Boy's Choir. There's a performance tonight at Ebenezer Church, where Martin Luther King used to preach."

He scowled at me. "I'm familiar with Ebenezer."

"Sorry. My roommate thought I was talking about Ebenezer Scrooge."

Cade snorted. "I'm hoping she's not from around here."

"Is that an excuse?"

"Not really. I was just thinking anyone who knows the city well knows Ebenezer."

"Anyway, Jamal asked me to accompany him on the organ. I didn't want to do it. The biggest performance I've ever done was a recital with maybe thirty people. This is huge."

"Take a deep breath, Prescott. I'm sure you'll rock the socks off those people."

"This is a night celebrating African American Gospel, not a

Guns N' Roses concert."

Cade dipped his head closer to mine. "Maybe you should sneak out of here a little early for some liquid courage."

I blinked my eyes at him. "You can't be serious."

With a shrug, Cade replied, "One or two tequila shots and I guarantee your nervousness will be gone."

"I can't go into a church after I've been drinking."

"Why not? Churches have wine."

"For communion, not for getting tipsy."

"Prescott, you have got to chill the fuck out. If not, you're going to combust before the performance.

"I don't know what else I could do to relax." I peered curiously at him. "What do you do to relax or calm down before a big game?"

"If I'm really nervous, like if it's a championship game or something, I find a quick screw really helps me."

And now I feel even sicker. A quick screw—gross. Although I shouldn't have been surprised by Cade's antics, it did bother me a little that he so willingly slept with anything with a vagina. "You are actually advocating for me to have sex?"

"Yeah, or you could rub one out. It's all about the release for me."

Warmth filled my face. "I can't…" I couldn't bring myself to say the word.

"I'm sorry. Would you prefer the word *masturbate?*"

"No. I would not," I hissed.

He held his hands up. "Excuse me. I was just trying to help."

"Yeah, well, I'm sorry I asked. Extremely sorry."

Cade scratched his chin thoughtfully. "Maybe you need someone to go with you, like to talk you down from the ledge," he suggested.

"I already tried bribing my roomie, but she has to work."

"I was thinking about me."

My mouth gaped open in surprise. "You?"

"Yep."

"You want to go to church on a Thursday night to watch a choir perform?"

"While it sounds mildly entertaining, I was thinking more that you could count it toward my community service hours. Then I'm helping you and me at the same time."

I shook my head. "That is so not happening."

With a scowl, Cade questioned, "Why the hell not?"

"Because your hours are mandated to The Ark."

Cade grunted. "Fine. Then you will just have to owe me for something."

"You mean you're still willing to go?"

"I said I wanted to help you, didn't I?"

"Yes, you did, and I really appreciate your offer."

"So it's a deal? I go with you tonight, and then you owe me a favor down the road."

"I'm not sure I like it being left open-ended like that."

Cade laughed. "Are you afraid of what kind of favor I might ask you to do?"

"It's more of agreeing to the terms when they aren't laid out before me."

"There you go thinking like a lawyer."

"Always."

"Okay, I think I know the favor."

"I'm scared to ask, but what is it?"

"Two weeks from Saturday, my fraternity is having a back to school '80s party."

"Why the '80s?"

Cade shrugged his shoulders. "Why the hell not? It was a fucking awesome decade in my opinion."

"And what about the party?"

"I want you to go with me."

I swallowed hard. Oh man, he was really sticking it to me with this one. After all, it was no secret to him that I hated parties. I mean, what true introvert does? Parties and socializing were the one reason I had never pledged a sorority—even the ones that were tied to the law school.

As I pondered the certain hell I would be in, Cade said, "You would also need to dress in an '80s costume. Most people come as famous people from the '80s—musicians, actors, sports figures, etc."

Well, didn't that sound peachy? I mean, could it get any

worse? When I looked into Cade's eyes, a mischievous glint burned in them. He was doing this on purpose to pay me back for not letting him get service hours. He also thought he would have an out to not go to Ebenezer because I would never agree to the party.

Although I was terrified, I decided to call Mr. Hall's bluff. "Fine. I would love to go."

The amusement drained out of Cade's face. "You would?"

"Sure. I mean, an '80s fraternity party, how fun!"

Cade snorted. "Yeah, right, Prescott. Like you actually mean that."

I held out my hand. "Do we have a deal?"

"Deal," Cade replied as he took my hand in his.

"By the way, you need to wear dress pants and a tie tonight."

He jerked his hand away. "Dammit, Prescott. That was a dirty move."

"It's not any dirtier than making me go to a *costume* party."

He growled. "Fine. I'll wear a fucking tie."

"Thank you," I said sweetly.

"Do you want to meet me there?"

I cocked my brows at him. "And run the risk of you not showing up?"

"I'm a man of my word. I would never ditch you. Just to prove it, why don't you come by my apartment and we'll go together?"

"Okay. That sounds good."

"What time does the thing start?"

"Seven."

"Then I'll see you at six thirty."

I smiled. "See you then."

* * *

When MapQuest led me to an average-looking apartment complex around the corner from Tech, I couldn't help feeling a little surprised. I knew Cade didn't live in the dorms, but at the same time, I imagined him living off his dad's money in some swinging penthouse, which was certainly not the case. It was, however, a lot nicer than the apartment Tori and I shared.

After I pounded up the stairs to Cade's second-floor apartment, I made my way down the hallway, counting down the numbers to 217. I knew I'd found it when I saw a blue door with a giant G and T painted in gold. Only Cade could possibly live behind a door so boldly sporting Georgia Tech colors.

When I started knocking, the sound of a baby wailing froze my hand in midair. I knitted my brows in confusion at the sound. Okay, maybe the door was a false lead. As my hand fell to my side, I glanced down at my phone in my other hand to make sure I had the right apartment number.

The door swung open to reveal a towering blond-haired hottie holding a red-faced baby girl. Tears streamed down her chubby cheeks as she continued wailing at the top of her lungs. "Yeah?" he yelled over the noise.

I took a step back. "Uh, I'm sorry. I must have the wrong

apartment."

Just as I turned to sprint away, the guy asked, "Wait, are you Avery?"

"Um, yeah, I am."

A friendly grin flashed across his handsome face. "Right apartment, wrong guy." He shifted the baby on his hip. "I'm Jonathan Nelson, Cade's roommate."

"Oh, I see."

With his free hand, he motioned for me to come inside. "Cade's in the shower."

"Oh," I murmured. An ache of longing shot straight between my legs at the illicit images of water trickling down the muscles of Cade's perfect body that flashed through my mind. Of course, it was quickly replaced by a feeling of extreme irritation that I was even remotely thinking of him sexually. Even though things were good between Cade and me, I still couldn't manage to fully let go of everything that had happened. The last thing I needed was to try to rekindle anything physical with him.

I breezed past Jonathan to step into the apartment. I was surprised not to find beer cans overflowing the tables or piles of laundry on the floor. For being inhabited by two guys, it was spotlessly clean.

My arrival seemed to have momentarily pacified the baby because when Jonathan shut the door, she peeked at me over his shoulder.

"Hi there, pretty girl," I said, wriggling my fingers at her.

Jonathan turned the baby around. "Say hi, Evie." He pronounced it Eh-v.

A gummy grin lit up Evie's face, and I couldn't help smiling at her. "I'm Avery."

"She's Evelyn after my mother, but we call her Evie."

When I looked from her to Jonathan, I grimaced. "Sorry about flaking out like that. I wasn't expecting a baby."

Jonathan chuckled. "Yeah, I can see your point. Cade living with a baby seems totally unnatural."

"Yes, it does, mainly because I imagined him in a swinging bachelor pad."

"Oh, it is when Evie isn't here."

"So she doesn't live here?"

"No, I'm just babysitting today so her mom could take the entrance exam over at Kennesaw. She's getting a later start going to college because of Miss Boo here."

"She's beautiful," I remarked.

"Thanks. She knows it too, dontcha, Evie?" He bestowed a smacking kiss on her cherubic cheek, causing Evie to grin again.

"How old is she?"

"Almost eight months."

"She looks just like you."

The pride radiating in Jonathan's eyes faded, and his expression became pained. "Actually, she's not mine."

"She's not?" I questioned incredulously.

"She's my niece, not my daughter. She belongs to my younger brother, Jake."

"Oops, I'm sorry." When I once again glanced between him and Evie, I couldn't help remarking, "Wow, you and your brother must look like twins."

"We did." He eyed Evie before swallowing hard, causing his Adam's apple to bob up and down. "He was killed fifteen months ago, before she was born."

Anguished grief rolled off of Jonathan in waves so palpable I had to draw a deep breath before speaking. "Oh, I'm so sorry."

He nodded and an uncomfortable silence fell over the room. Jerking his chin at the leather sofa, he said, "Why don't you sit down? Knowing Cade and his douche primping, it'll be a while."

A rude-sounding snort escaped my lips. "Well, it's partly my fault since I told him to wear dress pants and a tie."

Jonathan's brows popped up in surprise. "And he's really going to do it?"

"It's not so much about giving in to me as it is that the dress code calls for it."

"I see," Jonathan replied as he grabbed a bottle off the end table and started feeding Evie. "So Avery, can I tell you something?"

"I guess," I replied tentatively.

"You aren't like what I pictured."

I laughed. "Let me guess: based on Cade's description, I

should have warts and ride a broom, right?"

Jonathan laughed. "Well, that sounds like something he might've said in the beginning."

"I probably deserved that. I was pretty hard on him."

"Nah, he deserved whatever you gave him, especially with your history."

Warmth rushed to my cheeks. "He told you about us?"

"Yeah, the first day he came home from The Ark. Also, I sorta already knew about you before that because he sometimes talked about you when he was drunk."

I gulped. "He did?"

Jonathan nodded. "Usually I was drunk as hell too, so I didn't know a lot of the specifics of the story." At what must've been my horrified expression, Jonathan said,

"Don't worry, Avery. It wasn't like he described having sex *with* you. He just whined about missing you and shit."

"Oh, I see."

Oh. My. God.

Cade *talked* about me when he was drunk. Cade *missed* me when he was drunk. Jonathan's revelations had me feeling like I had stumbled into an episode of *The Twilight Zone*. I wondered what else talking to Jonathan would unearth about Cade. I guessed all I could do was ask and see.

Just as I leaned forward to get the dirt, I heard a door open down the hall. Damn. I would have to get Jonathan alone another day and ambush him with questions—and yes, I was totally and completely pathetic.

EIGHTEEN

CADE

After I got in from The Ark, I had about half an hour before Avery was supposed to pick me up. While she had left work early to get ready, I had stayed behind to play basketball with some of the guys and girls, which meant I was a sweaty, stinky mess. Ordinarily that wasn't an issue, but that night I was supposed to be getting my holy on while sporting a suit and tie. Because of that fact, I decided I better make the time to hop in the shower.

Somehow I managed to shave, clean up, and get dressed in a record amount of time. I had just come out of the bathroom and was straightening my tie when the sound of Avery's laughter floated back to me. Of course Miss Punctual would be early.

When I threw open my bedroom door, I froze at the sight before me. Avery and Jonathan sat on the couch together playing with Evie while smiling and laughing at each other and at Evie. They could've been the perfect picture of a couple, and that thought sent jealousy pulsing through me. It wasn't just about not wanting Jonathan to have Avery—I didn't want any guy to have her. I knew I was being stupid since there was no way Avery was going to be mine—*ever*.

Avery looked gorgeous as always. She had her hair down and it flowed in waves over her shoulders. She was wearing a simple black dress that did amazing things for her body.

"Hey," I finally said.

Avery snapped her gaze over to mine. Her eyes widened slightly at the sight of me in my dress pants and shirt. I liked the way she was looking at me—like she thought I was hot. *Yeah, keep looking at me like that, Avery, and we won't make it to the church tonight. We'll end up in my bedroom.*

"Hey," she replied.

"Sorry for keeping you waiting."

"It's okay." She patted Evie's cheek. "This little cutie was keeping me entertained."

"And Jonathan," I added curtly.

"Oh, yes. Jonathan's been very friendly."

I narrowed my eyes at Jonathan. "Thanks, buddy, for keeping an eye on Avery for me."

He gave me a shit-eating grin. "Any time. It was a pleasure talking to her." With Avery looking at Evie, he waggled his brows at me. Oh yeah, I would punch the hell out of him when we were alone.

"We better get going, Prescott. I don't want you to be late."

With a nod, Avery rose off the couch. She then leaned down to bestow a kiss on the top of Evie's dark head of hair. "Bye, bye, Miss Evie." She gave a wave to Jonathan. "It was nice meeting you."

When he gave her a cocky grin, a low growl came from the back of my throat. Jesus, why was I being so irrational? What was next? Pissing on Avery's leg to mark her as mine? I guess the better question was what it was about Avery that brought it out in me. She wasn't mine. There was nothing except maybe bro code to stop Jonathan from pursuing her. Avery and I were friends now, nothing more, regardless of how I felt deep down inside.

"Hope to see you again soon, Avery!" Jonathan called as I hustled us out of the apartment. Just before the door closed, I stuck my hand in and flipped him off.

"So Evvie's a real cutie," Avery remarked as we started down the stairs.

"Yeah. She has us all wrapped around her little finger."

"I never imagined you as a baby person."

"Oh, I totally dig Miss Evie."

"Just Miss Evie or babies in general?"

I opened the car door for Avery. "Most of the time, I like

babies. I'm not a real big fan of when they spit up on you or do the drool shit on you, but for the most part, they're cool." At Avery's surprised expression, I grinned. "Does my stance on babies make my blackened soul a little lighter to you?"

She shook her head as she slid inside the car. "I never said you had a blackened soul. In fact, I've always suggested the opposite."

"Even after what I did to you?"

Avery grimaced. "Okay, maybe I thought you were a soulless bastard then."

"I thought as much."

"But things change." She stared up at me. "People change."

"Here's hoping." I then closed the door and jogged around the front of the car. Once I was inside, I cranked it up and got us on the road. The closer we got to Ebenezer, the more Avery started to freak out. "Jesus, if I'd known you were going to get this worked up, I would have tried to score some Xanax for you."

Avery shot me a death glare. "I don't need drugs. I just need to think about something else." She inhaled and exhaled a few deep breaths. "Jonathan's brother," she blurted out.

"Evie's father?" I questioned. When she nodded, I said, "His name was Jake."

"What happened to him?"

"He got blown up on a tractor over in Gilmer County when he was visiting his grandfather's farm."

Avery gasped in horror. "Oh my God, how tragic. I was

thinking something like a car accident."

"Yeah, it was pretty terrible. It was just a freak thing. He and some of his cousins were shooting off guns and one nicked a fence and hit the tank of the tractor Jake was sitting on." Avery once again gasped while bringing her hand to her mouth. "It was a quick way to die for Jake, but it was horrible for his family. This last year has been hell for Jonathan. He and Jake were really close. Brandon and I have tried to get him through the best way we could."

"I'm sure you guys have helped him more than you could ever know."

"I hope so. He's a good guy."

"He seemed like it."

I cut my eyes over to her. "What's that supposed to mean?"

Avery gave me a funny look. "Um, that he didn't treat me like a douchebag like some guys would, and he was nice and welcoming."

"Trust me, you don't want to go there."

"Go where? What are you talking about?"

"You do not want to start anything up with Jonathan."

"Oh, my God, Cade, I didn't say I wanted to date him—I just remarked that he seemed like a good guy."

"He's a good guy and friend, but he's a total manwhore when it comes to girls."

"I see you two have a lot in common."

"Easy with the claws, Prescott."

"Only if you'll go easy with the wild assumptions about me and Jonathan."

I glanced away from the road to pin her with a stare. "You think he's hot, don't you?"

Avery giggled. "I'd have to be blind to not think he was hot."

I gripped the steering wheel tighter. I did not like the idea of Avery drooling over Jonathan. Being a selfish bastard, I only wanted her drooling over me. "Should I have put a towel down so your damp panties wouldn't wet the seat?"

Avery threw her head back and laughed. "Come on, Cade, you should know me well enough by now to know that regardless of how handsome he is, Jonathan is not my type."

A relieved breath whooshed out of me. "That's good since he's kinda seeing someone."

"You mean you just went through all that when Jonathan has a girlfriend?"

"They're not exactly dating, but they like each other."

"Good for him."

"I wouldn't necessarily call it a good thing."

"Is it the fact that he likes just one girl, or is it the girl in particular?"

"Nah, I'm cool with the girl."

"I see." Avery made a little harrumphing noise before crossing her arms over her chest. "So the idea of monogamy still scares you, huh?"

"Hold on, we were talking about Jonathan—how did this become about me?" I protested.

"I could just tell by the way you said it."

"And just how exactly did I say it?"

"Disdainfully and with disgust."

"Um, I don't think I said it any differently than anything else I was talking about."

"Okay, so if you didn't, then does that mean I'm to believe you're now okay with monogamy?"

"I'm fine with it." When I cut my eyes over to her, Avery cocked her brows challengingly at me. "Okay, so maybe I'm fine with it for other people, but not entirely myself." Taking my gaze off the road, I stared intently at her. "Not entirely doesn't mean never, ever. Like Jonathan, under the right circumstances and with the right girl, I probably could try."

"You were willing to try with me three years ago," Avery countered softly.

Oh, hell. She just had to go and bring that up. My left hand flew from the steering wheel to my collar to unloosen the button that felt like it was choking me. The truth was it was more like the conversation was strangling me. For the life of me, I didn't know why a simple conversation with Avery felt like I was tiptoeing through a minefield. With one false step, the conversation could explode in my face.

"Yeah, I was gonna give monogamy a whirl, and look how I

managed to screw that up. I couldn't even choose you over football."

Avery remained silent as she stared out the window. "It doesn't really count," she finally murmured.

"It doesn't?"

She turned her head to look at me. "Your father's ultimatum put you between a rock and a hard place. The choice you made then doesn't reflect your actual ability to be faithful to someone…to love someone."

"Yeah, I guess you're right. I mean, I hope you're right." An uncomfortable silence hung over us. Thankfully for me, we arrived at the church, and from the way Avery turned almost green, I was off the hook for the moment with the serious talk. I barely had time to park before Avery bailed out of the car. I was suddenly paranoid that she was trying to get away from me, but when I came around to meet her, she said, "Sorry, just needed some air."

"No problem."

When we started walking toward the church, I reached out for Avery's hand. The moment our skin touched she whipped her head around to stare wide-eyed and open-mouthed at me. I was sure that while she was shocked as hell by me doing that, she also wondered if I had any other motives behind it. "You're going to do fine," I reassured her.

"I wish I shared your confidence."

"Seriously, Prescott, you're way too hard on yourself. There is nothing in your life that you ever do half-ass. I'm sure that when you sit down in front of that organ, you will make it sing like no one's business."

Avery squeezed my hand. "Thanks, Cade, and not just for the words, but for being here with me tonight. You can't imagine what it means to me."

"Don't worry. I'll be collecting on it later on at the frat party."

She huffed out a frustrated breath. "Way to kill a moment."

We walked up the stairs and into the building where ushers were in the hallway handing out programs. Avery and I took one and then started into the sanctuary. "Do you have to go backstage now and meet up with Jamal?"

"No. I'll sit out here with you until one song before his performance."

I glanced down at the program in my hands. "Wait, there are like ten songs before Jamal's performance."

Avery groaned as we took a seat on one of the benches on the right side of the church. "Don't remind me. That means I have to be a nervous wreck through ten other songs."

"You know, it's kind of interesting seeing you unhinged like this. You've always seemed to have your shit together—" Avery elbowed me hard for my use of profanity. "Ow, you seriously have the boniest elbows."

"Oh, please, don't be such a baby."

"For your information, I'm not being a baby. My ribs are still tender from getting slammed at the scrimmage a few weeks back."

"Baby," Avery muttered under her breath.

"You try playing a contact sport and see how well you do," I replied.

Our bickering came to an end when Jamal and the choir took the stage. Jamal looked angelic in his choir robe, and it was certainly a change from how I was used to seeing him. When he met my gaze, he grinned.

The choir director took his place, and then the music started. Although I had originally thought the night would be a snooze fest, I was pretty intrigued by the performances. It wasn't all just holy rolling gospel. There was even a cover of Michael Jackson's *Man in the Mirror* as well as Simon and Garfunkel's *Bridge Over Troubled Water*. From the high notes some of the guys were hitting, I had to wonder if their balls had yet to drop.

After the performances started, Avery's nerves seemed to fade a little. She watched with rapt attention, although I noticed her doing chord progressions on her thigh. With one song left before Jamal's, she waved a quick goodbye and then headed backstage. When Jamal stepped up to the mic and Avery took her place at the organ, I couldn't help feeling a little nervous myself. What if I had reassured her all this time and then she blew it? How would I make up for that?

Jamal's song was a jazzy number called *Steal Away*. In the chorus, the choir would accompany him, but my man held his own on the rest. He didn't just sing the song—he felt the music. It was one of the most powerful performances I'd ever seen.

Once Jamal finished, applause broke out all around me. I rose to my feet to give him and Avery a standing ovation. The moment she stood up from the organ bench, I brought my fingers to my lips to let out a catcall. Even from where I was standing, I could see Avery's flush of embarrassment.

When she started off the stage, I hurried down the aisle to the back of the church to meet her.

"How did I do?" she questioned.

"Fanfuckingtastic."

Avery's eyes widened in horror as she glanced around to see if anyone else had heard me. "Cade, watch your language! We're in church."

I brought my hands together in a prayer pose. "My bad. Your performance was fantastic—a real heavenly experience."

Her brows knitted together. "You aren't just saying that to try to spare my feelings?"

I laughed. "No. You really did great."

A shy smile curved on Avery's lips. "Thanks."

After glancing around, I asked, "Does Jamal have any more solos?"

"No. That's it for him tonight."

"So now that you and Jamal are done, we're good to go, right?"

"Can't wait to get out of here, can you?" Avery teasingly

asked.

"Nope."

"Fine. We can go."

"Hallelujah!"

As we started down the church steps, Avery gushed, "Wasn't Jamal amazing?"

"He has a hell of a voice. He needs an agent."

"He really does." Avery's eyes widened in excitement. "Can you imagine if he got a recording deal and then became famous? We could say we knew him back in the day."

"We could." I leaned closer to Avery. "You know what his performance reminded me of?"

"What?"

"Remember that outside project we had in Dr. Paulson's class where we had to compare and contrast Zeferrelli's 1968 version of *Romeo and Juliet* to Baz Lurman's version?"

"Yes," Avery replied curiously.

"You know the scene when Romeo and Juliet get married, and there's a kid with an amazing set of pipes singing with a choir, something about being free."

"*Everybody's Free*?" Avery suggested.

"Yeah, that's it."

Avery smiled. "I do remember, and you're right. It was sorta like that part in the movie."

"I think Jamal was better than that other kid though."

"Me too. Now you have me wanting to watch that movie again or listen to the soundtrack."

"I think it was one of the few movies we had to watch for literature that I actually liked."

"Even though it was a little cheesy and over the top?"

"Yep."

"I liked the Zeferelli version a lot, too."

"That's because the Romeo dude looked like Zac Efron."

Avery giggled. "Oh, my God, he did, didn't he? But that's not the entire reason why I liked it better."

"I liked it because Juliet had a fabulous rack at fifteen."

Wrinkling her nose, Avery said, "Ew."

"That rack was amazing, and don't act like you didn't enjoy the butt scene."

"The butt scene?"

"Yeah, the butt scene, when Romeo gets out of bed and flashes his ass for like five minutes."

A dreamy expression came over Avery. "Oh yeah. That was a very nice scene."

"Ha, I knew you dug it. Of course, that scene sucked for the straight guys because the camera was on Romeo's ass way too long, and there's only a brief flash of Juliet's tits."

Avery laughed. "Whatever. I think we're losing points of intelligence by appreciating the film for the hotness of the stars and not its literary merit."

"You can jerk off to literary merit."

"Cade!" Avery shrieked.

I couldn't help laughing at her reaction. All the talk of Romeo and Juliet got the wheels turning in my head, and suddenly I had an idea. "Do you have to be anywhere else tonight?"

"No. Why?"

"Well, it's still early. I thought we could head over to the Shakespeare Tavern and catch a play."

Avery's eyes immediately brightened. "Really?"

"Yeah, why not?"

"I haven't been there since the senior year fieldtrip with Dr. Paulson's class."

"Me either." I glanced at my phone. "The show's probably already started, but we can catch the last couple acts. Since it's dinner theater, we could grab a bite to eat while we're there."

"Are you sure your head won't combust from having so much culture in one night?"

I laughed. "I think I could stand it."

Avery grinned. "I would love to."

"Then it's a date."

The moment the words left my lips, I instantly regretted them. They were just too loaded for the no man's land in which I currently found myself, and I felt even worse when Avery's face flushed a little. "Uh, yeah, we better go." I then ducked my head and made a beeline for the car.

NINETEEN

AVERY

Friday night found me holed up in my bedroom getting ready for Cade's fraternity party. Part of me wanted to feign some sort of illness to try to get out of it—nothing seemed like a more torturous idea than hanging around a bunch of drunk fraternity guys—but the other part of me didn't want to give Cade the satisfaction of gloating over my surrender.

As I was spreading blush across my cheeks, a low whistle came from the doorway. "Well, well, well. Look at you, Miss Hotstuff!" Tori exclaimed.

An embarrassed warmth filled my face, causing me to look like an overly made-up clown.

"Thanks," I replied as I tried removing some of the blush.

Tori collapsed onto my bed, sending her long auburn hair into her face. After she flicked it away, she asked, "What are you getting all dolled up for on a Friday night? If you don't go back home, this is usually your Netflix and chill night, isn't it?" She wrinkled her nose. "Jesus, did I actually just say 'Netflix and chill'?"

I laughed. "Yes, while I usually stay in when I'm here, tonight I'm going to a party."

My statement was met with the flailing of arms and rustling of sheets as Tori scrambled to sit up. "You're shitting me," she demanded incredulously.

"No. I'm not."

"But you never go to parties."

"As a wise—though often inebriated—roommate once told me, 'There's a first time for everything.'"

She laughed. "Well, it's the truth." When I glanced back at her reflection in the mirror, her full lips turned down in a pout. "But what the hell, Avery? There's a party and I'm not invited? I mean, I'm the one who loves parties, not you."

"Yes, I'm aware of that."

"Although I shouldn't speak to you any more tonight, I can't help asking where you're going."

I turned away from the mirror. "I'm glad you're sitting down for this one."

Her blue eyes widened curiously. "What do you mean?"

"Remember how Cade went with me to ease my nerves when I played for Jamal?"

"Yeah."

"Well, he sorta bribed me."

She snorted. "I knew there had to be a reason for him to go for a night of hymns."

I waved my hand dismissively at her. "Anyway, he said he would go with me if I would go to his fraternity's '80s party."

Tori blinked at me a few times. "You're going to a fraternity party?"

"Yes."

"With Cade Hall?"

"Yessss," I replied.

"Wow, Aves. This is…epic."

I swept a hand to my hips. "Is it really that mind-blowing that I'm going to a fraternity party?"

Tori shook her head. "It's more about fact that you're going with Cade."

Staring down at my heels, I whispered, "Because I'm not good enough for him."

My chin was unceremoniously jerked up. "That is not what I meant."

"It sounded like it."

"You are certainly good enough for Cade. If anything, you're worlds better than him."

I patted her shoulder. "I think it's safe to say you're shitting me, but I appreciate the effort."

"I'm serious, Avery. You got hella brains and beauty, not to mention you have one of the most giving hearts around. Cade should thank his lucky stars that you even lower yourself to speak to him, least of all go with him to a party."

While fighting the tears her compliments had induced, I couldn't help asking, "Then why did you seem so surprised Cade had asked me to the party?"

"My surprise came more from the fact that Cade wanted to go to the party with a date. Frat parties are hookup central."

"You know, I asked him the same thing."

"And?"

"It's payback more than anything."

"He's blackmailing you into being social? I don't get it."

"Cade knows how much I hate parties—especially A-list parties. So, in his eyes, it's payback for going to Ebenezer for Jamal's performance."

"Let me get this straight: Mr. Manwhore Hall is forgoing available ass just for payback?" When I nodded, Tori snorted. "Oh honey, I think it's about way more than that."

"What do you mean?"

"Cade doesn't give a shit about you hating parties or getting paid back. This is about him caring about you."

"I don't think so."

"Oh, I do. Guys like him don't give up free pussy just for payback."

I wrinkled my nose at the word *pussy*. I always had and always would hate that word. "He's also paying me back for being such a bitch to him at the beginning of the summer."

"Once again, I call bullshit." She cocked her brows at me. "You have lady-scaped, haven't you?"

A laugh burst from my lips. "Tori, please."

"I'm serious."

"I know you are—that's why it's so funny." I placed both my hands on her shoulders. "Trust me, there is no way Cade and I are having sex tonight or any time soon. Most likely never…again."

"It's a logical step. You guys are practically dating."

"We are not," I quickly countered.

"You hang out all the time and are constantly texting each other." Tori was right about that one. In the month that had passed since Cade's apology, we had spent an awful lot of time together. We would grab dinner after work at O'Malley's, and I would even stay with him to watch some of the Braves games on the big screen there. Besides dinner, we also caught an occasional movie, but I assured myself it didn't mean anything.

"Friends hang out together and text each other. We're just friends."

Tori threw her hands up in frustration. "Aves, you can't be 'just friends' with someone you have a sexual history with."

"One time doesn't constitute a history."

Tori shook her head. "Once is plenty to have a history."

"Whatever."

"Correct me if I'm wrong, but you had more than just a sexual history with him." Tori gave me a pointed look. "You loved him."

That comment hit me like a bullet to the chest. In the last three years, I really couldn't remember a time when I'd stopped loving Cade. It had always been there, and no matter how hard I tried to quit, I couldn't. It was like a flame burning within me that refused to be snuffed out. It had even remained flickering through my long-term relationship with Hal and during the two other short-term relationships I'd had.

After spending time with Cade recently, the little flame had begun to grow again. If I gave myself over to my feelings, it would become a wildfire that would consume me. Cade's rejection had burned me so badly before and I didn't know if I could survive again if things didn't work out. *Things didn't work out?* I was probably overthinking things a little. Once he was finished working at The Ark, that would be it, but while I could've argued a million and one reasons why Cade and I as a couple weren't a good idea, none of those reasons mattered to my heart. It had never felt for anyone else the way it had for Cade.

I exhaled a long, painful breath. "Yeah, I did love him, back when I was younger and much more naïve. I know not to start something up with him again."

Sweeping her hands to her hips, Tori countered, "Oh really?"

"Yes. Really."

"Avery Rose Prescott, you are lying through your fucking teeth!"

"I am not," I fired back.

"Yeah, you are, and no, it's not your perfect future lawyer poker face giving you away; it's the look in your eyes whenever you talk about him."

I closed my eyes. "Can we please drop this subject? I need to finish getting ready."

Tori held her hands up. "Fine, fine. I'll talk about something else like your costume. Where is it?" When I flicked my wrist at the black graduation robe hanging on the closet door, Tori gasped. "You can't be serious."

"What's wrong with it?"

"The better question would be who the hell are you supposed to be in that thing?"

I rolled my eyes. "Well, duh. Sandra Day O'Connor."

"Who?"

"Um, the first female Supreme Court Justice." When Tori continued staring blankly at me, I continued rattling on, "She was appointed by President Reagan in 1981, and she served until 2006."

Tori rose off the bed to come stand before me. Placing her hands on my shoulders, she shook her head. "My dear, sweet, delusional-as-fuck Avery, you cannot go to a fraternity party dressed as some old hag in a robe."

"That's really disrespectful considering she died in 2012. You shouldn't say bad stuff about the dead."

"Are you even listening to yourself? Unless you're going as sexy Sandra O'Connor with a red, white, and blue thong and American flag pasties, you will embarrass not only yourself, but more importantly Cade. The dude has a reputation to protect."

"Then just exactly who would you suggest?"

"It's an '80s theme, right?"

"Yes," I replied cautiously.

Tori momentarily pinched her eyes shut in thought. "Someone sexy from the '80s."

"Why does it have to be someone sexy?"

She peeped one eye open at me. "Shut up. You're ruining my concentration."

"Excuse me," I muttered back.

Her face lit up in a classic light-bulb moment as her eyes snapped open. "Oh my God. It's so simple I can't believe I actually had to think about it."

"Who?"

"Madonna."

I gasped and took a step back. "You've got to be joking."

"I never joke about parties."

"Tori, there is no way in hell I can pull off Madonna."

"Of course you can. You have a rockin' body."

Motioning to my B-cups, I countered, “These do not scream Madonna.”

“The bustier will fix that.”

“What bustier?”

“The leather one you’re going to be wearing.”

I grunted with frustration. “Cade will be here in less than an hour. I don’t have time to go to the store.”

“You can wear mine.”

“You own a leather bustier?”

“Three actually—a red one, a black one, and a white one. I’m just trying to decide what color for you?”

“Do I even want to ask why you own them?”

Now it was Tori’s time to grunt with frustration. “During my first year at Emory, I was in a sorority. Trust me, there was no way to escape sorority life without owning one.”

Since I was so not the sorority girl type, I replied, “I see.”

Tori bunched my hair in her hands. “Would you object to dying your hair?”

I jerked back from her. “I would object very much, not to mention we don’t have the time.”

“Let me call Jack and see if she has a blonde wig.”

Jack, or Jacqueline Bateman, was Tori’s best friend from high school. She lived a few floors down with her boyfriend and attended Georgia State. We hung out from time to time.

“Madonna is a natural brunette, you know.”

"Hmm, it might work. I'm thinking a bustier and fluffy skirt to look like the album cover for *Like a Virgin*."

As I pictured it in my mind, I swallowed hard. "I'm not so sure I'd be comfortable wearing that."

Either Tori didn't hear me, or she just chose to ignore me. Instead, she started furiously typing on her phone. Based on the dings in the air, she was getting quick replies. After a few seconds, a beaming grin stretched across her face. "Okay. It's time to get your Madonna on."

* * *

Jacqueline arrived with a white bustier, white crinoline skirt, white lace arm-length gloves, and the classic 'Boy Toy' belt Madonna wore. "How in the world did you find all that so quickly?"

"Oh, I had it in my closet." The way Jacqueline said it made it sound like it was perfectly normal to have a full Madonna costume just hanging among your leggings and tunic tops.

Any modesty I might've had was thrown out the window when they began to strip me. They helped me wiggle into the bustier and then put the skirt on me. I was basically a doll for them to dress up.

With twenty-five minutes on the clock, Tori and Jacqueline imprisoned me in one of the kitchen chairs while they worked their collective magic on me. The table overflowed with makeup and hair products. Tori had unearthed her hair crimper to give my hair the perfect '80s look.

When they were finally finished, Tori stepped back and

grinned at me. "Holy shit, Aves. You look ah-mazing!"

Jack nodded. "Just like the infamous MTV Music Awards performance, minus the wedding veil."

"How could you possibly remember that?" I asked.

"My mother worshipped Madonna, so I grew up idolizing her."

"I see. Well, if you don't mind, I think I'll have to judge how much I look like Madonna for myself—that is if you two will let me up to go look in the mirror."

Tori took me by the hands and pulled me out of the chair. "Fine. Go look at your epic transformation."

Jacqueline snorted. "Jesus, Tori. When you say it like that, you make it sound like she was some unfortunate hag before we got our hands on her."

"Thank you, Jack," I said.

"You're welcome."

Unlike Cade, Tori and I didn't have bathrooms of our own. Instead, we had to share the one off the living room, a Jack and Jill bathroom that joined our bedrooms. When I turned to gaze in the bathroom mirror, I seriously did a double take. I know that sounds cliché, but I seriously did the headshake of disbelief. I didn't know how it was possible that the reflection in the mirror was actually me. I had been totally and completely transformed.

"Holy shit," I murmured.

"Told ya," Tori said from the doorway.

Eyeing my pushed-up cleavage, I once again murmured, "Holy shit."

Jack's gaze zeroed in on my boobs. "Isn't it amazing what a bustier can do? Who knew you had tits like those?"

"I should wear a bustier more often," I mused.

"I bet Cade knows all about your tits," Tori said with a sly smile.

"Call me crazy, but I highly doubt after three years he even remembers my boobs, not to mention all the other breasts he's seen since then."

"Oh, I bet he remembers them fondly. I mean, I have two dicks that have stayed in my memory all these years."

"Seriously?"

Tori nodded emphatically. "When they're good both in their delivery and aesthetic quality, you tend to remember them."

Jack wrinkled her nose. "I'm sorry, but I don't find dicks aesthetically pleasing. It's chicks like you who have perpetuated the myth that women want to see dicks, and thus that it is imperative to send a dick picture."

I laughed. "Way to go, Tori. Thanks for inflicting the horror of dick pics on all womankind."

"Hey, just because I appreciate a large, veiny dick doesn't mean I started the dick pic revolution."

Our dick-pic argument was interrupted by a knock at the door. Immediately, my stomach did an Olympic-style somersault before twisting into knots. What would Cade think of my outfit? Would he think I was just dressing for the party, or that I had chosen my costume to try to get him to notice me? Oh, who was I kidding? I really wanted him to notice me, or at least desire me like he once had.

While my mind and heart waged a war over my feelings for Cade, my body was fighting its own battle—the battle of wanting to have sex, specifically sex with Cade. It had been six months since I'd had any type of physical action, and I was starting to feel it. Since I knew the type of sexual attention Cade delivered, it made me want him all the more. In the few times we had watched movies together on his couch, I had found myself fantasizing about him banging me.

Tori smacked me on my ass. "Go get him, girlie!"

I stumbled a bit on the stilettos as I made my way to the door with Tori and Jack close on my heels. I had a feeling it was going to be the three of us greeting Cade, rather than just me.

When I threw open the door, the breath I'd been holding wheezed out of my lungs. Cade stood before me in a white navy uniform complete with a hat. I was immediately hit with a *Top Gun* vibe, which made sense since it was one of my mom's favorite movies. "Maverick?" I questioned with a smile.

Cade gave me a cocky grin. "Yes, Madonna."

I laughed. "Come on in."

After Cade stepped into the foyer, he did a slow appraisal of me from head to toe. The way he looked at me warmed my skin like I had been out in the sun. He let out a low whistle.

"Damn, Prescott. That's some costume."

It wasn't just his words that lit a fire within my lower belly—and, if I was honest, between my legs; it was also the slow, sexy smile that stretched across his face after he said them that did it. I fought the urge to jump him right there in front of Tori and Jacqueline.

I glanced down at my outfit. "Oh this? It's just a little something I had in the back of my closet."

At Tori's snort, Cade tilted his head at me. "There is no way in hell you had that in your closet."

"I think you underestimate my wardrobe. I mean, I could totally sport this at one of the legal balls on campus."

"As what? A hooker someone was defending?"

"Ha, ha."

Cade grinned. "It doesn't matter to me how you got the outfit, I just like it—a lot."

My heart fluttered at his words while lust bloomed below my waist. "Score," Jack murmured behind me. Thankfully, I didn't think Cade heard.

"Okay then. Let me grab my purse, and then we can go."

"Have fun," Jack said.

"And don't do anything I wouldn't do." With a wicked grin, Tori added, "Which means there isn't an orifice off limits."

"Jesus Christ," Cade muttered under his breath.

I hustled Cade out the door before they could say anything else humiliating. Just before the door closed, I stuck my finger back in and flipped Tori off. Cade chuckled as we started down the stairs. "No offense, Prescott, but I totally wouldn't put you and your roommate together."

"She's more than just my roommate. She's my friend."

"Where in the hell did you meet her?"

"We had a corporate litigation class last year. I was thinking about moving off campus, and she had a room available. The rest is history."

"A very perverted history."

I laughed. "I guess you could say that."

We got quite a few curious stares from the residents as we made our way to Cade's car. Since it was an off-campus apartment, I supposed they weren't used to seeing a lot of costumes in the middle of summer.

"So how did you get the uniform?"

"My buddy Brandon has a connection to one of those army/navy surplus stores, so he hooked us up."

"Us?"

"Jonathan and me."

"Oh, he's going to be there?"

"Yeah, he is."

"I'm so glad I'll get to see him again," I teasingly said.

Cade clenched his jaw. "Don't get your hopes up. He's gonna be there with the chick I was telling you about before."

"Good. I'd like to meet the girl who got him to reform his ways."

Cade held the car door open for me. "I'm surprised you chicks don't have a secret club for taking down manwhores and making them commit."

"Oh my God. You just gave me the perfect idea."

Cade snorted as I slid across the passenger seat. As I worked at fluffing out my poofy skirt, he walked around the front of the car. After getting in, he cranked it up. Instead of his usual Jay-Z or T.I. thumping out from the radio, Aerosmith's *What It Takes* came on. I couldn't help wondering about the reasons behind his change in music and that choice in particular. After all, when the lines *Tell me what it takes to let you go. Tell me how the pain's supposed to go* came on, I couldn't help thinking how much they related to Cade and me.

Tuning out the song, I cleared my throat before turning to look at Cade. "You know it really would have made more sense for me to meet you at your apartment. This is like twenty minutes out of the way."

Cade cut his eyes over to me with a smirk. "And run the risk of you bailing on me? Nope. This is fine."

As I settled back against the seat, I huffed out a frustrated breath. "I resent the idea that I'm not a woman of my word. I told you I would go to the party, so you should have known I would."

"I know you're a woman of your word, Prescott. It wasn't a big deal to come pick you up. Just consider it the gentlemanly thing to do."

"Okay then. I appreciate your chivalry."

"You're welcome."

When we got to Cade's apartment, he had an Uber driving waiting for us. I knew it was so he wouldn't have to worry about driving after he had too much to drink. When I saw that it was just an average Toyota, I couldn't bite my tongue. "What, no chauffeur-driven limo tonight?"

Cade grinned. "Contrary to what you think, I don't ride around in limos, or chauffeured cars."

"How disappointing."

"I'm sorry if I've come down in your esteem."

I smiled. "It's okay. I like you more like this—you know, average."

With a smirk, Cade said, "We both know there isn't anything average about me." His gaze dipped from mine to his crotch and then back to me again. "If anything, I'm way above average."

My face flushed at what he was referring to. I jerked my chin at the driver. "I can't believe you just said that in front of him."

"Like he cares." Lowering his voice, Cade added, "Unless the comment made him feel inferior about his own equipment."

I crossed my arms over my chest in a huff. "Why is it that men always have to turn a perfectly innocent conversation into something sexual?"

"It's just our nature—that along with adjusting ourselves, burping, and farting."

I laughed in spite of myself. "That sums it up perfectly."

The driver pulled up in front of what you would imagine a Southern fraternity house would look like, complete with antebellum columns. I got out and was smoothing out my skirt, trying to quiet my nerves when Cade joined me.

As we walked up the front walk, Cade asked, "Do you ever listen to Runaway Train?"

"Sometimes. I like the band Jake Slater's wife is in better."

"Jacob's Ladder?" Cade suggested.

I snapped my fingers. "Yeah, that one."

"Well, it just so happens that the lead guitarist, Brayden Vanderburg, got his start playing in a band at this frat house."

"You're kidding."

Cade grinned. "Pretty cool, huh?"

"Yeah, it is. Was he in your fraternity back then?"

"No. Brayden went to Georgia State instead of Tech, but Jake Slater and AJ Resendiz lived in an apartment building down the road from mine while they were at Tech."

"I'll have to start listening to their music more."

"They have some great rock songs, but knowing you, it would be the ballads you would go for."

"I love Jake and Abby's duets."

With a groan, Cade said, "Why am I not surprised you go for the mushy stuff?"

"Because you know me too well."

Cade's eyes locked with mine. "Yeah. I guess I do."

I refrained from adding that I would love to listen to some of Runaway Train's love songs with him, that some of the feelings and emotions they sang about rang true with the two of us. I wanted to say that maybe once or twice when I'd heard one of the songs, I'd imagined listening to it with him.

But I didn't.

Since the front door was open, Cade motioned for me to go inside. A thumping bass from the DJ hit me the moment I stepped into the foyer. I'd only been inside one other fraternity house. My ex, Hal, belonged to a much more sedate one that had members who were way more serious and studious than Cade's. I half expected something out of the movie *Animal House*, but surprisingly, the house was in way better shape than that, and things weren't quite so crazy inside.

Of course, we'd barely gotten through the door before someone was shoving a red solo cup in my hand. "Don't drink that," Cade instructed.

"I'm not a total idiot, you know."

Cade laughed. "It's not so much about the fact that it's roofied, but about the fact that the good alcohol is stashed in the back of the pantry that only frat brothers know about."

He took the solo cup from me and set it down on one of the tables then grabbed my hand and started leading me down the packed hallway. My image of Cade being one of the "big men on campus" was confirmed by the way everyone spoke to him. Guys high-fived him and did the bro hug while girls fluttered their eyelashes and pushed up their cleavage. Cade took in all in stride, and thankfully, ignored the female attention. I couldn't help wondering if he was just ignoring them because I was in the room. Would he have done the same thing if he had been alone? Was Tori right that he was really serious enough about me to give up the opportunity for a hookup? Jeez, with all the questions swimming in my head, I definitely needed a drink.

When we got the kitchen, I noticed several beefy jocks standing in front of what must've been the secret pantry Cade had referenced. They fist-bumped Cade before allowing him behind the wooden door. I waited anxiously for him to return.

Finally, he reemerged with two solo cups. "A vodka and cranberry for you," he said as he placed the cup in my hand.

"Is there like a bartender in there?"

Cade laughed. "No. There are some things I can mix on my own."

"I see. I'll remember to tip you later."

He waggled his brows at me. "I'll be happy to be of service to you."

"Oh please," I murmured before taking a large gulp of my drink. Immediately the vodka seared my chest, and I succumbed to a coughing fit. When I finally recovered, I narrowed my eyes at Cade. "Is this basically vodka with a splash of cranberry?"

"Hey, I said I could mix drinks, I just never said whether or not I was any good at it."

"I guess I better remember to sip slow."

"Hey, there's Jonathan," Cade called over the music. He threw his arm over his head and waved. After leaning forward and peering into the crowd, he busted out laughing.

"What's so funny?"

"Apparently you and Presley have the same taste." He pointed to the girl standing next to Jonathan. She was also dressed as Madonna, except she had on a black bustier and black crinoline skirt. As she and Jonathan started over to us, I couldn't help feeling intimidated by her. She was the epitome of a sorority girl: tall and willowy with a fabulous tan and long blonde hair. She was the kind of girl I imagined not only Jonathan liking, but Cade as well. She reminded me a little of Elspeth, which didn't help my unease as I recalled how she'd assaulted me in the bathroom.

"Avery, this is Presley," Cade introduced.

While I expected Presley to turn her nose up at me, a warm smile lit up her face. "Oh my God, I *love* your costume," she said enthusiastically.

I laughed. "I love yours, too."

She grinned. "We have great taste, don't we?"

"We sure do."

"Presley is Evie's mom," Jonathan commented.

That remark made me like Presley even more. "Oh, she's amazing. I got to meet her a few weeks ago."

"Thanks." She turned her beaming gaze to Jonathan. "She loves spending time with her Uncle J."

Jonathan grinned. "I never thought I would admit this, but she has me totally whipped."

"I could see that the other day," I said.

For the next few minutes, Presley and I made small talk over the loud music. I found out she was starting at Kennesaw in the fall and wanted to be a nurse. Although she should have been a sophomore, having Evie had derailed her a year. At nineteen, she was the baby of our group.

The music changed over from a Beastie Boys song to Whitney Houston's *I Wanna Dance with Somebody.* The moment I recognized the song I squealed and jumped up and down on my feet. "Oh my God, I love this song!"

Presley's eyes widened. "Me too. I love just about every Whitney song. I hated when she went off the deep end."

"Crack is whack."

Presley swept one of her hands to her hips and then wagged a finger. "I wanna see the receipts."

While Presley and I laughed hysterically, Cade and Jonathan

exchanged looks. "Do you have any idea what the fuck they're talking about?" Jonathan asked.

"Nope, and I don't think I want to."

"We're talking about that infamous Whitney Houston interview," I explained.

When they both still looked clueless, Presley took me by the arm. "Come on, let's dance."

Although I pretty much never fast-danced in public, I let Presley lead me over to the dance floor. Each time we got to the chorus, we would belt, "Oh I wanna dance with somebody. I wanna feel the heat with somebody," at the top of our lungs. Cade and Jonathan didn't join us. Instead, they just stood off to the side, laughing at our antics.

Once the song ended, we rejoined the guys. "Want something else to drink?" Cade asked.

"No. I think I'm good nursing my vodka."

Jonathan clapped his hands together. "I wanna do some shots." He looked at Presley. "You up for some?"

I could see the internal battle raging within Presley. "No. I better not."

Jonathan's brow creased. "Really? You know you're off mommy duty tonight since Ev is with my mom all night."

"I know. You go ahead. Then I can be the designated driver."

"Okay. If you say so." Jonathan slapped Cade on the back. "What about you?"

"Oh yeah. I'm down for some," Cade replied.

Jonathan grinned at me. "What about you, Avery?"

When I opened my mouth to say no, Cade beat me to it. "Don't bother with Prescott. She isn't much of a drinker."

His comment fueled something within me. "As a matter of fact, I would love to do a shot, Jonathan."

Cade's eyes widened. "You have to be joking."

I jerked my chin up at him. "Make that two shots."

Jonathan laughed. "Two it is." He then started making his way through the packed crowd to the kitchen.

"Do you even like tequila?" Cade questioned.

"It's not my preferred drink, but I don't mind having some every once in a while." The truth was I hated tequila. I'd made the mistake of doing shots with Tori once, and I'd been sick as a dog the next day. Of course, I had done five shots that night. I figured if I stayed at two, I would be fine.

Jonathan returned with a tray full of shots and before I could talk myself out of it, I took one of the glasses and downed it. As soon as I put the empty glass back on the tray, I downed the other. The alcohol burned a fiery trail down my throat to my stomach and caused my eyes to water.

"Damn, girl," Jonathan murmured from behind his shot glass.

Cade also gave me a disbelieving look. "Who knew you had it in you, Prescott?" he mused before smiling at me.

With the two shots of liquid courage pulsing through my veins,

I was ready to dance again. A stone-cold sober Presley and a slightly tipsy me burned up the dance floor through several fast songs. I would have kept going, but Cade pulled me to the side to get me to drink some water. While I cooled off, the four of us chatted as best we could about college, Evie, and football over the loud music.

Cyndi Lauper's *Time After Time* came on, and Presley sighed and swept a hand to her heart. "Oh man, I love this song."

I nodded. "Me too. I love everything Cyndi Lauper. I must've been born in the wrong era. I love all '80s music and movies."

When Presley started swaying back and forth to the beat, Jonathan cleared his throat. "Wanna dance?"

A shy smile swept across her face. Instead of replying, she nodded her head. Jonathan held out his hand and she slipped hers in it. He then led her onto the floor. They stood there for a few seconds, just staring uncertainly at each other before he finally pulled her into his arms.

Cade and I stood watching them dance. More than anything, I wanted to be out there with Cade, but I didn't have the balls to ask him. I was just about to ask him to get me some water when Cade did something that shocked the hell out of me. "Come on, Prescott," he said as he took my hand. I didn't argue with him. Instead, I followed him onto the dance floor.

Our bodies melted effortlessly against each other. It didn't feel like any time had passed between us. We were right back in that moment at Rose's Garden when he taught me how to waltz.

After dancing silently for a little while, I knew I had to get my mind off the emotions swirling within me. Pulling back from Cade, I jutted my chin in the direction of Presley and Jonathan. "So what's the deal with them?"

Cade winced. "They're complicated."

I laughed. "Aren't we all? I mean, people in general."

"That's true, but let's just say they're extra complicated."

"Because of Jonathan's brother?"

With a nod, Cade said, "Jonathan won't make a move because he's not only afraid he'd be pissing on Jake's memory, but that it would make things weird in the family if things didn't work out between them."

"Hmm, that's a tough one."

"Since Jonathan's really never done relationships, he's worried about trying one with Presley and failing."

"What about Presley? It's clear she has feelings for Jonathan, too."

"Presley's deal is she's sworn off men. She was a mega slut in high school—"

"Don't call her a slut!"

"She's the one who told me that."

"Oops, okay, I'm sorry. Keep going."

"Anyway after Jake died, Presley decided to swear off men. Since Evie was born, she's really changed her ways. She doesn't party any more—tonight is probably the first time in a year. She's also not hooking up with random guys. She moved in with the Nelsons so they could help out with Evie while she goes to school."

"What about her parents?"

"She never knew her dad, and let's just say her mom was an enabler of the life Presley wanted to give up. Moving in with the Nelsons helped not only her, but them too. I don't think Jake's mom could have survived losing him if it hadn't been for Evie."

"Poor woman, losing a son so tragically like that."

"Jonathan lucked out. Evelyn is the type of mom I wish I could have had."

"Why is that?"

"She was the stay-at-home PTA mom who was around to make you something homemade for your afternoon snack and helps you build the volcano for your science project." Cade shook his head with a smile. "The woman knits for Christ's sake; you can't get more motherly than that."

"It sounds like Presley is very lucky to have her as a mother figure."

"She is. I think that's why, like Jonathan, she worries that if things didn't work out between them, she might lose Evelyn."

"What about Jonathan's dad?"

Cade rolled his eyes. "He and my dad should belong to the Asshole Fathers' Club."

"Wow, he's that bad, huh?"

"He's a pretty big douchebag, but even though he was a hard-ass on his sons, he's like a marshmallow with Evie. She brings out what little good there is in him."

"The more I hear about asshole dads, the more thankful I am I haven't had one in my life."

"You ever think about tracking yours down?"

I shifted uncomfortably on my feet. No one had ever really asked me that.

"Sometimes. I mean, I know his name, and that he still lives in Georgia."

"You should look him up. He sure as hell owes you and your mom some fat cash after all these years."

Shaking my head angrily, I countered, "It's not about his money."

Cade held up his hands. "I'm sorry, and I know it's not. It was just an observation."

"Like my mom, I'm too proud to take his money. I just want to know him."

"He should want to know you. Having a daughter like you is something to be proud of."

My heartbeat thrummed wildly at Cade's compliments. He had no idea that I had often fantasized about meeting my father. I dreamed that after he learned of my accomplishments, he would hug me tight and whisper, "I'm proud of you," into my ear.

"Really?" I choked out.

Cade nodded. "I mean it. Although none of the credit goes to him, he should be impressed with how you've turned out, not to mention that you're beautiful both inside and out."

The song changed over to Aerosmith and Run DMC's *Walk This Way*, but Cade and I remained intertwined in each other's arms. The world around us melted away, and we only had eyes for each other. My heart started thumping erratically in my chest; it seemed I had been waiting for this moment for so long.

When Cade dipped his head, I closed my eyes in anticipation of his kiss. Just before his lips met mine, my phone started going off in my cleavage. I gave Cade an apologetic look. "I seriously wouldn't take this, but that's Tamar's ringtone. I know she wouldn't be calling unless it was an emergency."

"It's okay," Cade replied.

After retrieving the phone from underneath my boob, I answered it breathlessly. "Hey Tamar, what's up?" My heart plummeted to my feet at the sound of her weeping. "Tamar? What's happened?"

"Darion's been shot."

"What? How?"

"It happened about thirty minutes ago. The paramedics called me on the way to Grady. The only number he had on him was The Ark's. We can't find his mother at the shelter or anywhere else. I'm forty-five minutes away if the traffic is decent, and it's a Friday night."

"It's okay. Cade and I are only ten minutes from there. We'll leave now." I was just about to hang up on her to fill Cade in when Tamar said, "Avery?"

"Yeah. I'm still here."

"I just wanted you to know that it doesn't sound good."

I gripped the phone tighter, desperate for her to quell my growing fears. "Like he might be paralyzed or something?"

Tamar's reply came in between her sobs. "They don't think he will make it."

My eyes pinched shut in agony as the realization washed over me. Darion had been shot. Darion was going to die. Darion was fifteen years old.

"Avery? What happened?" Cade asked at my side.

When I flipped my eyelids open, I stared into Cade's questioning face. My stomach lurched, and I fought to not throw up the tequila shots I'd had. I knew what I had to say was going to devastate him. Willing myself not to break down into hysterics, I said, "Darion has been shot."

TWENTY

CADE

There are moments in life that seem to defy all logic, where your world shifts on its axis so fast and so hard that you feel the world shudder around you, and you fight to keep your footing on the shaking ground. One moment I was so close to heaven, holding Avery in my arms, then the next, I plummeted down to the depths of hell.

Darion had been shot. Darion had been shot. *Darion has been shot.* Those words echoed over and over in my mind, yet I still couldn't seem to process it all. I shook my head a few times, trying to shake out of my disbelief, but the news still hadn't changed.

Avery still stood before me with blackened tears streaking

down her cheeks and her body trembling. I felt a hand on my shoulder and whirled around to see Jonathan and Presley. Both of their expressions were full of worry. "What's going on?" Jonathan asked.

"It's Darion."

"The kid you brought to the scrimmage?" Jonathan asked.

I nodded. "He's been shot."

"Jesus," Jonathan murmured.

Saying it out loud seemed to make it all the more real, and all the more devastating. "I have to get there…I have to see him." I started pushing my way out of the crowd toward the front door. By the time I reached the front porch, my chest felt like it was going to explode from the emotional overload.

Just before I could break into a sprint to the parking lot, I remembered I hadn't driven. "Fuck," I muttered.

"I'm calling another Uber," Avery said through her sniffles.

I jerked my hand through my hair in desperation. "It'll take too long. He could be…" I swallowed hard.

Presley dug her keys out of her top. "I'll drive you guys."

We started hauling ass across the lawn to the parking lot. "Which one is yours?" I called over my shoulder to Presley. The girls were having a hard time keeping up with us in their heels.

"The black Honda Pilot. Fourth row."

I nodded as I pushed myself a little harder. The SUV's lights blinked as Presley unlocked the car. When I reached for one of the back doors, Jonathan pushed me to the front passenger side seat. Presley started the engine as I closed the door. Once we were all inside, Presley threw the SUV into reverse and then gunned it out of the parking lot.

The car remained deathly silent as Presley drove like a madman through the streets of Atlanta. Although I wasn't overly religious or someone who prayed, I bowed my head and started asking for all the favors from God I could muster to save Darion.

We screeched into the ER parking lot at Grady Hospital on two wheels and I didn't even bother waiting on Presley to park. Instead, I bolted from the car before it fully came to a stop. I sprinted up the walkway and blew through the mechanized doors. In my Navy uniform, I got quite a few strange looks on my way to the front desk.

"Can I help you?" the receptionist asked.

"Yeah, I need to know which room Darion Richards is in."

After glancing at the screen in front of her, the receptionist narrowed her eyes at me. "Are you family?" she questioned skeptically.

"No, I'm not."

She shook her head. "I'm sorry, but only family are permitted in a trauma situation."

I smacked my palms down on the counter in front of me. "But you don't understand. He barely has any family. His dad is a junkie who disappears for weeks at a time, and the homeless shelter where he lives can't track down his mother."

"I'm sorry, but it's hospital policy."

My fists tightened with the rage that overtook my body. "Well, fuck your policy! If you think I'm going to just stand here and let a fifteen-year-old kid die by himself, you're fucking crazy," I bellowed.

The waiting room went deathly quiet as the receptionist reached for her phone. "Yes, we have a situation here."

At the feel of a hand on my shoulder, I whirled around and prepared myself to go ape-shit on security. To my surprise, it was Avery.

"They won't let you back?"

I clenched my jaw, fighting the tears of both frustration and pain that threatened to burst from me. "No."

Avery glanced past me and then nibbled on her lip. "Whatever happens, just get back there to Darion. Okay?"

Before I could question what she meant, Avery stepped away from me. She let out an ear-piercing shriek of pain before collapsing. At the same moment she hit the floor, Jonathan and Presley breezed through the mechanized doors. They met my frantic gaze for a brief moment before stepping into action.

"Help!" Presley cried a little overdramatically. Her heels skittered across the waiting room floor to Avery's crumpled body. "My friend is dying! Isn't someone going to help her?"

At Avery's continued screams of faked pain, members of the

ER staff came running from all directions. The chaos gave me the chance to slip back behind the mechanized doors without being noticed. *Damn, the girl is brilliant. This was more her kid, but she made sure I got back to him.* Once I was in the ER, I started reading the whiteboards outside the rooms to try to find him. Since Darion was critical, I didn't know where they might have him.

After a few minutes of no luck, I resorted to stopping the first white coat I saw. "Can you tell me where I can find Darion Richards?"

"Are you family?"

Jesus, these people never let up on the family bullshit. "Yeah, he's my stepbrother," I lied.

The doctor appeared momentarily skeptical, but then her expression became grave. "Your stepbrother was shot twice, once in the middle chest and the second in the upper abdomen. One of the bullets hit his inferior vena cava. While we tried to repair it, it had sustained too much damage…"

I tuned the doctor out. With all my premed classes, I knew there was nothing that could be done for Darion. He would just slowly fade away. It wasn't a horrible death when it came to levels of pain, but he was still going to die. "I want—I need to be with him."

"Of course. Follow me."

The doctor led me on down the hall to another area of the ER. It was part of the specialized trauma unit Grady was famous for.

When we got to the door of the bay, the doctor turned back to me. "We've made him as comfortable as we can. It's just a matter of time now."

"Thank you—you know, for everything."

She laid a hand on my shoulder. "My sincerest condolences." She then hurried off to the next emergency.

A nurse was eyeing the machine's in the bay when I stepped inside. Darion lay on a gurney with his eyes closed. His clothes had been cut away to access his wounds and they lay in blood-soaked shreds around his body. Lying there, he looked so small to me, like a child…nothing like the larger-than-life teenager he had been the day before when he was giving me shit while we played basketball.

As I made my way over to his gurney, it felt like I was trudging through quicksand. I had to work hard to put one foot in front of the other. The nurse nodded at me before stepping outside the door.

When I finally reached Darion's side, I took his bloodstained hand in mine. "Hey bro, it's Cade."

Darion's eyelids fluttered open. At the sight of me, a smile curved on his pale lips. "Hey, man." His voice was so quiet…so quiet. When he widened his eyes to take in more of my appearance, a bark of a laugh came out of him. "Hell you wearin'?" he coughed out.

I grinned. "It's '80s night at my fraternity, and I'm Maverick from *Top Gun*."

With a dizzy shake of his head, Darion mumbled, "Old movie?" Of course he wouldn't know what *Top Gun* was. It was made fifteen years before he was born. *When the hell did I see that movie?*

"Yeah, man. Even before my time."

Darion's eyes made a sweep of the room before they came back to mine. "Cade, I'm…done."

"Fuck that. You're gonna be fine."

"Always sucked at lyin'."

Tears stung my eyes, and I hated myself for them. These were Darion's last moments, and I didn't need to be acting like a fucking pansy during them. "Jesus Christ, I'm sorry," I whispered.

"Ain't ya fault. Shouldn't gone, block party."

I shook my head. "You couldn't have known anything bad was going to happen.

With a weak smile, Darion said, "Didn't like the scene. I's about to leave." He paused and his eyes became even more glassy. He grimaced and I wanted to do something that would take this fucked-up situation away. "Heard screechin' tires. *Pop. Pop. Pop.* I was on…the ground."

A grave expression came over Darion's face. "Tell Mama I love her."

My chest felt like someone had hit it with a sledgehammer. "Yeah, man. I will."

"And Miss P."

"Yeah, of course." *Yeah, of course?* I had to say goodbye from this kid to someone amazing who had been in his corner? Someone who had invested time and love into this kid? God, it was so fucked up.

"Don't let Marcus and Antoine…fight over my stuff. Ain't got much. Don't want them getting mad over it."

"I promise." Jesus, even when he was dying, he was thinking of others.

As if something truly important had woken him out of a stupor, he turned his dark but lucid eyes on me and said with more strength than just moments before, "Don't look so sad, bro." Darion gave a slight shake of his head. "Ain't afraid of dyin'. Gonna go play football with all the greats in heaven."

I choked on my rising sobs. "You're gonna give them one hell of a run for their money."

"Damn straight." He took a ragged breath. "Thanks…being there…for me."

"I should be the one saying that to you," I protested. He closed his eyes, but I wasn't ready, wasn't ready to say goodbye. Deep down, I knew I would never be ready to say goodbye.

"Had each other's back, right?" he asked me suddenly, his voice dull.

"Hell yeah."

"All good."

"It was good that I met you, D. I know it might sound like a bunch of bullshit, but you taught me a lot, man, like how to be a better person with a good heart."

Darion looked at me skeptically, but didn't utter a sound.

"You sure as hell did teach me that. I owe you so much."

"That's…tight," were his whispered words.

"It is."

He squeezed my hand. "Love."

The finality of his words hit me. Since I couldn't speak, I merely bobbed my head as I knew he was coming to the end. I'd never been with someone when they died. I'd wanted more than anything to be with my grandfather, but my parents wouldn't let me. Instead, I'd had to sit in the waiting room. I didn't know what to expect. Would it be like in the movies where the body shook a few times, or would Darion gasp for breath as he clutched the chest where his heart was ceasing to beat?

Instead, it was one of the most peaceful things I had ever seen. After turning his head away from me on the pillow, Darion tilted his gaze to look up to the ceiling. The corners of his lips quirked up in a smile, and then he was gone.

The long *beep* was a sound I never wanted to hear, but it stormed in and eradicated the momentary peace.

Darion was gone.

There weren't words to describe what that moment felt like. It was like five different emotions crashing together in a head-on collision that rocked me both body and soul. "No! Please no!" I cried. Even though I had known it was going to happen, I wasn't prepared for the actual moment. The agonizing pain in my chest grew even more intense, and I had to fight hard to breathe.

Pulling Darion into my arms, I began to cry so hard it shook the both of us. I threw my head back and wailed. "Oh God, no, no, no!"

The noise drew some nurses to the doorway. When they tried to pull me away from Darion, I fought against them. "Sir, please. He's gone. There's nothing more you can do," a nurse said.

"Turn off the fucking noise. *Turn it off.*"

When she hit the button on the machine, the silence was almost louder than the incessant beeping.

Although I knew she was right, that there was nothing more I could do, I still just wanted to hold on to him. It felt like as long as I could touch him, he wasn't really gone.

Then it was like I could hear Darion's voice in my ear. *Dude, enough with the waterworks. Pull it together. Man up and let me go. I promise it's okay.*

So I did what he asked.

I let go.

Twenty One

AVERY

Once I saw Cade enter safely through the ER's doors, I stopped my crazy screams. I calmly rolled into a fetal position and remained on the floor. Inwardly, I fought the extreme mortification of what I had done, but I had to get Cade back to Darion. If one of us could be back there, it needed to be Cade.

"Miss?" one of the nurses questioned.

"The pain…it's better."

"You still need to be seen by a physician. Let us help you up and then we'll get your medical information."

"No, really, I'm fine."

"But you—"

Presley held up one of her hands. “Look, lady, she said she was fine.” She then swirled one of her fingers around her temple like I was crazy. In a low voice, she said, “When she has one of her episodes, we just try to humor her. I’m sorry we bothered you. We’ll leave now.”

“Perhaps she needs to be checked into the psychological facility for evaluation?” another nurse suggested.

I threw a panicked glance up at Presley and Jonathan. “She’s good. We’ll get her home and get some medicine in her,” Jonathan said before he lifted me up off the ground and started hustling me outside.

“Sir, wait!” the nurse called, but Jonathan ignored her. He practically broke into a sprint getting us out the door. When we were around the side of the building, Jonathan sat me down. “Jesus, that was a close one,” he said with a grin.

I fluffed my skirt down. “Tell me about it. You weren’t the one about to be committed.”

“In these costumes, we probably all looked like we had escaped the loony bin,” Presley joked. I welcomed the laugh that came bubbling out of my mouth; it had been such a tense last half hour.

“What do we do now?” Jonathan asked.

“I guess we just wait around here for Cade to come out. If we stay here on the corner, we have a good view of the emergency room exit,” Presley suggested.

"That sounds good."

Wringing my hands, I said, "Dammit, I hate that he's back there all alone with Darion."

Jonathan nodded. "Me too." He swept one of his hands over his face. "I was all alone when I got the call about Jake. I was in the middle of a bio lab, so when my older brother Jason texted me a 911, I got up and went outside to take the call."

Shaking his head, he said, "As long as I live, I'll never forget standing outside that lecture hall as Jason told me Jake was dead. I broke down right then and there. I guess I was crying so loud the professor came out in the hallway. He was really nice when I told him what had happened. He got someone to go get my stuff, and then he let one of my buddies leave to help me over to my dorm room. Cade didn't have a morning class that day, so he was at our dorm. Since I was such a fucking mess, he drove me home."

Tears shined in both Presley's and my eyes at his story. Presley closed the gap between her and Jonathan and wrapped her arms around him. They both wept for Jake, and I couldn't help crying along with them, except my tears were for Darion, and for Cade.

After they recovered, Jonathan said, "I'll go get the car. That way we can be ready to leave when Cade…when Cade comes out."

"Okay." *When Cade comes out.* When Cade came out, that would mean Darion was gone. Oh God, how was it possible this was happening? Darion was too young. He had his whole life in front of him. Fresh tears sprung to my eyes.

Although I would have understood if she had gone with Jonathan, Presley stayed by my side. She held my hands in hers as we waited. We were both teary, which was understandable. When Jonathan came back with the car, Presley got into the front seat, and I got in the back. We drove around to the front of the ER and parked a few feet away from the entrance.

The waiting was agony and broken up only by fielding texts from Tamar, who was still in traffic, as well as other members of The Ark's staff. The news about Darion had spread like wildfire. I had just finished texting with Kevin when Jonathan said, "Jesus."

I glanced up to see Cade stumbling out of the ER. His white uniform was covered in blood. I fumbled with the handle on the door before hurrying out of the SUV to meet him. "Cade!" I called.

His head jerked up as he turned in my direction. The agony of Darion's loss was etched across his face. I immediately began to cry as I walked up to Cade. "He's gone, Avery," Cade whispered dejectedly.

I threw my arms around his neck. "I'm so sorry." Even though Darion's loss was also my own, I felt it more for Cade. I had known Darion longer, but I had never experienced the bond he and Cade had. What the two of them had might've been for just a short time, but it ran deeper than anything I had seen for some time.

While my body shook with sobs, Cade remained frozen. He didn't wrap his arms around me to comfort me. When I pulled away, he appeared stone-faced, just staring ahead. From the disaster training I'd had to go through to work at The Ark, I knew Cade was going into shock. "Come on, let's get you home," I said.

After I led him over to the SUV, I opened the backseat door for him. He slid inside without a word to me or the others. I went around the other side; although I would have liked to sit closer to him, Evie's car seat served as a buffer between us.

We made a silent drive back to Cade and Jonathan's apartment. Without a word to any of us, Cade got out of the car and climbed the stairs. Unsure of what to do or say, Jonathan, Presley, and I trailed behind him. When he got to the front door, he unlocked it and went into the apartment. I hurried ahead of the others to be at Cade's side. As Cade started for his bedroom, I glanced back at Jonathan and Presley.

Jonathan nodded. "We'll be here if he needs us—if you need us."

"Thanks."

As Cade trudged across his bedroom floor, I hung back in the doorway, uncertain of what I should do. His steps didn't seem to have any purpose, but then he ended up in front of a tall bookshelf. It overflowed with more with trophies and plaques than it did with actual books. It appeared to be a shrine to the accomplishments of his football career. Back home in my old bedroom, I had something similar, but my awards were all for academics.

Cade placed his palms on the sides of one of the shelves. His head drooped down and his shoulders bowed as if under the pressure of his grief. Then came a dizzying flurry of flailing arms and crashing objects as Cade swept all the trophies and plaques to the floor. As soon as one shelf was empty, he swept the next clean. He didn't stop until everything lay in a heap in the floor.

"A waste. It's all a fucking waste. All these trophies I coveted…a fucking waste. What does any of it matter in the end?"

He dropped to his knees and began to weep. Gut-wrenching sobs tore through his body, causing him to shake violently. "Why?" he shouted in agony.

I was so rocked to my core by the events of the evening that for a while I could only stare in disbelief, but then I began to weep as well. I didn't just cry for the pain Cade was experiencing; I cried for my own pain from Darion's loss. I fought my own guilt that I hadn't spent as much time with Darion as I had some of the other kids. I wished I'd taken the time to hang out around the gym more. I would have a lot of regret where Darion was concerned.

Rushing across the room, I dropped down beside Cade and pulled him into my arms. "Shh, I'm here. It's okay."

Cade jerked back to glare at me. "It's not fucking okay. Darion's dead."

"I'm sorry. I'm sorry for everything. I'm sorry Darion is dead. I'm sorry I don't know the right things to say, but more than anything, I'm sorry you're hurting so badly and I can't do anything to make it better. You have to remember I'm hurting, too. I'm going to miss Darion too; I cared for him just like you did."

"I know you cared for him. He knew you cared for him. He told me to tell you goodbye."

Tears once again stung my eyes. "He was so very sweet."

"He was. He sure as hell didn't deserve to be killed," Cade lamented.

"No. He didn't."

He swept his nose with the back of his hand. "It shoulda been me."

"No, Cade. Don't you ever think that."

He gave a shake of his head. "He had a light about him, a goodness I don't have, will never have. The world needed someone like him; I'm a fucking waste, just like my father said."

"That isn't true."

"Yeah, it is."

I cupped Cade's chin in my fingers, forcing him to look at me. "There is so much good inside you. The change that has come over you since you started at The Ark is amazing. I've seen it, and Tamar has seen it. You can be like Darion and carry on his light. I know you can."

Cade stared disbelievingly at me. "You really believe that?"

"I do, more than anything."

"But I hurt you—"

"That was in the past, and you apologized for it. You're a different, better person now."

"I don't think I can ever be better. Just a waste," he murmured.

It was then I realized he was in a place of such extreme shock that my words of comfort and reassurance couldn't reach him. It was something I had experienced when I lost my grandfather. When my mother came to tell me my grandfather had died, I had gone to a dark place I never knew existed before, a place where all light was snuffed out and there was *no* hope, only desperation.

I surveyed the blood staining Cade's arms and hands. "Come on, you need to get cleaned up." Cade didn't respond. "Let's get you showered and changed."

Rising up off the floor, I held my hand out for Cade to take. When he continued staring into space, I gripped both his arms and tugged, hard. "Oomph," I muttered as I tried dragging him to his feet.

After sliding one arm around Cade's waist, we started lurching toward the bathroom. With my free hand, I flipped the light switch. As best I could, I steered him over to the toilet. I put the lid down before easing him onto the seat.

I opened the shower door and turned on the water. Sticking my hand into the stream, I tested the temperature. "Okay. It's ready." When I threw a glance over my shoulder, I found Cade with his head in his hands. "Cade, do you want me to get Jonathan to help you get undressed?"

"No," he murmured.

"You're going to do it yourself?" I questioned skeptically.

"No."

"Then how are you going to get undressed?"

Cade slid his hands away from his face. "Will you help me?"

My stomach dropped to my feet. Oh God. Of all the things he could have asked me. I had said I would do anything for him, but I didn't know if I could do this. "Um, okay."

He stood up and faced me. With trembling fingers, I started working on the bloodstained buttons on his uniform top. When I had them undone, I slid it off his shoulders. I gripped the fabric of the white undershirt he had on and pulled it out of the waistband of his pants then pushed it up his abdomen and over his chest. When it got to his neck, he raised his arms. Pressing myself against the warmth of his skin, I eased it up over his face. I had to stand on tiptoes to get it up the length of his arms.

After I dropped it on the floor beside the uniform top, I reached for the buckle on his belt, then froze. I was no longer in the bathroom with Cade. Instead, I was lying on a velvet settee as Cade worked his belt off. I slammed my eyes shut to shove the memory from my mind. I couldn't believe with everything going on, I could possibly think about us having sex.

"It's okay," Cade said.

I yanked my gaze from his pants to him. "What?"

"What you're thinking about…it's okay."

Warmth flooded my cheeks, and it wasn't from the steamy shower. Cade's fingers came to grasp my chin. "It's okay, Prescott."

"No. It isn't. This is a time for mourning, not—"

"I was thinking about it too," Cade whispered.

My brows shot up in surprise. "You were?"

He nodded. "I think about that night a lot."

"Me too," I answered honestly.

He jerked his head at the door. "I've got it from here."

"Are you sure?"

"Yeah."

"Okay. I'll wait for you outside."

"Thanks."

When I turned to go, Cade grabbed my arm. I whirled back around to face him. The look on his face caused my heart to flutter rapidly and as he dipped his head, I sucked in a breath. He placed a tender kiss on my cheek that was filled with all the emotions he couldn't seem to say.

Once he released me, I went back into the bedroom. Presley stood in the doorway, eyeing the wreckage. She had changed into a pair of leggings and a t-shirt and her gaze snapped from the mess on the floor to me. "Is he okay?" she asked.

"I guess as okay as he can be."

She held some clothes to me. "I thought you could use these. I always keep a spare pair in the car in case Evie spits up or poops on me."

I glanced down at the t-shirt and shorts. "I hate to take your clothes."

"It's okay. I don't mind."

"Thanks. I really appreciate it."

Presley closed the door behind her and I got undressed. As I looked at the costume, it was hard to believe the course the night had taken. What had started off so light and fun had turned so dark and painful. I knew I would never be able to hear another Madonna song without thinking of Darion.

While Cade showered, I worked at putting his shelves back together. Some of the frames had cracked and would have to be replaced, but I set them back up. I had just finished when I heard the shower shut off. After waiting for what felt like an eternity, Cade still hadn't appeared.

My knuckles rapped against the wood. "Cade?" When he didn't respond, I said, "Cade, are you all right?"

The doorknob was unlocked when I tested it. I braced myself and threw it open. Cade stood in front of the mirror with a towel wrapped around his waist. Both his palms were flattened on the countertop while his head was tucked against his chest.

I cautiously stepped into the room. "Cade?" I questioned again.

He jerked his gaze up to meet mine in the mirror then shook his head forlornly. "Christ, Avery, I feel so dead," he murmured.

"I'm know…I'm sorry." I placed a hand on his back. "I know it sounds trite and cliché, but Darion wouldn't want you feeling like this."

"I know. He told me."

I gasped. "He did?"

"He was still lucid when I was back there."

Swallowing hard, I asked, "He wasn't in any pain, was he?"

"No. He was really peaceful." A bark of a laugh came from Cade. "He even said he was going to heaven to play football."

"Sounds just like Darion."

With a shake of his head, Cade said, "I can't believe he's gone."

"Me either," I whispered.

"I don't know what to do. I just don't want to feel dead any more, Avery."

In that moment, I stood at a crossroads. I could have told him to take his time grieving alone, that I would just wait for him in the bedroom, but I didn't want to leave him. I wanted to somehow ease his pain and in the same token, my own. To do that, I would have to step over the line I had so carefully drawn between us. I would have to let him feel something—something physical.

I dipped underneath his arm to wedge my body between him and the vanity. The warmth of his body singed my skin beneath the flimsy material of my t-shirt and shorts. As I met Cade's questioning gaze, I slid my hands up his chest to encircle his neck. I pulled his head down to where our mouths were just inches apart. "I want to make you feel alive again."

The grief in Cade's eyes faded and a burning lust replaced it.

His reaction was all I needed. My hands fell from his neck and came to rest at his waist. I jerked the towel away and then tossed it to the floor.

I pressed my lips to the center of his chest before kissing my way down his abdomen. Once I had dropped to my knees, I took his growing erection in my hand. I slowly worked my hand up and down his shaft.

Licking my lips, I then slid the head into my mouth. Cade groaned and threw his head back. "Jesus, Avery," he muttered.

I'd never had the chance to do this for him the first night we were together. Now I planned on making up for that. I swirled my tongue around the tip before sucking it hard, giving special attention to the pulsing vein underneath. I took him into my throat as deep as I could while my hand worked up and down on his length. His groans of pleasure fueled me on. I wanted him to truly feel every lick and every stroke. One of Cade's hands came to fist the strands of my hair while the other went to grip the edge of the vanity. His hips began to slowly rock back and forth.

With my free hand, I reached underneath to cup his balls. I massaged them gently at first before adding more pressure. "Fuck, Avery," Cade moaned.

After a few minutes, I started to feel him tensing, and he abruptly pulled away. He gazed down at me over his heaving chest.

"You could have finished."

He gave a firm shake of his head. "I want to finish inside you."

Reaching underneath my arms, Cade pulled me up off the floor. He then whisked my t-shirt over my head and his hands came to my knead my breasts before his mouth settled on one of them. He licked and sucked my nipple into a hardened point before trailing warm kisses over to the other. While driving me wild with his attention to my breasts, he pumped the hard ridge of his erection against my core. It was all too much. "Please, Cade."

"Anything, baby."

"I need to feel you inside me."

"And I need to be inside you. I need it more than anything in this world," Cade murmured against my nipple. His hands left my breasts and came to the button on my shorts. He practically tore them off, and my panties went next.

When his cock rubbed against my exposed clit, I gripped his shoulders so hard my fingers left marks on his skin. He fumbled in one of the drawers and somehow produced a condom. After he slid it on, his hands came to my waist. He lifted me up and sat me on the edge of the sink. As he moved between my thighs, I widened my legs for him.

With one harsh thrust, he was inside me. "Oh, fuck," Cade groaned while I gasped at the intense feeling of both pleasure and pain. As he began pounding into me, I wrapped my legs around his waist. "I need you…so…much," Cade murmured against my neck.

"I need you, too. God, have I needed you," I replied as I tightened my arms around his shoulders.

Once again, it felt as if time and distance hadn't even occurred between us. Everything was just like it had been before: the feel of his skin against mine, his hands on my body, the feel of him deep inside me.

Well, it was almost all the same. He had made love to me our first time together. This wasn't the slow thrusts of making love. This was the hard pounding of fucking. It was raw and desperate. It was a frantic coupling.

And I loved every minute of it.

Cade might've needed to feel alive again, but I needed it just as much as he did. I'd never had this with any other guy—this connection, this level of lust and need. In the end, I didn't care if we only had this moment. I would enjoy what we had and worry about the rest later.

Cade abruptly slid out of me. Pulling me down from the vanity, he spun me around. As Cade pushed my legs apart with his knees, I placed my hands on the granite counter in front of me. One of his hands came to my waist while the other guided his cock into me. I cried out with pleasure when he slammed back into me. With both his hands now on my hips, Cade pulled me back against his harsh thrusts. Sensing I needed more, he slid his hand around my hip to come between my legs. As his fingers rubbed against my clit, my cries of pleasure grew so loud I was afraid Jonathan and Presley would hear.

When I came, it was harder and more intense than I had ever

experienced with a guy. Cade followed close after me then his head collapsed forward against my back. "Oh Avery," he grunted as he continued to pump into me.

Once he was finished, Cade began pressing kisses onto my sweat-slicked flesh. He kissed a trail from one shoulder blade to the other. After he slid out of me, he continued to kiss my skin as he turned me around. He then kissed his way up my neck and to my lips.

Cade's eyes met mine and he smiled. My heart, which I tried to keep in check, instantly melted. In that moment, words seemed inadequate. Instead, Cade cupped my face in his hands before bringing his lips to mine. This kiss lacked the desperation of before. It was sweet and tender, the kind of kiss a lovesick girl would dream of.

When Cade pulled away, he stared intently into my eyes. "Will you stay the night with me?"

I didn't even hesitate before replying, "Yes."

While Cade went about disposing of the condom, I did a little cleaning up myself. Although it could have felt awkward being so intimate around him, it didn't. The familiarity between us seemed to erase all of that.

Once we were finished cleaning up and redressing, Cade took my hand in his and led me out of the bathroom. When we got into the bedroom, he went over to the bed and pulled back the covers before motioning for me to climb inside. Where I had a double bed back at my apartment, Cade had a lush king. I practically melted into the mattress, not having realized how tired I was until I actually laid down.

Cade climbed in behind me and I scooted closer to him so our bodies were touching. He raised one of his arms so I could prop my head on his chest; listening to his heart beating beneath me made me felt safe and secure, and very alive.

"Darion's mom probably doesn't have any money for a funeral."

His comment had taken me by surprise. "I'm sure she doesn't."

"What will happen to Darion?"

"From what I understand, people who die at the shelter are often buried in one of the indigent cemeteries outside the city."

Cade's body tensed. "You mean they'll just throw him in a pine box with nothing but a number on his grave?"

The thought of that happening to Darion caused stinging tears to pool in my eyes. "I guess so."

"Fuck that. It's not going to go down like that."

I rose up to look at him. "What do you mean?"

A determined expression had come over Darion's face. "I'll pay for his funeral."

My mouth gaped open in surprise. "Seriously?"

"Hell yes. I'll make sure he goes out with dignity."

I swiped the tears from my eyes. "Oh, Cade. That's so sweet of you."

"I just wish I could have done more for him while he was alive, maybe get him and his mom out of that shelter. Maybe then he wouldn't have been hanging around with some of the people he was."

My hand rubbed over his heart. "You couldn't save him from the world, no matter how hard you tried."

"I know. It's just wishful thinking." A curious look came over Cade's face. "Maybe I can't save Darion, but what if I could save other kids like him?"

"What do you mean?"

"What if I started a foundation to help at-risk youth?"

"Something like The Ark?"

Cade nodded. "Maybe I could team up with Amad Carlson and make more Arks."

"That would be amazing." I smiled at him. "Anything you do will be amazing, I know it."

He leaned up to kiss me. "Thank you for staying with me, Avery. I needed you now more than you'll ever know."

"You're welcome." I then motioned to the TV. "Think we could find a John Hughes classic on Netflix?"

"It wouldn't hurt to try."

TWENTY TWO

CADE

When I woke up Tuesday morning, my stomach felt as though it was clenched into a barbwire ball of grief and anxiety. It was the day of Darion's funeral. His mother, Denise, had been so overcome with grief that she had handed over all the arrangements to me. It was both an honor and a burden. His funeral was the last thing I could do for Darion, and I didn't want to fail him.

With Avery's help, I'd organized a wake at one of the downtown funeral homes close to the shelter where Darion had lived. We had held the visitation the night before, and my heart had overflowed at the number of people who came out. The line to see Darion went out the main room and overflowed into the hallway.

Not only did the support and love of Darion's friends touch me, I was amazed at my own friends really stepped up to support me. Jonathan and Brandon stayed at the funeral home with me from the time the visitation started until it ended. I couldn't fathom how Jonathan did that given it hadn't even been two years since he'd buried his brother. Presley helped Avery with some of the more girly funeral details like making sure the room was filled with beautiful fresh flowers as well as catering in food. I couldn't believe it when I walked into the funeral home's kitchen to see a whole sit-down dinner for the mourners, most of whom hadn't had a decent meal in a long time.

In the last three days, I'd come to realize I couldn't have survived without Avery. She wasn't just there to make phone calls or bounce ideas off of; she was there for me emotionally. After staying with me Friday night, she hadn't been back to her apartment except to grab some clothes and toiletries. She was a truly calming presence, and she never left my side. I came to realize then why it was so important to have someone not just in the good times, but in the bad. I guessed that's what real love really is.

Even though I had felt such love for her, I still hadn't managed to say those three little words to her. I wanted to, and I didn't know why they wouldn't come out. I had no problem saying, "Man, I love this sandwich," or "Damn, I love this song." Why was it I couldn't say the words to the girl who meant everything to me?

"Hey," Avery whispered.

I glanced over at her. "Hey."

She gave me a sad smile as she snuggled her body closer to mine and brought her hand to my chest. "How are you feeling?"

"Like hell," I answered honestly.

"Are you nervous about the eulogy?"

I nodded. "I should've had someone like you write it—someone who knows how to express their emotions. You could make a hell of an argument for how amazing Darion was."

"But then it wouldn't mean as much because it wouldn't be from here." She rubbed the skin over my heart. "Whatever you say will be beautiful because it'll be how you truly felt about Darion."

Avery had more faith in me than I deserved; she always had and always would. "Thanks. I hope so."

"I know so." She placed both of her hands on my cheeks and gave me a long, lingering kiss. When she pulled away, she smiled. "Come on, we need to get ready."

I reluctantly nodded. While we showered together, nothing X-rated happened. I hadn't touched her sexually since Sunday morning. It wasn't that I didn't want her that way a million more times; it was more about the fact that we had both been so exhausted that we'd fallen into a deep sleep the moment our heads hit the pillow.

After we finished showering, we went our separate ways to get ready. Once I had shaved, I went to my closet. As I pulled out my tailored black suit, Avery came out of the bathroom in a short-sleeved black dress with a simple strand of pearls around her neck.

"Can you zip me?" she asked as she held up her long dark hair.

"Sure." I moved the zipper up from her waist to the top of her shoulders then turned her around to face me. As I stared into her questioning eyes, I placed a chaste but sweet kiss on her lips. "Thank you."

She smiled at me. "It should be me doing the thanking since you just zipped me up."

"But you're the one who kept me going these last few days."

"You don't need to thank me for that. I wanted to be here for you."

"And for that, I'm eternally grateful."

Avery's soft hand cupped my cheek as she gave me a kiss. Her breath warmed against my lips as she said, "I'll always be here for you, Cade. All you have to do is let me."

"Why?"

Her brows furrowed. "Why what?"

"Why do you want to be here for me?"

She nibbled her lip as if she was unsure how to respond. "Because I care about you."

"How much?"

"A lot?"

"Do you love me?"

"Of course I do."

"I mean, do you *love* love me?"

"Cade, please." She started to brush past me, but I pulled her against me.

"Why won't you answer the question?"

"Because now is not the time."

"Then let's make it the time." I wrapped my arms tighter around her. "Avery Prescott, I love you. I've loved you since I was eighteen years old. There has never been anyone else for me but you, and walking away from you was the worst mistake I ever made."

Avery blinked at me in disbelief. Her mouth opened slightly as she made a little strangled noise. "Oh Cade," she murmured as tears pooled in her eyes.

"Well, that wasn't quite the reaction I was going for."

"They're happy tears, I promise."

"They are?"

"Of course they are." Her fingers came to tangle in the strands of my hair. "I've waited so long to hear you say those words."

"I meant them, and I swear it's not the grief talking. I mean them from the bottom of my heart. I love you."

"I know you do, and I love you just as much. I have since I was a seventeen-year-old girl. No one has ever made me feel the way you do, physically or emotionally. You are everything to me."

I bent my head to kiss her. There was no lust behind the kiss; it was only love. It was sweet, pure, and honest. I'd never kissed another girl like that in my life, and I never would again. Avery was the only girl for me. I knew that without a shadow of a doubt, and as long as I had a breath within me, I would never allow anyone or anything to ever come between us again. I would work my ass off so she would never have to doubt my love.

A knock at my bedroom door interrupted our moment. "Yeah?" I called.

"Hey man, we need to leave in five minutes," Jonathan replied.

"Okay." I reluctantly pulled away from Avery. "I guess I better finish getting dressed."

"I'll go put my hair up." As she started to go to the bathroom, I took her hand in mine. "I love you."

She smiled. "I love you, too."

As I pulled on my suit jacket, I thought about the last time I'd worn it: the night I'd taken Avery to Jamal's performance at Ebenezer. Never would I have imagined that the next time I would be wearing it would be to Darion's funeral. It's amazing how quickly life can change.

Of course, something good had also happened since the last time I'd worn it. I'd finally told Avery how I felt about her. I knew if Darion were there, he would be stoked. He'd always ragged me about Avery and I ending up together. Knowing him, he had been working on getting us together from above. Tilting my head, I looked up at the ceiling with a smile. "Nice job, man."

Once I had my suit on, Avery and I went to the living room where Jonathan was waiting on us. "Presley just texted me that she's running late because Evie had a bad night. She's just going to meet us there."

"Okay." Although it was the last thing I wanted to do, I grabbed my keys and headed out the door. After we came down the stairs, I saw the long black limo waiting for us. Jonathan lowered his sunglasses. "Did you seriously rent a limo?"

"I did. The funeral home doesn't provide one, and Denise and most of Darion's friends don't have cars."

Jonathan clapped my back with his hand. "Good idea, man."

Avery smiled. "Yes. It was very thoughtful of you."

"Darion would have loved it," I remarked as a familiar pang of grief washed over me.

Before I'd met Darion, my life was focused on one thing and one thing alone: me. It was amazing to think how much you can change in just two months, and I was definitely changed. My heart had moved past its selfish focus, and my life felt full because of it. Currently, it was overwhelmed with grief, but it still felt full. Avery thought my decision to hire a limo was thoughtful, but I never would have considered it had it not been for her. *All because of Avery.*

We then headed to The Ark. Although Darion had a church he attended, it seemed to make more sense to have the funeral in the gym at The Ark. It was a large enough to seat everyone as well as somewhere he had loved spending time. The kids who weren't comfortable attending the funeral would just stay in the other parts of The Ark.

Once we arrived, members of Darion's family met us. Some had driven over two hours to make it. After talking with them for a few minutes, I went inside. I needed to be with Darion.

An agonized grief entered my chest when I walked into the gym and saw his casket sitting in the center of the floor. On top was a blanket of flowers made to look like a football. Although Avery had initially tried talking me out of it, I wouldn't give up on the idea. It might have been tacky to some, but it represented Darion. Football was his life, his ticket to a better future, his joy, and his dying wish.

I remained standing by his casket for the next hour until it was time to start the funeral. I then took a seat in one of the chairs behind the podium in front of Darion's casket. Even though she wasn't speaking, Avery sat beside me to lend me moral support. On the other side of me was Darion's minister, Reverend Prentiss.

Jamal, along with the other members of the Innercity Boys Choir, stood on risers to the right of Darion's casket. Their angelic voices filled the air with old hymns like *Amazing Grace, Take My Hand, Precious Lord,* and *You'll Never Walk Alone*. After they finished, Reverend Prentiss walked over to the podium. He spoke about how Darion never missed a Sunday morning service. When he'd realized Darion was walking almost two miles to get to church, he had started sending the bus to get him. Although I appreciated everything he had to say, it just made feel even more gutted over Darion's loss. It certainly reiterated the fact that the good died young, and in Darion's case, it was way too young.

When Reverend Prentiss finished, Avery squeezed my hand in encouragement. I drew in a deep breath as I stood up from my chair and made my way over to the podium. After adjusting the microphone, I cleared my throat.

"I met Darion in May when I was mandated by Georgia Tech's athletic board to volunteer at The Ark. Over the last three months there, I've gotten to know a lot of kids, but from the moment I met Darion, there was always something about him that stood out. He had a megawatt smile that could light up a room, and a laugh that warmed your heart. Even though life hadn't dealt him a very fair hand, he was never bitter or discouraged. He never complained about the things he didn't have, like a car, or even a home. He just seemed to live each day in the moment and with a focus not on material things.

"His teachers could stand here and tell you how hard Darion tried in school, that although the cards were stacked against him, he always managed to have his homework or prepare for a test. Coaches could stand here and talk about what a gifted athlete he was—how as a sophomore, he was already being scouted by colleges. I have no doubt that after playing college ball, Darion would have been drafted to the NFL. He was just that talented. He had a bright future ahead of him."

Tears stung my eyes and blurred the lines on the paper. I glanced out at the mourners.

"I stand before you today not only sad, but mad, really really mad. I don't understand why someone like Darion was taken, someone who had so much to give this world, but life isn't fair and bad things happen to really good people. Although I know Darion is scoring touchdowns in heaven, I selfishly want him here. I want to be able to sit on the sidelines and watch him play for an NFL team. I want to take him for his favorite chili dogs at The Varsity. Most of all, I want to watch him grow older with gray in his hair, but he will remain forever young."

I swept the tears from my cheeks. "His loss is something I will feel for the rest of my life." I glanced down at Darion's casket and called upon a line from Shakespeare's *Hamlet*, which I had read many years ago. "So goodnight, sweet prince. May hosts of angels sing you to sleep."

As I stepped away from the podium, the choir once again rose to their feet to sing. When I went to sit down, Avery popped out of her chair to give me a hug. "That was so beautiful," she murmured into my ear.

I was so overcome with emotions I couldn't speak, could only nod my head in acknowledgement of her compliment. When Avery pulled away, she kissed my cheek before slipping her hand in mine. We then fell in line with the procession filing out of the gym.

Nothing could have prepared me for what I saw when I entered the rotunda.

"What are you doing here?"

Dad glanced from Avery back to me. "She called to tell me your friend had died."

My head whirled to stare open-mouthed at Avery. "You did?"

She nodded. "I thought he needed to know what a hard time you were going through."

Jesus, I couldn't believe this amazing girl. She had a million reasons to tell my father to go fuck himself, but instead, she had called him. Almost as surprising was the fact that he had shown up.

My father fiddled with his cufflinks before clearing his throat. "She also told me about how you stepped up to pay for the young man's funeral along with planning it."

"Her name is Avery, Dad. Avery Prescott. And yeah, I did."

Dad ignored my correction. "That was very mature of you, Cade."

I shrugged. "I just did what needed to be done."

"I'm very proud of you for stepping up and taking responsibility."

As if my emotions weren't already frayed, my father telling me he was proud of me sent me over the edge. "Thanks. It's *nice* to hear you say that."

"Miss Prescott also tells me you want to start a foundation in Darion's name."

"I do."

"I would be happy to give you the money to get that started."

What the fuck?

"You would?"

"Yes. Of course."

While I wanted nothing more than to enthusiastically take the money, this was my father. He didn't do anything out of the kindness of his heart. "What's the catch?"

"Excuse me?"

"Come on, Dad. You don't do anything without having an ulterior motive."

Dad pursed his lips. "Fine. I want you to sit down for interviews with the media. Mention my name and how I influenced you to see the error of your ways. I could use the boost."

I shook my head slowly back and forth. "Unfuckingbelievable. You're such a cold bastard that you would come to my friend's funeral to bargain for something to benefit your political career."

"It doesn't just benefit me. It benefits the youth of this community."

"Forget it. I'll start the foundation—without you."

My father's face clouded over in anger. "Good luck with that. You'll never be able to get it off the ground without my help."

"You might be right, but even if it fails, I'll know I didn't sell my soul to the devil to make it happen." I turned to look at Avery. "I already made that mistake once. I won't do it again."

As Avery's eyes widened, my father growled, "Fine." He wagged a finger in my face. "The next time you find yourself with your ass in a bind, don't bother calling me. I won't help you."

"Good. Don't need or want your help."

"We'll see about that." He then stormed out the door.

"Are you okay?" Avery asked.

"You know, I'm actually good."

"Really?"

"I am. More than anything, I'm determined to prove my father wrong. I will get that foundation going."

"I believe you, and I'll help you."

I smiled. "I know you will."

"Do you know why?"

"Because you love me?"

"That's right. I love you very, very much, Cade."

I brushed a hand against her face. "And I love you very, very much. Like Jake Ryan loved Samantha. Like Blane loved Andie. Like Romeo loved Juliet. Like that utter shit Hamlet loved Ophelia."

Avery grinned. "You had me at Jake Ryan and Samantha."

"But most of all, you are the Fairy Queen to my Bottom."

Tilting her head in thought, Avery said, "You're comparing yourself to the half-man, half-donkey from *A Midsummer Night's Dream*?"

"Face it, I'm an incredible jackass."

Avery threw her head back and laughed. As the noise echoed through the rotunda, she quickly cupped her hand over her mouth and flushed red. Although she seemed mortified to be laughing after a funeral, the sound helped heal my troubled soul. The last few days had been so dark, and it was good to hear laughter again. "Don't feel bad. Darion would have liked you laughing. He wouldn't have wanted us to bury ourselves in mourning. He would want us to live and be happy."

"I know he would."

I drew Avery into my arms. "He would want us to live every moment to the fullest, and that's what I intend to do, with you and only you."

Then I brought my lips to hers.

EPILOGUE

AVERY

Five Months Later

With a VIP lanyard around my neck, I stood on the sidelines of the Georgia Dome. A few feet away from me, Cade was looking very sexy outfitted in his Georgia Tech uniform. We were just an hour away from the kickoff for the SEC championship game between Georgia Tech and the University of Tennessee. The stadium was already packed, and the air was filled with buzzing conversation.

Cade was standing next to a tall, balding reporter from ESPN. “If you’re just joining us, I’m here at the Georgia Dome with Georgia Tech senior running back, Cade Hall.” The reporter gave

Cade a toothy grin. "So you've had an amazing season—probably the best of your career."

Cade smiled. "Yeah, I have. It's been a real blessing to have my final year be such a successful one."

Although I'd never been a huge fan of football, I had been to every home game of Cade's, and I'd even made it to some of the closer out-of-town games. I would never be someone who lived and breathed for the blue and the gold, but it was growing on me.

The reporter's lips curved into a smirk. "I understand that you came close to not being part of the Yellow Jackets' football program this year."

A sheepish expression came over Cade's face. "I got myself into some hot water after doing a really stupid and childish prank, and it looked like I might be suspended from the program unless I completed community service hours at The Ark."

He turned to wink at me as the reporter filled the audience in about The Ark and its founder. Even though we'd been back together for months now, I still got butterflies in my stomach when he winked at me.

"And it was because of your time at The Ark that you started the Darion Richards Foundation."

A look of immense pride came over Cade's face. "Yes, while I was at The Ark, I met an amazing athlete and gifted young man named Darion Richards. He was killed in a drive-by and because of the life lessons he taught me, I wanted to do something to give back to at-risk youth."

True to his word, Cade had started the foundation without any help from his father. He had managed to pair up with Amad and some of his financial donors, and I was so proud of the amazing transformation he had made. The goodness I had always known was within him had come shining through.

The reporter nodded. "From what I hear, the foundation is off to a great start and doing great work here in the inner city."

"It's still in its infancy since it has only been up and running for about two months now, but I have a lot of support, and I look forward to seeing what the future holds."

"And what does your personal future hold?"

"Well, after graduating this spring with a premed degree, I'll be attending Emory next year to begin pursing sports medicine."

"That's very impressive."

"I'll be off the field in more ways than one."

The reporter's blond brows furrowed. "What do you mean?"

"I mean I'll soon be out of the dating field—permanently."

With a beaming expression, the reporter asked, "Does this mean you have a special lady?"

Cade stared past the camera to me. "I do, one who has stood by me during the darkest time of my life and who shows me love like I never knew existed. I'm a better man because of her. I don't know if I could make it without her, and that's why I want to ask her to be my wife."

When Cade started walking toward me, I thought my heart was going to explode right out of my chest. Oh. My. God. Was this real life? Was this actually happening? I swept my hands to my face and covered my mouth in absolute shock.

Cade knelt down before me. “Avery Rose Prescott, will you marry me?”

“Yes! Yes, of course!” I cried before throwing my arms around his neck. He stood up and wrapped his arms around me. I kissed him all over his face before my lips finally met his and we sealed the deal of our engagement.

Cheers and applause erupted throughout the whole stadium, although it was hard to notice the crowd while being held by my beautiful man. Normally, I would have been mortified by the attention, but in this case, I loved every minute it. I mean, how many people get their proposal witnessed by thousands of people—maybe even millions considering the television audience. Okay, so maybe the thought of millions of people made me a little queasy, but it was still amazing.

“There you have it, folks. Even if the Tech Yellow Jackets lose the game tonight, Cade Hall is a still a winner,” the reporter said.

Even though we were live on national TV, Cade and I didn’t stop kissing. I wanted nothing more than to stay in that moment, wrapped in the arms of the man I loved for the rest of my life. We had come a long way from two teenagers from opposite worlds. We’d been to hell and back.

Like the man who brought us together said, the course of true love never did run smooth. We'd learned some of life's lessons the hard way, and now we had nowhere else to go but up.

About the Author

Katie Ashley is a New York Times, USA Today, and Amazon Best-Selling author of over twenty titles across many genres. She lives outside of Atlanta, Georgia with her toddler daughter, Olivia, and a spoiled mutt named Duke. She has a slight obsession with Pinterest, The Golden Girls, Shakespeare, Harry Potter, and Star Wars.

With a BA in English, a BS in Secondary English Education, and a Masters in Adolescent English Education, she spent eleven years teaching both middle and high school English, as well as a few adjunct college English classes. As of January 2013, she became a full-time writer. She is a hybrid author with both indie and traditionally published titles.

Keep connected with all things Katie Ashley by signing up for her Newsletter.

CPSIA information can be obtained
at www.ICGtesting.com
Printed in the USA
FSHW021314210920
73984FS

9 781539 849223